Sary and the Maharajah's Emeralds

by

Sharon Shipley

Love, Lust, and Peril:
Sary's Adventure Series, Book 3

Sary and the Maharajah's Emeralds

COPYRIGHT © 2018 by Sharon Shipley

Cover Art by *Diana Carlile*

The Wild Rose Press, Inc.
PO Box 708
Adams Basin, NY 14410-0708
Visit us at www.thewildrosepress.com

Publishing History
First Tea Rose Edition, 2018
Print ISBN 978-1-5092-2292-6
Digital ISBN 978-1-5092-2293-3

Love, Lust, and Peril: Sary's Adventure Series, Book 3
Published in the United States of America

Dedication

For Skip and for my fearless editor, Nan Swanson

Prologue
Fatal Arrival

I would never distinguish if Tommy and I made love with such fevered recklessness that last time because we had a premonition…or if it was our usual unquenchable desire. The thirst to behold each other's bodies, reveling in sweet musk, moist heat, the silken feel of limb entwined with limb, while searching each other's eyes, and forgoing the explosive coupling, because it was all the sweeter…

Tommy approached me that last time, in our cramped dressing room in the costume truck as it lumber-rattled about India's ferociously hot province of Rajasthan. We had arrived in the city of Bharatpur overheated and slick with sweat-dew as usual in India's torrid climate. At first, I laughed and tried to wriggle out of Tommy's embrace.

"I'm all perspiring!"

"But I want to taste you, m'dear," he growled in his best villain's voice. "You remember how I relish salty sweets."

"Like salt water taffy?" I laughed, backing off.

"Don't interrupt my elucidating…" Tommy continued murmuring huskily. "Nibble your ear and bite your lips, and a few other choice bits, and…"

"Tommy!" I cautioned. "The audience awaits." But my protest was half-hearted, my fever building as he renewed grazing down my neck, arched in what I hoped was a swanlike pose.

"Whet their appetites. It will get you in the good temper for Katerina's bitchiness," he goaded. He was speaking, of course, of our hugely popular version of *The Taming of the Shrew*, with abject apologies to Shakespeare. In Tommy's estimation, Shakespeare never had it so good.

"As if I need it with *you* around…" I breathed, brushing kisses over his Irish-fair chest, following the black silky line feathering down to his taut belly, until Tommy thrust me into the colorful rack of saris.

By that time, I viewed the top of Tommy's wayward black chrysanthemum curls, as he slid down, feeling his mouth against my bare tummy, snagging my silky underthings and drawing them down with his teeth.

"Mmmmm." He mumbled something indistinct, never guessing it would be the last time he took me, and I him, without grace or restraint, before that last showing of *The Taming of The Shrew*. We pressed hard against the walls of the truck, amidst swirls of flamboyant silks replacing the heavy, stuffy velvets of past tours.

Entangled like colorful maypoles, chuckling and gasping, we fell to the floor amongst the masses of filmy material, searching for mouths to kiss as gossamer silk stuck to our faces.

"Stop! You will muss them!" I giggled, meaning the delicate silk, after we had enjoyed each other a second time; truth be told, they needed to be replaced soon. I was instantly sorry, for Tommy sat up, with a fillip of rose-colored silk over his head.

"Methinks thou dost protest too much, thou lustful wench." Grinning lasciviously, Tommy helped me up.

"And as always, your prudence is correct, love. Let us now stun the audience with our wit, charm, and talent. Eh?"

Damnation! He did not even have the grace to mind. I pouted.

****

Tommy was correct. Our lovemaking brought color to our cheeks as I checked our looking glass before going on, and a hooded ardor to Tommy's eyes as we went through the antic paces of *The Taming of the Shrew* for delighted Hindi audiences. They needed little English—Old English or otherwise—to revel in Katerina's comeuppance, especially when Petruchio upended me and rendered an all-too-realistic spanking on my scantily clothed bottom.

Women covered their mouths with their *ghoon ghats*, while menfolk, with heads thrown back, roared approval—a bit too heartily. I scowled, which brought more laughter.

I remember fondly how Katerina wore violent red saris to match her temperament while Bianca wafted about in ethereal whites and Petruchio wore a tunic of riotous Saint Joseph's colors and a sloppy oversized turban.

How could I foretell, that torrid night at the end of the wildly popular *Gangaur* Festival, celebrating the goddess Gauri, that I would be torn from my beloved Tommy and my adored scalawag of a son, and sent to a torment of fear, and ultimately, the zone of forbidden, irresistible desire?

All we hoped for was that the festive spirit would

make the audience greedier and thus put more money in our pockets…though in reality, I was flush with diamond riches from my last foolhardy escapade, as Tommy so lovingly referred to it.

Money measured only success, not livelihood…

If I had had premonition that this would be the last time where sanity reigned, I would have burnt the saris and driven our Rolls Royce caravan of trucks off their axles in fleeing to the Tibetan border.

The spectacle of twenty-three stately Rolls Royce vehicles—trucks riding high and proud, trailing flatbeds of props, long-snouted busses, high-topped Barker Tourers, and the Barker enclosed cabriolets—had fatally entered Bharatpur, in the province of Rajasthan, two days before.

The glittering Rolls Royces were not gleaming black, Silver Ghost gray, or even hunter's green, but bright jewel colors like wrapped sweets, bright as macaws—richly enameled school bus yellows, fire engine reds, the blues of turquoise and robin's egg, and oranges that put sunsets to shame, all embellished with painted flowers, balled fringe swinging from every window, and trumpet horns polished to a blinding silver.

Long used to a maharajah's gaudy opulence—one maharajah owned an automobile resembling a long-necked swan, its sweptback wings enfolding the occupants—our parade entering Bharatpur that fateful day was startling even for Indians, the flamboyant banner heralding the caravan:

Sir Thomas's Traveling Thespians,
Lovely Maidens, Acrobats, Magicians,
and

Feats of Astounding Strength!

If that wasn't enough, a gussied-up siren—me—
rode a silver howdah, embossed with lions, atop a
garishly painted elephant. My foreign corn-silk hair
must have shimmered under the scorching India
summer sun that day. My over-lush bosom was barely
encased in its pearl bustier, and flowing pantaloons,
scandalously slit to my hips, revealed legs I hoped were
still slim and shapely. My skin gleamed pearly white
with sweat under the canopy, for my fair skin tended to
burn. Better I should have been covered in sackcloth
and ashes, for the horrors that followed.

At the time, all I could think of was, *Another show!
Another town! Adventure!*

Yet as I swayed high in the howdah, the first
prickle of doubt began in my tummy.

Merely the heat, I shrugged—heat was a living
beast in India—or perhaps those spicy *chapattis* the
troupe lunched upon. Pungent smells, too. Whirling
dervishes of dust and storms of sacred cow dung did not
help over much.

I blinked from one such and missed the golden
sandstone palace, so vast it filled the horizon. Nor could
I have seen the two figures on a high parapet.

Just excitement. Yet why this chill prickling my
arms despite the heat?

I felt dizzy. *Damn those chapattis.* A thousand eyes
were on me. The odd feeling hit that *one pair* tracked
me, eyes one could scarcely see between the immense
rolls of fat—but I could not know that then.

My unease must be from the *chapattis*. That was
all.

****

Little could I know that, in the palace, word spread thick as amber trapping insects. Whispers from fawning eunuchs reached the Maharajah of Bharatpur's ears.

"A pearl-skinned goddess? If you will!" He sniffed to the handsome man who lounged beside him, and dipping into a bowl of honeyed figs, loudly sucked his fingers. He licked his thumb where the stickiness dripped down. His brother winced at the explosive smacking.

"With hair of spun platinum, no less?" the maharajah continued undeterred. "Eyes rivaling emeralds! Please. Emeralds? I have emeralds!"

However, the maharajah's eyes glittered, belying his scorn.

The striking man flicked a grimace. Beside the immensely fat man he was shapely in proportion— broad shouldered, sculpted chest and abdomen, lean hipped, long strong thews, handsome in a lushly exotic way, he could have been a pirate, or a Parisian gigolo…

His skin reminded one of ripe pomegranates, smooth and highly colored, the face long jawed and arresting beneath onyx black curls, carelessly resplendent even in his less formal gear.

He could read his brother's mind—unfortunately.

"It is said she does acrobatic tricks in the nude." The maharajah, grubbing in the bowl for more figs, gurgled his eagerness. It sounded like a clog going down a drain. "I will have her." He cast a smug look at his brother and lifted the bowl, draining the dregs of honey.

The rajah glanced at him derisively. "As you will. I take my leave now." He said it more heavily than he intended.

"Precisely. My will." The maharajah mocked his handsome brother's retreat.

Chapter One
The Burning

I felt heat. I opened my eyes and wished I had not. I could see into the white heart of Hell—a wall of live flame dancing to the sky—the brilliance burning, burning, evaporating my garments.

I looked down. But what am I wearing? Through it, I could see my rosy nipples plainly. Confused. What are these diaphanous wisps whipping about in the vortex?

White silk, trimmed in red-gold of the setting sun. Or was that orange shimmer a reflection of the fire to which I was propelled—such a wispy barrier to the furnace before me.

Held by many arms, I twisted and turned, felt the sheen on my face, my body, as they, the unseen, prodded me toward the enormous pyre.

Yes, I whimpered. That was what it was. I recognized it now—a funeral pyre.

The blaze. The wood piled high, crisscrossed, like the stacking of a log cabin and narrowing at the top.

The conflagration had a mouth that roared and hissed my name. Flame-fingers snapped at the wisps trailing my feet. I touched my veil stuck with jewels. I could feel them cold, even in the intense heat, on top of carefully pomaded hair. I could smell the coconut oils. Oils to attract fire…

A cloth-bound man lay atop the inferno. His chest

was covered with yellow flowers. Hungrily licking tongues had not reached him yet.

I pushed back, skidding my heels in the earth. Many hands shoved me forward. The press of bodies, smells of perspiration, patchouli, sandalwood, and garlic smothered me.

No! *I shouted. Already my face blistered. The least spark could catch my veil on fire.*

"This is a mistake!" I screamed until acrid heat scorched my throat, choking my voice with cinders.

Still they relentlessly pushed. I was heating up hellishly now. I saw the edge of my sari flicker, spark, and flare.

"Stop it!" I screamed. "I will not follow! You have it wrong! I am not the one! A mistake! It isn't me!"

My clothes twisted around me then, binding me like a shroud as hands grabbed at me, mauling me this way and that. I could not breathe; the scalding air shimmered with sparks before my eyes...

My veil, lifting in superheated air, loosened my hair and let it waft freely in the hellish updraft.

"Sary!" the flames called as they crackled and spat encouragingly. "Sa-ryyyyy. Cooooomme...."

Chapter Two
Captive

I bolted upright, still feeling intense heat.

I squeezed my eyes tight, and then opened them quickly to see if the horrific view changed. No. Still veils upon veils—but cool veils, languidly drifting in a humid breeze from windows shaped curiously like keyholes, across a vast room. No flames, no scorching heat. I kicked at clinging sheets twining like damp coils of snakes.

"Where the pluperfect hell am I?"

Something filmy—a bed drape this time, lemony—the finest silk as blissful silk worms could possibly spin, floated across my eyes, obscuring my vision.

I swatted it irritably away. Something was terribly wrong.

But this is India, silly. Of course, I am overheated.

India!

Oh, yes, India.

Why did that not seem strange?

"And why would I be here? Wherever here is!" I looked dazedly about. One mystery at a time, please. I somehow sensed it was not a fancy hotel or a private home.

My hand slapped a gleaming twisted trunk—a bedpost trying mightily to be a gilded tree, its branches forming a canopy of, yes, more silk, lofting lazily.

Delicate gold formed twigs, each twig studded with gems, lest one's eyes, roving the ceiling, became bored.

I pushed off the bed, tumbling four feet with a spine-jarring thump. I sighed. Naturally, one does not take these silly steps, looking like a decorated cake, to get off the bed.

"This whole room was surely decorated by deranged angels besotted on fermented honey." I spoke aloud to ease suspicions I might not know exactly where I was.

Barefoot and naked, I raced across an acre of marble to the queerly shaped windows. Sultry air brushed my nose with frangipani and jasmine.

I felt a tickling on my neck.

Cold fingers teased my spine.

Suddenly aware of my nakedness, and crossing my arms over my breasts, I checked the endless room. Then I leaned out the window, shaped like an alabaster keyhole—to view a sixty-foot drop and twenty-foot walls that imprisoned acres of green velvet mazes, macaws in a breadfruit tree, and a fountain's lazy *plish-plash*.

I dropped back, disquieted.

It is a prison. I stand here as God made me. And someone watches.

Flipping my tangle of hair, I knotted a sheet at one shoulder, and pattered across to a wood door that looked like it might have been formed from the ark. "Hey!" I pounded. "Blast it!" I tensed at a low grunting as if someone on the other side breathed through his mouth.

Yanking at the door, I fell onto a man imitating a wall, or at least another door. Five feet tall, four feet wide, mostly shoulder and hard belly, and naked save for pantaloons tucked between beefy legs and a curved sword with nothing ornamental about it.

Eyes black as currants in a pudding face, blank as a windup toy, gazed stolidly back.

Somehow I knew what he was by the breast-like pouches where his muscles should be. A eunuch.

Mute, the eunuch placed one blocky hand on my chest and shoved me back.

"Hey! You blasted—you great—you plug-ugly—you—!" I kicked more from nerves than anything else. He didn't move. "Ow-waw!" I hopped on one foot. "Dad blast it!" It was like kicking a tree stump.

In answer, he swung the door closed in my face. A lock grated like an iron hand fitting into a mesh glove.

"Well, that went well." I kicked at the door—but gently, sensing my guard dog was indeed a tree, rooted until moved, and had no authority to release me. I studied the room resembling something from the Arabian Nights, or a brothel—an *expensive* brothel.

"Buck up, girl! Get some sand."

I heard the words from someone I once knew, yet the name, the face remained scarily, stubbornly blank.

"I have 'sand'!" I gritted.

Whoever you are, an imp smirked.

My head swam. The overbearing room glittered and whirled. Still, smarting from bruised toes, it was too real to be a dream. I was suddenly hungry—hungry as one who hadn't eaten in days.

Still that prickling sensation of being watched. Irritating as all get-out!

I looked behind me—at the ceiling, cradling my arms over the armor of my sheet, gazing at carved friezes of fanciful birds and flowers embellishing even the ungodly ceiling.

****

Close-set flat black eyes watched the pale-haired woman through a spy hole set among those same carved lotuses and fanciful birds. The immensely fat man, supreme despot of the vast northern province, had struggled down onto his knees, blaming the woman below for his humiliating position. "At least she's stirring," he grumbled. Yet," he gurgled softly, "does not a bit of spying add spice for the meal that is to come?"

At the faint sound of laughter, the woman below frowned at the ceiling with eyes of startling green, as luminous as water, and terribly keen.

The maharajah flinched as if she judged him. He rejected that notion. *Good, good.* He liked them that way. Cowed. Afraid of his mighty sword…

He giggled again, but softly.

****

"Silly goose. No one is here!" I checked the ceiling again. I wondered if I should scream.

Then, glimpsing a riot of silks through an archway, I slipped into a dressing room crammed with embroidered slippers, drawers spilling over with jeweled pins, combs, and gaggles of bracelets and earrings; I grabbed a silk thing in panicked indecision and plainer slippers and fled. I needed food, but first a bath, sensing I had not bathed recently either, judging from the musky sheen on my body.

Through another arch, I stared at flagons of perfumed oils and baskets of lemons ranged about a mosaic pool as large as a pond and fitted with spouts resembling golden frogs with jeweled eyes. "What is this—a dad-blasted bawdy house?"

I halted, wondering at my speech. *Dad-blast?* Where had that come from? How do I recognize a bawdy house, elegant, over-decorated, or otherwise? Was I one of…one of those?

****

The ungainly man shuffled to the other peephole above the bathing pool. Drool fell from his meaty chin as his flat black eyes looked directly down on the female, viewing two glistening breasts rounded above the water, shiny pink points of knees and shimmering hair piled in a mass of curls like pale wood shavings.

He edged around the hole, trying to see her face, that which he could see—fierce golden brows drawn to a scowl, straight nose over a pouty rosy mouth, as she contemplated her surroundings, tapping fingers on the edge of the pool.

His lustful gaze traveled her slim back as she leaned for an oil flask. He frowned. She had an odd puckered scar on her shoulder! Ugly! He thrust out a lower lip, resembling a boiled sweet. She was not perfect. Ah, well, it scarce mattered for his purposes—but still…

He petulantly wiped his mouth, unconscious of the puddle beneath his chin, re-fixing his eye to the spy hole. "Ah, yes!" he breathed. Her rounded bottom was the color of two ripe peaches above long slim white legs as she climbed out and roughly toweled her feet dry.

Yes, she would do nicely. His plump hands knotted in anticipation.

He relished the way her taut thighs, smooth as

cream velvet, met in the middle, cupping that sweet delta covered with downy yellow fluff like a baby chick's.

The legs were too long and slim for the torso. That was how he preferred them, though—long. Long legs were more—he choked a laugh—*acrobatic*.

Her breasts lifted as she thrust up her hair and allowed the silken waterfall to drop in a platinum tangle.

How dare she entice him, the sluttish baggage! She did that gesture deliberately to enflame him!

Scowling, the maharajah screwed his eye tighter to the hole and viewed her cheeky bottom once again as she bent to pick up the towel, showing off a scut of peach silk. "Oh, most certainly seducing me! She will pay for her shameless ways!"

Of course she knew he was watching. His nether regions stirred from—if truth be broadcast about—a very long slumber.

He giggled again.

She'd be the one to awaken him.

The pink-soled feet slapping across chill marble below left damp prints as the maharajah of all Bharatpur began the laborious undertaking of getting back up onto his own swollen feet. His effort was rather like that needed to place an elephant in a sling.

Quite ready for afternoon tea, he decided, already conjuring up hot English scones, five or six at least, lavished with thick clotted cream, strawberry conserves, and heavily sweetened *chai*…

"Only thing superior about the invading Brits," he sniffed, pushing up from one elbow. "High cream tea!" He giggled, halting as he viewed sturdy arched feet planted before him, hearing an impatient, "Tcha!"

"Supposed I might find you here." His devastatingly handsome brother drawled, watching him struggle to his feet.

The fat man stiffened. "I need no aid, brother. I can scarce rise with you standing there like the great Lord Shiva." He snarled, getting one plump knee under him, and gasping like a fish, managed to lever himself up. "How dare you spy on me!"

The striking man, raising one dark brow, ironically toed the spy hole in the floor.

"Paaah! I was merely seeing if she was ready. I am indeed growing impatient. As a lusty and virile man, I have special needs. Have a care, brother!"

The rajah watched his elder brother waddle off and, once he'd vanished, rolling his eyes at his own voyeurism, strolled to the spy hole.

The exquisite man's burnished walnut face seemed made for seduction, for subtropical nights and indolent days filled with the most sensual appetites bordering on the prohibited, not for lurking in niches—or anywhere, for that matter. A man who strode, sat upright, lounged gracefully, and did all with purpose and unintended flair.

However, now that broad-shouldered man lay flat on the coolness of the stone in a very un-princely fashion.

The woman below stilled like a doe in the woods.

Feeling ludicrous, the rajah effortlessly rose.

Disturbed, he touched himself briefly as if gentling a wild stallion and nodded a salute to the woman below with a certain melancholy.

"Mayhap this exquisite creature, if she is fortunate,

will not have so much trouble after all…"

****

I glided to a vanity, muttering, "This bloody vanity is six feet long, with a mirror that outshines bleeding bloody Versailles!" I was nervy. I knew it.

Dabbling in caskets of face paint to quell unease and take my mind off my empty stomach, I finally raised my eyes and took stock.

The face staring back was terrifyingly unfamiliar.

Who am I?

Oval face. Pointy chin.

Full mouth darker than a tea rose, tucked into folds like half a dimple. High cheeks. Narrow nose. Nothing to write home about there. A bump on one side as if broken at one time—but it was the great troubled green eyes staring back that arrested me.

The eyes. Faintly familiar. True green, not hazel or flecked with yellow or blue but luminous, like sunlight through waves. Not too unattractive, I thought.

I peered closer at the wavery image. "I know this face." I had looked into these same eyes in a looking glass—somewhere.

"My name is Sary…," I breathed. "I'm Sary. I am called Sary!" But Sary what?

Congratulations, my disagreeable imp goaded me. *You know your name.*

"No. That's not right." I pressed my nose to the glass as if I could see the other side…my other self. "My real name is Sarabande. I think."

I sighed. Further knowledge retreated into shadows on the other side of the looking glass and could not be coaxed back.

Restless and troubled, I held up lengths of silk I

thought were called saris—why did they seem familiar? I experimented with hairpins and tiara-like things with bangles over the eyes, and a profusion of massive neckpieces, and finally shoulder-knotted diaphanous peach silk in time to hear the lock cracking like a walnut, and the wall of a eunuch ushered in a pretty little thing with a small burn scar on her cheek.

She set down a tray of food and scurried off while I gawped like an idiot.

"Wait! Don't leave! Who—?"

The girl looked back curiously before the eunuch hustled her out. "Asha," the girl, casting worried eyes at the eunuch, whispered.

"Hey there! Wait…! Damnation!" I stamped my foot as the door slammed shut.

I wandered back, troubled. Deciding I was starving, I inspected the tray. Chicken in a spicy cream sauce. Crispy bread. Almonds, dates, a fruit much like peaches, and heavily sugared spiced tea. Heaven! I halved the peach thing, staring at my nails as I did so.

I kept them clipped. Now my nails were noticeably longer. I knew this instinctively. A time-marker, of sorts, indicating weeks. How odd. Now I was afraid.

****

His brother's face held the same gloating triumph as it had when he was a boy setting fire to a trail of ants.

"I of course do not question you, brother," the rajah soothed. "Yet would it not be wise—"

"Hah. What care I for the English? I could have her shot or hung or…"

"Of course," he said patiently. "Yet the woman may not be English. I detect no accent. She may be some one—diplomatically important. She may be—"

"So much the better. A nobody!" The maharajah sprayed crumbs. "No one will miss her." The maharajah returned to his afternoon tea. The rajah looked away. His brother had a huge clot of strawberry jam dripping from his chin.

Slathering cream on the fourth scone, the maharajah—now it resembled an enormous boil—crooned complacent. "We shall see how she pleases me and if she pleases me—ultimately." He giggled, taking on a sly coy cast, which set the rajah's teeth on edge.

"As you will," he answered tightly, hiding his disgust.

"Yes! You seem to forget that!" The maharajah's words came, muffled and petulant, through the loaded scone, and wiping his hands on the seat cushion, he waved his troublesome brother off.

Tonight would be her undoing. Tonight he would show the uppity sorceress what a real man was!

****

Just dusk, when the sky turned limpid turquoise, after a scrabbling of the locks, as if rats gnawed on metal cheese, my eunuch-bulldog stumped in, staring stolidly.

I clutched my sheets. I had been moping in bed, planning fanciful escapes—and/or murdering the eunuch with a hairpin. Groping for something heavy, I scowled at him, who might have changed his mind regarding women in general. Instead, women flooded in bearing boxes and pots.

Mindless of the sexless eunuch, I leapt from bed, making a beeline for the door, intercepted by a tall harridan in slubbed brown silk, her gray hair, painted to her scalp, ending in a severe bun. She wordlessly set to work with the solemnity of a hanging judge, pummeling me about as if I were an unfeeling doll.

Their liquid chatter eluded me as they rubbed my skin with rough lemon rinds, leaving me silky and smelling of lemons and roses. I tried to communicate, but Gray-Hair sternly jerked her head.

Next came a massive untangling, until my hair was a platinum sheet hanging to my waist; murmuring approval, the women let it run silkily through their fingers.

Then the older female, apparently named Padmavati, snapped fingers, and aides traced designs on my hands and arches of my feet with pots of henna. "Am I going to a party?" I tried, just to say something inane.

Padmavati stilled me with a buffet, and all business, elongated my eyes with kohl, a thick black paste.

I settled down to spy a way out of this mad hatter's tea party, looking up cross-eyed as she painted a red dot between my brows. Satisfied, she draped a gossamer sari with gold beads dancing about the hem, fastened saucer-sized pearl-and-gold earrings that banged my neck, and hung a ruby diadem low over my forehead.

The face shimmering back from the looking glass was not mine.

I stared at the alien image and near-nude figure. For all the covering, the transparent silk afforded little to modesty. My lips glistened like cherry cordial, and the huge black-rimmed eyes stared back a stranger.

I heard the word, "*Dulhan.*" One girl eyed me, pointed, and giggled.

I was ready. Ready as a dulhan. Whatever that was.

The girls made rude, easy-to-translate gestures, interspersed with irritating titters and snickers. I felt my cheeks flame and my stomach tighten like a fist. I *was* in a brothel! That explained all the frippery, gilding, and whatnots. A brothel!

I had been kidnapped and sold into—what did they call it? Then, as I stared furiously at my near-naked image, they tossed on a face-covering veil I later learned was a *ghoon ghat*.

Padmavati imperiously snapped fingers. The handmaidens withdrew. Two eunuchs, scimitars braced bandolier-style over hard bellies, strode in, staring blankly at me.

I skirted past with a look back.

My jail seemed a haven.

I checked my unbound breasts as Tweedledee and Tweedledum herded me along. My nipples betrayed me, peeking through the filmy gauze like puppy noses. I giggled from nerves.

One eunuch snorted contempt at my apparent humor.

I stifled more laughter. "Where—where do you take me?" I looked back. Padmavati watched me—I thought sadly—from the door. Sadly? Why would she feel anything? Obviously, she was a madam. I stared coldly back. Now to concentrate, to seek out any escape through my veil.

Yet the two half-lifted me when I dallied.

I tried a word of Hindi. "*Rukho!* Stop! I can walk!"

Wait! I recognized that word, Rukho!

My feet lagged again as I pondered this.

"Tell me. What is this place? Do you speak

English?"

Might as well speak ancient Aramaic for all the notice they took.

Corridors stretched like wings to freedom. Certain I was fleeter than these lumbering potbellied behemoths were, I contrarily planted my heels. I was not going to make this a cakewalk!

The two uprooted me as easily as they would pluck a dandelion. Alternately, I lay back, skidding my feet against smooth cold marble, merely aiding them, as they slid me along without comment. I noted one quirk his mouth in a hint of a grin.

Human, after all. Filing that away.

Outside. Good.

It was getting on dark with only a golden fingernail of a moon to scratch the warm velvet sky. I tried to look about, but one placed a hand on my skull and firmly turned my face forward. They lifted me up wide marble steps and hustled me through courtyards, passing turbaned guards and servants skittering about like water bugs on a pond.

I could not countenance the vastness of this place, with its muddle of rooms, corridors, open atriums, each more lavishly decorated than the last and stuffed with gilded furniture—I lost count.

My minders halted before doors studded, cross-braced, and guarded by burly sentries in red, with epaulettes, puttees, gold satin turbans, carbines, and curved swords. I sighed.

A heavily guarded…*brothel*?

A eunuch flicked a cool, appraising glance. Presentable?

I raised my chin. *Don't dare touch me.* Even so, he

flicked straight a fold of the peach sari. Impulsively, I swatted his hand and snatched an arm soft as putty. "Wait! What is this place? You can talk!"

I nudged him. *Look at me!* It was like nudging a stone wall. "They did not remove your tongue, too, did they?" I snapped.

The eunuch faltered, grunted, and shoved me into absolute blackness. The door dragged closed with the finality of a mausoleum.

When I regained my balance I tensed, knees bent, hands out, the room thick with a fetid smell, like a swamp, yet my nose detected another scent overpowering all, a cloying perfume overlaying moist, none-too-clean flesh, like meat left overlong in the sun.

"Is—is anybody here?" I muffled through my palm to keep the odor at bay, whirling. Ponderous footfalls like the shuffling of an old elephant thumped behind me. I could almost feel the marble floor shake.

A disembodied giggle accompanied a rustle of cloth. The swishing of my sari betrayed me. The wet chuckle now came from a different direction.

By a stirring of fusty air, I knew the gurgling presence sidled closer, sensing moist heat close to my arm, a whiff of breath on my face. More dead meat smell. The stench was indeed old perfume overlying body odor; it was as if I had entered a cave of bats. I noiselessly swerved aside, still sensing the presence ponderously seeking me out.

The reek was worse. There was a faint stirring of warmth on my shoulder as the heavy being shuffled past in the dark. Scarce breathing, I clutched my elbows, making myself small, making myself silent. Not daring to flounder for fear I'd stumble into whatever it was, I picked up a strangled chuckle like grease poured down a drain, and a coarse rasping like mighty thighs brushed together. The unseen thing in the silent war of hotter/colder tracked me in a dance of blind man's bluff, accompanied by a whistle of strangled windpipes.

My heart stopped. Somehow the…he…it had circled.

I backed.

The thing collided with something. Furniture, judging by curses and scrape of wood on marble.

A splinter of light striped my face. I ducked to keep from view, sending something crashing. The male, I assume, got my bearings with pig-like snorts of disgruntlement.

I let the midden smell of body odor and heat sidle past, then—a hint of fresh air! Movement from a stirring tapestry! I groped toward it. Almost there. Flatten—slip through…too late.

A round shape manifested in the gloom. A moist, squishy hand gripped my upper arm. The hand, nearly slipping off, squeezed harder, drawing me inexorably nearer. The fatty hand, a firm grip for all its puffiness, slip-slid to my wrist. Fingers dug into my other arm, snagging at my sari. I earned a phlegmy chuckle, flooding me with hot sticky breath, sour and garlicky.

The moist squishy hand, bristling with coarse hair and with mountainous weight behind it, pulled me up wide shallow steps with angered snorts and wheezing. My knees and shins bumped along painfully. It…he… was losing patience and no longer chuckling.

I lost the battle, yanked headlong into a fever-hot body as if I sank into risen bread dough, soft, puffy, yeasty with body odor.

One slippery hand fumbled for my face, grasping my chin. In turn, using a free hand, I wedged it between us, forcing the man's chin up, feeling wobbly flesh slip-slide beneath my palm.

Muttering curses, greasy lips smeared my cheek, seeking my mouth…a blubbery hand tangled with mine as I blindly flailed. I tried to punch him but only succeeded in sinking a fist in blubber. Then I heard him speak.

"*Kuttiya!*" The epithet needed little translation.

I felt a shock to my toes as one hand gripped my breast, slicking off my now damp silk, while the other yanked my long hair painfully back, tearing it loose from its pinnings. The unseen creature attempted to reach my face again. I prized at fingers—fat slugs of iron—as the man dragged me toward himself. I skidded, clawing the hands. The remarkable thing was that, beyond the one curse, we still warred silently.

I eeled away, leaving my hair in his fist. I desperately wanted to reach those draperies. I must see this thing—then he swung me through and I got my wish.

A garish lantern barely piercing inner gloom caused a sickish glow through inset gems, enough however, to catch the first glimpse of my adversary.

My knees turned to pudding, frozen by the vision of the corpulent man before me, barely my height but as wide as he was tall.

Some short garment left open across a pendulous chest and bulbous belly barely covered the man's dignity. What grotesquery was he trying for? Seductive innocence? Confidence? Was he truly ignorant of his appearance? The fatty chest, perched shelf-like atop a belly mottled with a black pelt, glistened with perfumed oil.

Patchouli, I vaguely thought. Its thick reek sickened.

I looked off, not before the pumpkin face split into a randy grin, bunching pocked cheeks and jowls where a sketchy beard sprouted in clumps and the eyes—the eyes fixated on me like carrion birds.

The man clumsily backed me to a bed the size of a small park. I suddenly became aware of sharp pricks on my arm. I looked down. His fingers were clad in sharp ornamental points that scraped my skin.

That was the tipping point.

I did not care what happened.

I was fighting for, if not my life, then my dignity, or whatever you call "sand." I screamed, using my voice as a weapon, sharp and brittle as strands of glass.

The meaty arm twirled me about, his belly to my back, clamping my mouth and part of my nose with the other hand. "*Saali kutti!* Bloody bitch!" He muttered in English, in case I failed to recognize the insult.

I did not wait to smother but bit hard, gagging, sensing the fleshy palm would taste and feel like uncooked rotted meat.

He screamed, high-pitched and childish. The slippery hand released so suddenly I tumbled to my knees. I felt behind me, watching him suck the heel of his hand.

The back of my knees bumped into the bed. I stared wordlessly at the depression in it, as if a body habitually sank into its depths. I imagined myself beneath such a weight, taking the place of the mattress, enveloped by that globular body—for surely that was his intent—suffocated, if not crushed to death.

I sprang from the bed as if I were a cat and it was a tin roof in August.

But he had other plans...

I saw the blur too late.

The arm with its sagging dumpling flesh slashed out—I heard the swishing as if an ax cut the air.

I ducked. Fear lent power behind my own blow, surging down my shoulder to my palm and connecting in a stinging wallop, jolting my entire body, sickening me as the wobbly jelly of his cheek slid sideways.

My blow did not move the mountain. I drew my smarting hand back, yet I felt tremors of rage—or simply dislodged fat. The space reverberated with the high scream of unaccustomed pain, reminding me of a small child's temper tantrum.

The vast brass-and-wood door exploded open.

Sentries poured in like palmetto beetles, from bright light. In the sudden brilliance, I caught a sad snapshot, as from a Kodak Brownie, of a very ugly man, purple-faced, half-clothed, and diminished. Only his insane rage gave the man status—that, the bowing, scraping guards, and rough handling of myself. He must be a king or something. *No. In India, they call them maharajahs.*

I viewed him in full as they dragged me before him. The matted chest, a gold satin kimono that would do nicely for a circus tent—sashed, barely, about the corpulent waist by a garish leopard belt, one paw dangling. Fortunately, the robe covered whatever inadequacies cowered beneath. No doubt his choice of wardrobe had been meant to be seductive, even rakishly boyish.

Yet the most telling ornament was a flaming handprint on his jowls. Eyes half hidden in smug folds now spoke volumes. It was a death warrant.

I tried to speak, to explain, cajole, flatter, anything! My tongue stuck to my teeth. My lips felt wooden.

As guards looked on, he drew back a wobbly arm and plunged his fist into my chest and, swiveling with the grace of a ballet dancer, jammed his elbow into my stomach and stood heaving, red-eyed and triumphant, spraying the words, "*Kuttiya! Rundi Ki bachi!*"

Then, as if I wouldn't understand—oh, I did, if not words, the intent—he repeated in English, "Bitch! Daughter of a whore!"

A guard snickered.

That was low. I may have been a bitch, but certainly not the daughter of a whore.

Paralyzed from the first blow and retching, I had desperately opened my mouth to suck air when the second blow came—nothing moved now, not my diaphragm, lungs, or heart. It stopped mid-beat. Tiny squares enlarged. The hiss of jubilation was my last sensation as I floated to earth…

Chapter Three
Prison Most Foul

I rubbed my nose and scrubbed my face. My nose
wrinkled up with stench, but not like before. This was
damp and mildew. Dirt and grit rolled under my body
where I lay curled with my knees under my chin.

They'd heaved me in, the night before, regardless
of where I landed on slimy stone felted with something
spongy, like layers of rubbish slightly moist with what I
didn't wish to contemplate. I was terribly thirsty.

Propped on one elbow, I detected a plash of water
somewhere, aware my mouth was glued shut.

To cry is defeat. I cannot cry! And I was afraid I
could not stop, once started.

I prodded my ribs. Not broken. Bruised. It felt
good, nevertheless taking a deep breath, even sucking
in the mildew.

"Best move," I muttered.

Move about, where? my imp asked. As I scanned
the space, my eyes took in what my head would not. A
dismal cell, about eight feet by ten. Dirt floor. One door
with a grille inset. A tiny window thankfully open to
the air. A bucket in the corner, a pile of jute sacking in
the other.

Oh, yes? my evil imp inquired. *The window is so
small. How can you get through that?*

My imp nudged me. *Cat got your tongue? So is*

this a dungeon?

"No. Dungeons do not have windows. They are underground." I railed at myself.

Same thing, sniffed my imp.

Wanting to stop crazed imaginings, I hobbled over to where water dripped from a banana palm outside. Drops bounced off leaves. I pressed my cheek to the bars, then put my tongue out in an attempt to catch rivulets dripping from the fronds.

I studied my cell in the greenish light, sensing it would rain tomorrow at the same time. It was something. I sagged below the small opening and, for the first time, wondered how long I would be here.

"I did something unforgivable. But how could I do else?" I asked myself forlornly.

I heard my imp. *A short stay—means execution? A kangaroo court, it is called. No judge. No jury...taken out at dawn...*

"Oh, shut up!"

I tensed for footsteps of coming executioners, relaxing when I heard nothing but the drip and soughing of banana palms.

In a corner sat a bowl by the bucket.

Not good!

However, not bad, either.

Unless they want you healthy for your execution, my imp carped. *You did strike the maharajah, didn't you? The supreme ruler over all things living? You did strike him most grievously!*

I angrily shook the imp off as I would a leech sucking the lifeblood of all hope, sinking back under the bars, where a ray of sun dyed my platinum hair silver.

I didn't eat that night.

****

Rolling thunder pushed rain through the bars, blood-warm and soothing—still, it dragged me from healing sleep.

I willed my eyes open to watery dawn. My long hair was dripping and muddy now as I lay on the bare ground. The wet under me was a puddle. Chronic damp crawled the walls. I finger-combed my hair, twisted the water away, and knotted it on top. I gathered rainwater, finger-scrubbed my teeth, then scrubbed my face and lady parts. Ablutions completed, I waited.

Footsteps and a metal clicking! A bowl of chickpeas and a chapatti thrust through a slot under the door I had not seen.

So much for rushing a guard, my imp chortled. I fell on the food, too stunned to call out and too hungry to care.

Two days…

My ribs did not sting now. I inspected the bruise between my breasts and midriff. The purple had turned a dirty yellow-gray, another marker of sorts. Bruises healed in about two weeks, I thought.

"I might be here long enough to escape—or at least to plan for it."

My imp woke up. *Hopeless. One door? A window small enough for a monkey, perhaps? Thick walls? They feed you through a slot! Really? You suppose you will escape?*

"I can try!"

It rained again.

I brushed fingers along moist walls. Were they crumbly? I had already chipped away flaky plaster,

31

thinking they might be frangible, yet they seemed solid beneath the first crumbly wetness. I traced where unknown beings had scratched names in green and black scum down to bare brick.

All names were feminine sounding.

"Who are you?"

I could see them, digging fingernails to the quick through moss.

I was here. My name is…

"How long before I scratch my name?"

I am here. My name is Sary. I resisted the urge to dig my fingernails into the green scum.

****

Gazing past drawn knees, I viewed dirty toes, with their faint tracery of red henna still showing; I drew my feet tighter under my grimy once-peach sari as filmy as poppy petals. Ten days of scratches were on the wall behind me.

I whimpered, sorry for myself. *I smell bad. Hurts. Glad I slapped him. Glad!*

Sensing the ache in my clamped jaw, I vowed, "I will not cry. I will not!"

As I did each morning, after guzzling gray tea and soggy naan shoved through the door, I called out to retreating footfalls and grumbled spiteful comments when they did not answer. I paced off ten steps, fifty times, wall to wall. I performed pushups against the door. Then I slumped with my head back in the beam of sun, drearily surveying the squalid room and preparing for one more day.

Boredom seemed worse than hunger. I explored every inch. If there were other inmates, they were ghosts. I heard not a whisper but from palm fronds, except when whoever brought food and water, and took my bucket. Each day a butterfly or a bird's trill was cause for joy and speculation.

As I sat in misery, sweating in the humid cell, I had time to ponder. "I am in India...somewhere. I know that much. This place I am in is more than a rich man's home or fancy hotel, far more than that. Almost a town enclosed in a wall." With its own zoo. For I heard animal roars.

That repulsive man is the key. An important man, with soldiers and servants thick as thieves. He has to be—must be—a king, or a maharajah as they call them here. If so, why on God's green earth had he decided to torment me? Yet every time I thought I could leap over that wall of forgetfulness, it was as if something in my head skidded to a stop and I ran smack into it.

Rarely, the tiny window in the door slicked open and a face looked in. Each time, I creaked up, appalled at my condition. I had no strength, my legs growing stiff from damp and inaction, despite my efforts at exercise.

"*Arrey!* Hello!" I banged on the door. "*Kya aap meri madad kar saktey hain?* Can you help me?"

I did not wonder how I knew the words. I had ceased caring long ago.

I even enjoyed a cold corn porridge shoved under the door that night as a reward. Frightened, I looked forward to the small treat. A highlight, after becoming used to deprivation. At times, I panicked. *Am I forgotten?* I looked anxiously at the food slot. What worried me was that, for two days in a row, I had not even been given tea for breaking my fast.

"Get up!" I commanded myself. "Walk, you

useless lazybones!"

"But I can't. I am hungry! I am hurt!" I answered myself.

"Yes, you must. Back and forth twenty times, stretch—push against the wall. Stand in that patch of sun! Scrub your teeth!"

I hardly noticed I talked back to myself now. It was soothing to hear a voice.

"Later," I grumbled. "Let me rest in this dry patch where the sun reaches me. It only comes once a day!"

I awoke to the scrape of metal as a pan was shoved through the usual gap, the source of food—and nightly discomfort, for wind whistled under the door when I fitfully tried to escape reality.

This time, though, it was a step up from the sticky rice and gray tea with scum on top or red beans and naan. I crawled over. Lentils with slivers of hot peppers and some kind of meat. Goat, I thought, with a tiny ball of rice and a chapatti, tasteless but surprisingly fresh. I made it last, recalling all the food I had shoved aside, half-eaten, not wondering at my good fortune.

Dark again.

****

I scratched green walls. Thirty-two lines and cross hatches, now. I allowed warm rain to lash my face. Almost an appointment. Time to take my bath. I scrubbed my hair and removed the stained silk each morning and twisted away brown water between my hands until it was rags.

I awoke one night, preternaturally attuned to the slightest noise.

Something slid back! That was different.

Galvanized, I leaped-crawled-stumbled to the door

as if to press to the other side. Dropping, I craned to see underneath, frightened I would scare them off. Nothing—no shifting of light. No feet. And nothing slid through the bottom. Only the breeze soughing through palms. The sound came from the little door and grille at the top, along with jasmine-scented breeze. Suddenly unnerved, I tensed.

"Have you had enough…?"

I tumbled back on my bottom. The voice was in my head.

"Have you had enough?"

No. It was real, and the words in English.

I scrambled up, pressing the door.

"Yes. Yes! I have!"

Silence.

"Please, answer! Please, don't go away. Please don't!"

A sighing sound as if someone outside sucked a quick breath.

I stood tiptoe to peer through where it didn't fit tight, and viewed a sliver of hall; by shoving at it, I, and possibly others, had loosened one side.

No one was ever there.

And no one was there now.

"Have you had enough?" It reverberated in my head until I wasn't sure I heard it.

The next night, along with the gruel—Christmas! The Fourth of July! My birthday!—a small package was thrust through the slot, wrapped in a strip of cloth that I recalled.

"Asha…" I breathed. That small girl with the burn scar, that first day. A strip from Asha's sari, with its distinctive elephant border. I recalled it well.

The bundle held three balls of sugary sweetness. Fighting tears of gratitude, I did not eat them. I held them to my nose, fondled, and licked them before taking tiny nibbles. Too soon gone.

Asha remembered me. Asha knew where I was. Hope flared for a time. I could wear the cloth as a sort of scarf. It seemed more extravagant than the bedraggled silk sari ever was.

Despite this, days dragged with the slowness of a sloth. Fear bubbled from a deep well of dark imagination—is this a cell for the condemned only? How will I be executed? Each footfall tortured. Perversely, I—Sary—My name is Sary!—dredged up a hundred gruesome ways. Trampled by elephants—left to grow old, half-mad, with a shriveled face and stringy hair, thin and gray.

A bowl slid through.

I studied the red rice and beans, sickened at my relief, flinging myself at the door and scattering the food.

"Please! Wait! Talk to me! Who are you! My name is Sary!"

****

The striking rajah, so out of place, his white satin clothes glowing in the dank surroundings, brushed the bowing jailor off, waiting impatiently until he was gone, his strong face unreadable. He gripped the grille. Sighing, he slapped his palm against the wall.

I heard new footfalls, strong and measured, but receding.

"Please. Take me out of here. Please stay—talk to me…" My voice floated after the unseen person.

****

The plate of sweets flew past his ear, clanging off the wall, spraying jelly.

"I do whatsoever I wish! When so ever I desire! And for whatever reason and for how long I might fancy!"

The rajah stepped out of range of his brother's flying spittle as the ruler's face seemed to swell to bursting like an overripe eggplant. "In case it escaped your mind, this royal personage was meanly, outrageously, traitorously treated! As do you also, if you...if you suppose otherwise!" He watched his handsome brother through mean little eyes.

The rajah in turn studied the mottled butter-yellow face with the alarming eggplant-colored splotches, surprised his brother recalled the woman at all. He had shut up so many and forgotten them, if they were lucky.

He mused. His brother's latest bout of addiction left him even more paranoid—with what substance, he could not hazard a guess—but not, apparently, forgetful.

If he did not watch it, he might suffer a stroke. That was not necessarily a bad thing. "Does not one need to be a citizen of Bharatpur to be a traitor?" He asked as if he could not have cared less. The rajah grinned roguishly, as one man to another, popping a grape and spitting seeds carelessly. "Let's see if I can hit that vase," he drawled.

His brother would not dissemble, however, continuing, "A blatant assault. And by a female assassin!"

"Assassin? Oh, surely!" The rajah scoffed. "A trifling attack by a woman? Some would call it love-play." He winked broadly, feeling the fool in a play. "In what dank hole have you shoved her, anyway?" he asked with a wink and a nudge hoping to gain more information.

His brother glowered, his little eyes suspicious below eyebrows sprouting like caterpillars. "Why the interest?" He sulked. "It was a while ago, now." Suspicion pinched his face into an oily little ball, like a fistful of suet.

As the rajah had suspected, the maharajah had forgotten her until now.

It seemed the days of jollying his brother were fleeting, buried under narcotic dreams and blind indulgences. The rajah went inward, recalling all the times he had defended this man he now watched with distaste. "You like it when they fight. Especially if they are young. Very young," the rajah added heavily.

The mottled face puckered in a grin, preening as he stroked his wispy goatee. "True enough."

The rajah dug an elbow at him, sharing the jest. "Right you are! She is beneath your notice. The wench learned her lesson and may yet be used." He laughed carelessly. "But not if she's kept in a wretched hole much longer, I'd wager." He idly yawned, popping another grape. "Ah, well. I would imagine she is properly subdued, either way."

The maharajah sneered, *"Pah! Kahe ko kha raha hai chut ki chapati aur lund ka beja!"*

The rajah answered, "I regret my idle curiosity and questions bore you, brother dear, as you proclaim." He stretched and put on his best jaded expression while his brother surveyed him like a mongoose scrutinizes a cobra.

"You would betray me, too."

"Brother! Such a dramatic word—betray! You wound me." He nodded a bow. "You are supreme. The woman is but a weak-minded, silly female. Her strength is in those strong loins you so admire. Eh?"

Feeling a right fool, the rajah winked and waggled his brows. Sweat trickled his forehead. His brother had never gazed on him with such evil calculation. *Tread easy. Is she worth it?* Yes. For more reasons than he could sort out.

The rajah twirled at his own head in a universal gesture of insanity. "All females are prone to hysteria and maidenly shyness. She was overwhelmed, the poor woman, never having seen a royal being such as you— much less your exalted company. Come, brother! Have pity."

The maharajah, stuck out his pillowy lips, eyeing him slantwise. "You think so?"

"It was plain to see. The poor girl was dazzled, even frightened out of her—" He grinned, man to man. "Well. Obviously, not her knickers."

He waited to see which way the coin dropped.

The maharajah, chewing his thumb, went inward and muttered slowly, with a silly grin, "S'pose so."

His face took on a sulky look, as though he were loath to dilute his umbrage, scrubbing his jowly cheek in remembrance. "Shyness was not what I felt!"

The rajah pressed. "Most likely the female, under the rule of a sad recluse like the elderly Queen Victoria, never beheld such majesty. What can she know of our glorious heritage and customs? You were a shining light, dazzling her into making foolish blunders."

His brother observed him over a finger-smeared glass of honeyed chai, his eyes little black pellets, flat and as deadly as rat turds.

He had gone too far. Shining light? Dazzling?

"British? You said you did not know."

"I don't have that knowledge," he answered truthfully.

"You want her for yourself!" His brother jabbed a fat finger.

The rajah mused. The finger looked like a white slug.

"Hardly, dear brother. I cannot keep up with all the juicy young cherries in the hareem as it is. While you...A bull! A stallion! A lion king of the bedroom! Eh?"

The maharajah looked mulish but reluctantly pleased. "True. They all fear me." The rajah knew the look well. He had won some small victory, but not all. He waited.

"But you never visit the hareem. They told me," the maharajah accused.

The rajah didn't answer.

The maharajah pouted. "We shall see. Surprisingly, there is much truth in what you allege. Either way, she may not come under my full graces quite yet." He sniffed, groping for his water pipe, which the rajah knew was laced with the tears of the poppy. Sticking the stem in his mouth, like a babe's pacifier, was the last conscious thing his brother would do for the while. There would be no danger today.

A plume of musky smoke masked his brother's face and his intentions.

Outside, the rajah blew out relief. All his other brothers were dead. He did not wish to join them.

Chapter Four
Pride Goeth

My torment did not end there, but at another place altogether.

They came for me.

I straightened, as much as limbs bent from inactivity and pacing or crouching in a corner could manage. I lifted my chin and walked upright as the door grudgingly opened, holding my tattered sari, now an unrecognizable color, like a queen's robes.

My jailors, two men in turbans and rough breeches, waited. I did not wish to leave—I was wild to leave.

Was this my last walk, my last day—hour?

I swept hands over my sari, mangled as it was, glad I'd kept it clean if irredeemable, that my face, teeth, and hair were as fresh as I could make them, hating my bare dirty feet and cracked nails.

Chapter Five
Auntieji

The old woman slapped the rajah's hands as he plunked brashly down on a stool, so old and wobbly it gleamed from the many buttocks that had polished it over its decades, including his own. He scooped two fingers in a pot of *dal* and brought them to his mouth.

"Owww! Hot!" He winced.

"Of course hot! You great fool!"

"*Mujhey bhookh lagi hai, auntieji,*" he mumbled past his fingers, looking ten years younger.

"Naturally you are hungry. You always are, you great ox. Just a growing boy." Raising her stir spoon questioningly, she continued, "*Kyaa aap ko yeh accha lagta hai?*"

"Indeed, I don't like your cooking, auntieji," he answered her. "That is why I am always sampling, hoping even though you are old as grandmother's goat, you might improve."

She grinned, toothless, and whacked her wooden spoon on his knuckles, sniffing dismissively. "It's just lentils."

"Ahh, auntieji Madhuri, but you make them savory just by sticking your little finger in the pot."

The rajah swept up her gnarled hand and gave the wobbly veined back of it a loving kiss.

The old woman jerked her hand away with a

reproving twinkle and made to rap him on the head.

He swerved aside and industriously began lifting large copper and brass lids, questing and sniffing. "What is sweet, now?"

"What sweets are you after?" She raised corrugated brows to her grizzled hair parting. "My poor kitchen wenches?"

"Too much like you, old hen. Cluck, cluck, scold."

The striking rajah, the prince, with the gleam of a boy intent on mischief, lifted another lid, spooning milky broth. "*Khandvi*! You always made the best *khandvi*, you old hag."

"Don't we sweat and slave and work our poor fingers to the bone?" She displayed knobbled brown hands. "To make you and your well-fed brother satisfied." She emphasized "well-fed" ever so slightly.

It was enough. She felt her bony arthritic knees knock.

The rajah's eyes threw a glint like a spark from tinder. The old retainer knew when to quit. She did not wish to stir a riffle simmering in any pot she might own. She was as sure of his affections as one could be in her position, but still... She couldn't let him get by without a final verbal switch on the rump. She grumped, "You are not too big to swat, young man."

"As you yearn to do, wrinkled old auntie."

They mutually grinned with a fondness breaching generations, status, and sex.

In truth, she—the scold and his once-upon-a-time amah—was as close to a mother as the rajah ever had known. His birth mother had been a neurotic, lovesick woman, years younger than her age, who obsessed over the inattentions of his father, the old maharajah.

"Oh, sit you down, and I'll serve you proper. No more sticking your dirty fingers in my pots…"

"Some of your rice pudding, then, auntieji," he said humbly. His soft words did not match the cold rovings of his eyes, which, as she was very much aware, had occurred during their entire banter.

What could he be looking for? Her crafty eyes reflected her inner question. Not my kitchen wenches, surely. There was only that scrawny, weak-as-skim-milk female.

The rajah squinted past curdled air wavering over braziers and ovens. The steam was a virtual stew as the old lady stirred and ladled, still grumping as his gaze bored into dim corners, past curtains and stacks of firewood. He halted his gaze, veering back at a flick of a pale moving head, alien amidst bright saffron strings and hanging chilies.

The old woman glanced up to see his broad back slipping behind a hempen curtain on his way to the scullery.

"Haven't you enough sweet *laddoos* at your disposal?" she groused. "Why pester my poor kitchen slavies, eh?"

****

I knelt, almost upended in a basin as big as a washtub, the rim jamming my stomach, and I am certain my rump was clearly outlined in my dingy cotton shift for any wag passing. I complained under my breath, "Ooooph!"

My project was to vigorously attack the pot's dried-on fava bean residue, though my back ached, my hands were raw, nails broken to the quick, and my hair, stringed with dried bean scum, swung in my face like a metronome in time to my scrubbing.

"Let them look," I complained.

Damnation! Dad-blast bean-eaters!

On good days, I supposed this was a step up. I now had plenty to eat—when I had stomach for it after checking the mountains of teetering pots, littered plates, and smeared glasses.

"Have you had enough?"

I thought the voice was in my mind, so much did reality blend with the ramblings in my head, doggedly reapplying rags and bristle brushes.

Ignore it.

"Have you had enough?" A hint of humor in the words.

I scrubbed harder, cursing. "Be quiet, drat you!"

"Well? Have you?"

Slowly, I dared look up. My face drained, I am sure, to as white as bean curd.

The most devastatingly stunning man I had ever beheld lounged on a hundred-pound sack of rice. Not handsome exactly, in the ordinary sense, but thoroughly male. Curved hawkish nose, eyes heavily hooded and black, smoldering under jet brows taking off like wings. A pirate, or a gypsy.

My second impression was clean—loose cotton pants of blinding white linen, knotted low on a taut, bare bronzed torso. A rough turquoise pendant dangled on a leather thong almost as far. I looked away—not before catching a glimpse of his satiny, copper-burnished chest. One strong wrist showed, from a carelessly rolled linen sleeve, a modern Swiss time-piece, the other wrist sporting a wide silver native cuff. A simple cotton turban topped his hair which, with the gloss of licorice, sprang with life, unruly.

I'm afraid my mouth gaped.

I sat hard on a stool, scrambling up and smoothing my bean-stained cotton to dirty knees, wiping clotted stringy hair from my face and sensing the red flooding back to my cheeks. What cared I what I looked like? I was me! He could take me as he found me.

"It was you!" I accused. His presence was the last straw, the spoon that stirred the pot of confusion, pain, and isolation into boiling over. Perhaps something on my face made him step away, neither denying nor explaining.

****

Looking past the grimy, sweat-streaked face framing those eyes reminded him of stormy seas. The foreign woman was a beautiful wild animal staring out from a hedge of wild hair, but charcoal smears could never spoil her beauty. He took in grubby toes and the now-tarnished pale hair knotted and hanging like loops of old rope, the thinner face with its high cheeks sharper now than when he'd first beheld her, her lips curved as an archer's bow—untamed even after, or because of, her time in the cell.

His brother apparently sought to humiliate rather than destroy. Uncommon. Increasingly unpredictable, his brother's mind. The rajah smiled cautiously, as though soothing a half-tame animal.

****

If he thought I was swooning over him, he would be wrong. He saw it too late in my eyes that I narrowed like an alley cat's. He, smelling of tuberose or jasmine or some pungent fragrance, failed to impress. Did men smell of jasmine, I asked? His clean, polished nails and jackdaw black hair gleaming with oils only added fuel to my ill-banked fires.

Brushing my knotted hair back with one hand, I reached into the pot with the other.

I saw the irritating man's eyes open wide as he jerked back, scrambling to rise from the sack of rice as he saw what I held.

I gripped the wet rag dripping bean-juice scum and dirty water, and I hurled it, smacking his pristine shirt square in the chest, where it made a satisfying squelch sound.

I stood back, hands on hips, my eyes sparking green flint. If you can't stand the dirt, stay out of the kitchen, my eyes said.

Then the revolting man made the mistake of laughing.

I flung a greasy sea sponge next and picked up a hefty stone pestle. "This isn't a zoo! Leave me be! What? Are you somebody important?" I sashayed and swayed my hips. The effect was lost, in a stained, coarse, cottony thing. I could not seem to stop. All my anger seemed to boil up, rattling the lid, like one of Madhuri's pots of lentils.

He ducked, checking the splotch on the wall beside his head. I pranced back, curving a cat's smile designed to curdle the strongest man's will. Then, noting his enraged look at the stain ruining his crisp shirt, I disciplined my expression. Subdued—even contrite.

Sort of.

This never happens—I saw it on his face. He sprang up.

I looked for a way past him. My back was to the washing tubs.

Snatching a broom, I swished it at his legs. Distracted by the old woman, my latest scourge, looking on, he stopped my downward swing with one strong brown hand.

He looked back.

"Leave, auntieji!" He roared.

She scuttled off.

"You won't take me back!"

His eyes burned as if memorizing my face.

"Take you—where? Where in God's name would I if I wanted to?"

"You! Me! That—cell! I didn't mean to hit you."

Only once. In a pig's eye!

I back-peddled, clanging into the copper caldron. "But you shouldn't—*look so clean*—waylay me! I have work! Madhuri!" I called to the old woman he called his auntieji. Madhuri would be a match for this peacock! But Madhuri, somewhere safe in the kitchen, didn't respond beyond a "Harrumph!"

"I'd like to take you to the whipping shed," the handsome man threatened. "I would like to bend you over my knee for acting like a *bach cha*." His face threatened such was imminent as he looked down at his spoiled shirt.

"*Bach cha*? What is this Bach cha?"

"Child!" He said in English with a decided posh accent.

"Don't you need to catch me first? For I will never"—I swatted the broom, reaching blindly for a dirty plate—"allow you…" I lifted my arm and stopped, dropping the plate. It broke into pieces at my stained feet. Madhuri cursed in the background at the sound of the smashed plate.

We both grinned involuntarily. I was close to hysterical—it had been so long since anything approached being comical.

"Have I—" I swallowed the grin before I shattered like the plate. "Do I know you? Have I seen you somewhere?"

I was stammering. I did not trust my memory. I saw faces in my head. Yet perhaps this man resembled slightly he who wronged me. The "greasy man," as I thought of him. Not in looks. The voice. Not even that. Maybe the downward slanted eyes, only his were large and almond-shaped, like dark amber with the sun shining through. Not small and piggy like the other's.

I pulled back. I dropped the broom as one large hand encircled my wrist, drawing me to him. He gently clasped my face with elegant bronzed fingers, from my cheek to my chin, searching my eyes, thumbing my lips. Then, dropping his head to mine, he kissed me thoroughly. I was conscious of the garlic I had eaten for lunch.

My body responded, however, telling me it had been a long while.

I smelt of garlic. However, so did he. Garlic, tobacco, spirits, and fragrance. His body felt good, and I cupped myself into his strong supple frame that smelled of crisp linen and *man*. His arms felt—safe.

I pressed him away to breathe. What was I doing! He abruptly moved me against the wall amid brooms and mops, drawing the curtain, denying Madhuri's interested eyes and bending his glossy pirate's head to my pale tousled one.

He plucked a bean from my hair.

"Should be pearls," he whispered, grinning his

crooked smile.

I could only stare dumbly.

That first kiss was an electric current, however. My knees knocked. I would have fallen had he not had a firm clasp of my waist.

"I did not mean to upset you with my warning. I was not tormenting. I wanted to find your mettle."

I flared again. "I have"—I pulled back sharply— "mettle and metal in my person."

He looked at me appraisingly. "Very good. You will need it." He stroked my hair from my forehead. He nuzzled my ear, speaking, "Courage, *Bach cha*."

I ducked, slipping from his embrace, armed now with a copper saucepan but not quite ready to hurl it.

"Leave me be. Have not all of you done enough?"

"I rescued you," he informed me. "I placed myself in harm's way." He said it without pride or reproach.

I cocked my head. His voice was that of an educated Englishman. Formal—a toff. He used full verbs, not contractions. I looked from his bare chest, between two slices of the spoiled white linen, into his face, so out of place in this grubby scullery among scraps of decaying garbage that attracted flies and rodents and apparently handsome males.

I did not want to feel.

Yet I wanted this man to kiss me again and take away the real world, where bewilderment reigned, if even for the moment.

The saucepan clattered to the floor. I could feel the tickle of impending tears. "Should I bow? Curtsey? Prostate myself in grateful thanks?" My voice cracked. "Be damned!"

He backed. Slowly his gaze traveled my disgusting

rags. "Cleanse yourself, for Lord Shiva's sake." Then he melted away, leaving me standing there befuddled.

"That's the pot calling the kettle black!" I yelled belatedly. A puzzled crease formed between those black brows as he turned back. Meaningfully I flicked his shirt, cocking a hip and elbow in uneasy defiance.

"The pot calling…?"

He looked down where I pointed. "The kettle black. Oh!" He threw his head back, laughing. Then in a confusing change of attitude, he abruptly said, "Enough! This is serious, Bach cha."

"Stop calling me Bach cha!"

"If you behave as a child you will be called one. Now! You will pleasure the maharajah if he so chooses. As he so wishes. You are to have another chance. Do not waste it. I can do no more."

He pushed me aside, leaving me with the broom, the wet rags, and dirty dishes.

To me, it appeared he fled—and left me with the ghost of the brush of his lips on my mouth and an ache where it should not be.

Chapter Six
Seraglio

Two eunuchs, Tweedledee and Tweedledum, one placid as a cow, the other grim with invisible lips, came for me where I slept in a kitchen alcove. *Do they order them by the yard?* asked my imp. One nudged his block of a chin, stumping after me like a squat footstool. My heart froze in my throat. They would take me back to the maharajah…he was right.

Madhuri, with a knowing look, made no protest but gave me a small nod and smile that reached her sad, drooping eyes.

As they herded me, I noted my surroundings this time, coming from the kitchens, even though opulent and staggering, seemed different from before, though I had only the sketchiest notion of the vast palace's outlay. After a half hour of parading through colonnaded corridors and gardens, and after the unlocking of an unusually stout, padlocked, barred entry, I heard the twittering of many birds as we entered an atrium beneath candy-bright canopies lofting in the torrid air. The twittering, which reached a crescendo when I stepped inside, ceased as the eyes of many women turned to watch me with bird-like interest.

Involuntarily, I scanned twenty-foot walls for an overhanging tree or a breach of some sort and saw none. Still, I was freer.

I've come up in the world.

The garden was alive with beautiful women of exotic plumage, chattering like a swell of gulls swooping over a sea of words.

The dungeon cell and palace kitchens had left my hair dull and dun and my skin mottled from steam, hands chapped, legs bruised, and bare feet calloused from the flagstones. No wonder these lovely creatures stared.

I recognized the place as a seraglio, or hareem, where women dwelt—some as young as twelve, I surmised, and achingly lovely as only the young can be. I moved hesitantly among them. They parted like the Red Sea, holding their fragile silks close. Older women eyed me with amusement or, if from rural areas, indifference. They'd seen worse, and been spared the poverty and premature aging by the lottery of their birth-beauty. A few followed with dead eyes from cold slabs of faces, and these bothered me the most, but most smiled, with lovely almond eyes of acceptance.

Then I saw little Asha.

Chapter Seven
Dangerous Games

Asha crouched beside me, my mascot, my champion, my friend as days passed. Asha's tittle-tattle wasn't malicious but more to school me. "Watch out for Chandrakanta," she whispered. "She will take your combs." Or, "Lakshmi will say you cheat at Parcheesi!"

That's tolerable. I will not be lingering, I vowed. Asha innocently explained which city lay outside the walls, and in what state, though it brought me no closer to remembering or being able to plan an effective escape.

And just how will you manage that? my imp sneered.

"Never mind. I'll find a way. Give me time. Let me think!"

I timed the eunuchs prowling the perimeter walls, playing up to one slightly more amenable, which was like wooing a stone. His eyes didn't flicker below my forehead.

Asha clung. Having her follow me was the last thing I wanted, fearing she'd draw attention, or wish to flee with me. There I was wrong but could not ken it then. Ferreting chances of escape was solitary work.

I studied her little monkey face, despairing as I repeated, "*Meri Hindi kucch khaas nahi hai!* My Hindi is bad!"

However, I learned, "Can you help me? *Kya aap meri madad hain?*" Not knowing with what. I needed help with everything.

Little Asha shyly told me her name meant either Wish, Hope, or Desire, possibly all three, and introduced me to the pitfalls of being enclosed with females all fighting over the same shiny object, mainly the maharajah's affection and—his seed.

I shuddered as I covertly studied them.

Most were supple, lovely, with huge slanted eyes as black as olives. Skin tones ranged from a russet peach, to hickory, to even a Chinese girl as pale as yellow roses.

I stood out like a hulking sunflower in a field of poppies, or so I imagined.

"From what country are you?" an older woman named Damayanti demanded.

"I—I don't remember."

Damayanti looked disenchanted.

Another poked my chest, giggling, "*Choochii!*" mimicking a large bosom with cupped hands. I crossed my arms. True, I was larger than most with their silk saris riding their jiggly little bumps.

"What *chudai khana* did they drag you from?"

I turned at the sound of spite in any language from a sloe-eyed lovely marred by a resentful face. Asha retorted something sharp. Apparently, being in a *chudai khana* was no place good.

"Oww! She pinched me," I hissed as the beauty swept by. "*Chudai khana?*" I queried.

"A...a place where men go to women...for... for..." and Asha made a universal gesture to indicate what took place there.

"Oh." I subsided. Then, hotly, "And what makes this place any different than a tarted-up brothel?"

Asha cocked her head. "Bro-thel?"

"Oh, never mind!" I said crossly, eyeing a monkey as it stole a date and scampered over the wall. I sighed. "So easy if one is a monkey."

A willowy girl little more than a child, with a jewel hanging from a diadem between her eyes, seeing my distress, spoke gently. "You will see the maharajah soon. *Chinta mat karo!* Do not worry! He will surely want you. You are…"

"Different?" I snapped, feeling like a proper grump. Oh, yes, very, I thought mutinously. I caught Asha's sweet face, usually half-hidden under her *ghoon ghat*, or her large earrings, or with a loop of ebon hair hiding the small burn scar, and uncharitably wondered what she was doing here. Little insignificant Asha.

"You want to leave? To escape?" Asha stared with dismay when I confided.

I sighed and surveyed the seraglio. "Indeed," I breathed. Yet a traitorous part of me saw the wretchedly handsome man from the kitchens everywhere from the corner of my eye, and felt the strength and warmth of his lips on mine when I least expected it.

****

The ladies of the seraglio occupied themselves with hairdressing, body painting, armfuls of bangles, spats, and endless games. Boredom manifested itself in gorging, fighting over stolen combs, cutthroat Parcheesi, *Ganifa,* or *Raja Rani*, where players using slips of paper guessed who was named.

Restless as a cricket on a spring night, I viewed the girls' roughhousing, longing to join them for once—just to run. *Kho Kho* meant chasing from one side to the other, where one hoydenish team, saris tucked up, knelt in a line cheering, "Go Aaditi!" Get up, Kushi!" "Don't be crybaby, Lakshmi!"

Or so I translated. I entered a simpler game called *gilli danda*, where girls ran with sticks flicking the *gilli* with what was apparently the *danda*, soon laughing as if I were one of them.

"We used to play that when we were children," Asha said wistful.

You still are a child. I studied Asha. *And you will forever stay that way until you are a toothless crone with no life beyond this gilded cage.* I vowed I would not be among them, running about with a stick to pass the hours.

Treacherously, between searches for weak, untended spots, my thoughts increasingly winged back to a dreary scullery—and the devastating gypsy and his strong, muscular arms, lithe body, and full lips pressing mine, wondering if I would ever behold him again. By accident, of course.

As I meandered, smiling prettily, innocently, I observed patterns and cliques, even attempting to enter a game like *Mah Jong* to listen to gossip, now I understood a few words, but it came to nothing. The rules were thick as sticky rice.

Surely, some had trysts or secret places, even outside the walls. But with whom? A sentry? Some eunuchs were handsome, and if one were lonely enough, an unlikely liaison might be compelling. They must have a way out.

Chapter Eight
Maharajah's Birthday

My chance came unexpectedly. At dawn, ladies abandoned games to feverishly apply cosmetics and try on parades of saris, jettisoning what they didn't like as if they were dust rags. Hot eyes gleamed, and even though my Hindi was on a child's level, I caught the spicy chitchat until eunuchs herded us off, keeping us close together in case any foolhardy male would attempt to sweep away with a bit of sari-clad crumpet.

The passage through the palace, with me gaping in wonder at the fairytale splendor, ivory and marble whatzits, jewels, tapestries, swags, fringes, mosaics, and ceramic urns taller than myself, eventually numbed, and we came onto a pavilion of billowing white silk canopies snapping in the humid breeze while shielding us from a cobalt hot sky.

"You will like this, Sa—ree! Wait and see," Asha chirped happily as we filed to floor cushions across from a dais with three throne-like chairs, one of them enormous.

I hid behind my *ghoon ghat*, the silky half-veil tossed over the face at the approach of a male not a close relative—which in my case was every male in the known universe.

Chapter Nine
Weight in Rubies

Across from us were ranged women in descending order according to their age, it appeared. They resembled Easter eggs in a gilded carton. "The wives!" Asha whispered, overloud. "And there's the maharani!"

I directed my eyes toward the dais. The young, enchanting maharani looked up once. Her elongated dark eyes were as opaque as stones.

The throne chair, big enough for an elephant, was still empty.

"He will come soon! He is a very great man!" Asha giggled behind her veil.

Not missing Asha's childish joke, I felt the earth move.

Asha nudged. "You may look now." I sucked in, shutting my eyes.

"Sar—eeee!"

"Okay, Asha!"

"Yes, he does affect us all. You see!"

Yes, I saw him, all right, in daylight. He had not improved. Six massive aides strained under a palanquin where he squatted cross-legged, looking like nothing more than a pumpkin beneath a turban, in turn, resembling a silk squash—a heap of slag inside a sumptuous tent circumnavigated by a sash that a row of waiting dancing girls could fit within. He sagged with sashes, badges, braid, and gilt, all held with an enameled brooch as big as my fist. A forest of white plumes swayed above his massive head, fastened with another jeweled trinket surmounting the turban like the top of a gilded teapot.

The supreme being of all Rajasthan heaved to his feet, aided by two enormous eunuchs, and stumped up to the dais. I watched in suspense as they, with trembling limbs, lowered him to the throne.

Eyes lost between rolls of fat like slabs of butter, the maharajah surveyed his fawners, even from my humble place, I imagined waves of perfumed heat as from a midden on a hot India summer day.

I softened. Poor man, to be so disgusting.

Even then, his pudgy hand, clotted with rings, pawed a platter of sweets the size of a small table, blindly stuffing in the entire handful as he raked the crowd with a gaze of serene malevolence.

I shivered despite the humidity as anthracite eyes slowly rolled over the lovelies, each more lithesome than the other, all arrayed in front of him like more sweets.

Asha sighed, contented. "It is good to be part of the hareem. Otherwise, I would miss this." She waved her tiny hand. I struck it down. "Don't! You will be noticed."

"But I…?"Asha opened her lips, astonished. "But that is why we are here!" I did not catch the rest. Checked by the petal smoothness of Asha's right cheek and the way her lips glistened as if smeared with honey, I looked from her to the maharajah.

Oh, the poor thing. Most assuredly, this monstrous tub of lard will want her even with her scar, eventually.

I would almost take her place. The maharajah's mouth enveloped a glob of something yellow and sucked his fingers.

Maybe not.

Even the maharani cast a sour sideways glance.

The pumpkin-like head pivoted. His eyes moved on, then rolled greasily back and, as marbles clicking at a roulette table, dropped and stared straight at me.

I shivered, drawing the whisper of silk more across my face and ducking behind little Asha, no easy thing.

"What are we doing here?" I whispered faintly.

"Oh!" Asha chattered happily, explaining while I sorted through my sad vocabulary.

Anniversary? Celebration?

"Day of birth," the child elaborated. "The maharajah's birthday! We weigh him! The maharajah is worth his weight in pearls. Or diamonds!" She clapped tiny hands. "This year, rubies! Oh! How lovely it will be!"

The small one blushed and nudged me, and my world forever changed. "The rajah is here!"

I squinted, vexed that I was growing slightly nearsighted, and expecting a younger but still grossly heavy version as overindulged as the birthday boy.

Instead, my gypsy navigated the throng like a sleek yacht parting the seas. As filtered sun hit his arresting face, his walnut complexion changed to the russet of a ripe peach.

I scowled.

He was at once beautiful and masculine, his beard and mustache trimmed in a pattern unbecoming in the West, full lips pressed forbiddingly between. His eyes, darkly gleaming as obsidian, were heavy, hooded, drooping at the corners—"bedroom eyes" in some quarters.

I watched the striking figure stride, graceful as a jungle panther, to the dais. An iridescent peacock feather, fastened by a large pearl surrounded by emeralds, was the only color he wore. It swayed atop a satin turban. A wide pearl choker clasped his neck. More pearls swagged down his broad chest. Again, the simplicity of white against white was perfection.

I started, looking down at Asha's small hand, shaking me.

"The maharajah's brother! Next in line—his favorite. Mine too!"

Oh, yes, I knew him well. He who was last seen skulking around the scullery, groping any women he fancied. Ohh! Drat!

Miserably, I studied the man as he neared the dais. I despised him.

Oh, really? Is that why you keep watching? Is that why you crane your neck so?

"Oh, do shut up!" I spoke aloud.

Asha regarded me oddly. "Sar-eee. I do not understand."

"Neither do I."

I squeezed Asha's hand. "I meant nothing." It did not stop me peeking through the *ghoon ghat*, however.

The carnal lines of the full lips that had brushed my own were now pressed as if disavowing the spectacle as he bowed slightly to both the maharajah and the maharani.

I tore my gaze away and watched the maharajah dig a finger in his ear. I winced and quickly switched back to the prince—or whatever the Hades he was called—as he effortlessly composed himself on a throne slightly below the maharajah's, one pointed slipper in front, presenting an elegant line. The audience rippled with admiration.

Mimicking Asha's excitement, I turned. Murmurs rose, and with one intake of breath, the throng craned at the creaking groan of cartwheels.

The maharajah's small eyes slanted impatiently sideways at four men laboring to haul a garlanded cart toting a huge brass balance scale like one in a butcher shop, if ten times larger. From a sturdy post, large flat pans swung wildly, clanging, from thick metal chains. *What on God's green earth...?*

I watched, mystified, as the maharajah ponderously rose in quiveringly gelatinous stages, tottering in thunderous steps as aides, not without peril, lowered his immense bottom onto one of the pans.

Chains creaked. The pan with the maharajah clanked to the floor, while the other shot up. Another cart groaned up, hauling five bulging velvet bags as large as hundred-pound rice sacks.

Asha clapped her hands. Excited murmurs rose. I watched, perplexed, as bearers shoveled from the bags rattling heaps of glittering stones. Pink, violet, blood-red to almost black-garnet, faceted or smooth as quail eggs, the scarlet pebbles were tipped onto the empty balance while the maharajah jerkily rose inch by inch with each shovelful of jewels.

"Sa—reee, look!"

I assessed not one stone of this fiery pile was less than five carats.

As the stones clattered higher and higher, the maharajah yawned...and as the saucers balanced, quivering under the strain, they added one last ruby. The balance swayed and settled.

"You see!" Asha timidly patted me.

More than you think, child.

The audience applauded.

The maharajah's perilous way back to his throne was difficult to watch.

The murmuring crowd groaned with satisfaction. After more ceremony, and after the dancing girls danced and the rest of the gifts were bestowed, everyone prepared to leave.

"Come, before the sweets are demolished!" Indeed. Spectators flooded discreetly to the food pavilions.

Asha insinuated her tiny body through the restrained stampede to a sumptuous array of food like a needle through cloth. A bangle with tiny bells caught my veil, pulling it aside. As I looked back, automatically smiling forgiveness, my gaze caught on the wretchedly handsome rajah—or prince or whatever he was.

Flustered, I lost Asha but found her plastered to a buffet, inhaling hot breads, curries, and sweets. I threw both appetite and waistline to the fates, despite realizing it was vital on some important but vague level that I remain reasonably attractive. To Hades with that!

Drowning disquiet, I selected coconut dumplings that looked like rows of tiny yellow turbans, with the unlovely name of *modak*. Plucking two *modak*, I moved on to towers of cherry-bright balls of *gulab jamun*, reluctantly turning to plainer trays of *pani pori*.

I need meat. Seraglio fare leaned heavily to sweets, oily fried goods, rich vegetable curries, squares of potato dumplings, and peas. I moved on to spicy *kachori* balls, *djhal muri* and *dahi vada* with yoghurt sauce, and tureens of pork *vindaloo* and duck. Nibbling as I grazed, I felt the eyes of the "sisters of the veil" amazed and disapproving. Lovely! Grimacing a smile, I mugged while gulping a lentil ball.

"Always did have a robust appetite," I mumbled, stuffing another pearly globe of sweet *sohan papdi* in my mouth…and froze.

I revolved, taking in the vast pavilion.

What in the Sam Hill am I doing?

You are stuffing your mouth, my imp suggested helpfully.

I dropped the other pearly globe, smashing it underfoot in my heedless scanning of the crowd.

Stupid, stupid! There may be no other time! Everyone is fixed on food and gossip. No one will notice! Go—Go!

I choked down another *sohan papdi* and pulled at my veil, hiding my telltale hair. The crowd was lulled and dulled by food and that peculiar weighing ceremony, yet opportunity fled like a thief. Knotting a bag made out of the hem of my sari, I tossed in mostly breads, recognizing from somewhere in my prudent past that it was needful to be prepared. A shame to leave so many sticky treats—I eyed the pork *vindaloo*. Aware of a few noticing my odd behavior, I stopped…

The crowd perversely pressed closer. I forced my way through, craning for the nearest exit, already planning my escape.

I would nip across greenswards, hide in foliage, and sneak past sentries until I stumbled on an unguarded gate. I looked up at the freedom of the sky, now a water coloring of evening flowing into India's inky darkness. *Soon,* I promised, *I can easily melt into India's shambolic street scene. Let the devil take the hindmost. There, I'll surely figure out who the Hades I am; recognize someone. Something!*

In my agony to be gone, seconds dragged like an errant child yanking my skirts as I swam, like a fish upstream, through the chattering throng massed about the tables.

There—ahead, past that knot of elderly aunties. I could taste freedom.

"Sar-eeee?"

I heard my name with the shock of ice down my neck.

"You don't need to take food!" Asha looked reproving. It would have been comical on one so young if I weren't so distracted. "What are you doing? They will feed you!"

The broad open arch just ahead. I can almost touch the wall hanging... Asha raced alongside, looking back, worried. "Sar-ree! What is wrong?"

I studied the innocent with the schoolmarm frown. Beyond Asha, I saw the rajah staring blank-faced at me, and a sentry forcing his way through the crowd. "Asha! Let go!" I hissed. The sentry knocked the aunties aside. I screamed inwardly, "Let go, you wretched girl!"

You are creating quite a little drama, nagged my imp.

Giving an exasperated yank, I edged outside. "Asha!" I looked at her helplessly.

More turbans bobbed toward us, cutting through the crowd.

I pulled her away when guards, looking back for instructions, finally surrounded us.

"Go, Asha." I looked meaningfully at the guards. "You'd best go."

So much for discretion. Haven't thought this out, have you? You will now, my girl, I heard my imp nag.

"But—Sar-eee!" Asha reluctantly backed up an inch, refusing to abandon me even then.

****

On the dais, the maharajah stared sullenly at the disturbed mob. His birthday was spoiled. What was this outrageous disturbance? All eyes should be on him.

The maharani wasn't certain of the cause, but the pale, unattractive foreign girl was in distress, and her esteemed husband was about to hurl thunder and lightning her way. So far he hadn't seen the cause of the ripples.

She smiled. Looking in a calculating way at her husband, the maharani gestured to the servants to bring the next course.

The maharajah's understanding had almost arrived as to what was occurring—when arrived in front of him a steaming plate of honey-roasted duck. Fanning herself, the maharani looked on, amused, watching her husband tuck in. It wasn't often she got her own back.

Her brother-in-law shared a quiet smile. She nodded at Sary. He bowed from the waist and gestured. The guards, noting the rajah's careless wave, released Sary, stiff with uncertainty.

****

Deep in the seraglio, a discreet note on foolscap, penned in block print in black print, affixed with a splotch of red wax, lay on my pillow when we all returned, bedraggled and abounding with gossip and excitement of the day. It advised: *Is this what you seek?*

Next time will not be so agreeable. Take heed of your actions.

I paced like a caged tiger. Time stretched like a scarf knitted by inexpert knitters, not knowing quite when to quit. Little did I guess my days were to become even more knotted and incomprehensible.

Chapter Ten
Broken-Winged Butterfly

They came as before, amid the hareem's intense speculation, old Padmavati and her handmaidens. A cold snake of bitterness coiled deep in my belly. In the past weeks I had been dulled by the sameness of stodgy fare, gossip, routine, and spiteful childlike squabbles over trifles, high drama here but irksome for me yet as I endlessly stalked the perimeter without seeming to, trying to spy out any breach. The seraglio or hareem provided an exquisite view of a large artificial lake to one end, through sheltered colonnades where one strolled in cooling breezes, a respite from the heat. Some of the ladies even swam or waded, affording me also an artificial sense of freedom, tantalizing and adding to my frustration.

So now I foolishly quarreled with Padmavati, more to be irritating than for any other reason. "Why me? No one raves about my beauty. I am not young and nubile as most! I have no special skills." I felt my face grow red over what some of those special skills involved.

After the first startled look, since she knew no English, she decided I was touched. "I don't want to be made pretty!" I raged on. "Your beautifying routines put witches' covens to shame!" I knocked a few pots off the table and stomped away to be returned by a eunuch to a stoic Padmavati with a blank expression on her face. I sat bolt upright with a grim expression and let them pommel me. I would not make it easy.

Smoothing turmeric paste, called *uptan*, on their skin, they washed it off, leaving their flesh blooming with the peachy glow of a nectarine. They warmed coconut wax, rubbing it in their thick black hair, and combed until a gleaming satin shawl hung to their waist, then sat in the sun.

I had fought those attempts to beautify me. The same treatments would leave my face yellow and my hair a greasy dun hanging in pathetic strings. Now I wished I had let them.

High above, the maharani observed me from a cloistered walk. I thought she cast a sympathetic eye before moving on. I stood up abruptly, stung by that look, knocking over the cosmetic tray, sending bright powders and paints flying, hauled back by Padmavati's steely fingers, and plunked on the stool—repeatedly, until the elder summoned the eunuch, who placed hands like sandbags on my shoulders.

I clenched my mouth, twisting my face until Padmavati threatened with a wicked-looking hairbrush. *"Chinta mat karo!"*

"You tell me not to worry!" I had learned some halting Hindi and now looked daggers at the older woman.

Choice seems to be a luxury, my imp prodded as the eunuch eyed me speculatively. Holding me fast while I clenched my jaw, they rimmed my eyes again with thick kohl until I saw a green-eyed cat staring back from the mirror. They crimsoned my mouth and anointed knees, ears, and crooks of my elbows with jasmine. I felt lightheaded, as if the pungent fragrance soaked up all the oxygen.

"Mujhey samajh mein nahi aataa?"

"I do not understand," I pleaded. "Please do not take me back to that loathsome creature you hold in such…" I floundered. "Such dumbfounding esteem."

I was near screaming as they floated over me another filmy sari, gossamer as dragonfly wings, expertly winding it about my trembling body.

Why not a winding sheet and let me die?

I stared at the copper mirror. The wide-eyed face looking back was as wavery green as I felt inside.

I smiled grimly. *Perhaps the maharajah will suffocate from the overpowering reek of my perfume…* And I picked up a small sharp fruit knife.

Looking down at the rest of me, I though what a pity it was, to waste all this finery. Gilt threads wove through diaphanous pink silk, and gold embroidery embellished a hem studded with rubies, pink pearls, and crystals that danced about my ankles.

I gasped—ashamed I should think so well of myself.

Padmavati casting a dark warning eye as though to say, "Don't move!" and daubed the red dot between my dark painted brows.

This is where I began. Tarted up, like a Christmas goose. I had gained nothing.

Even so, I shrank when they brought out henna and traced designs on my hands—like they would for a bride. Padmavati fitted a pearl choker on me from chin to breastbone. "Pearls before swine" had never had so much meaning.

Assessing me as if I were furniture they contemplated buying, they nodded, tucking in stray hairs, re-crimsoning lip paint I'd bitten off, and dabbing more perfumed oil. Padmavati, shaking her head, removed the fruit knife from my nerveless fingers.

I stood, stoic, while the seraglio drifted by ogling, assessing, offering unwished for advice as they transformed me to semi-goddess.

"Be compliant," they whispered shyly.

"Don't look at him…close your eyes," a soft voice offered with a hint of laughter.

"Raise your hips—the baby will take!" An older inmate cackled in my ear.

I swiveled as a heartbreakingly lovely girl tapped my shoulder. "But you are so old! The maharajah will never want you!" Genuinely concerned.

"I'm only twenty-six!" *Am I?*

"Your hair is yellow like dead grass!" This from a woman I thought was called Ravinder, who cheated me at the game of *dehla pakad*.

Asha helpfully translated. I scarcely heard. I wanted to sink like rain into sun-cracked earth.

I fixated on the ornamental knife on a copper tray holding fruit, stealing it back. I did not wish to leave this earth, yet I knew equally well I'd never again let the maharajah touch me. One way or another, my future was cast.

The other women receded. Even little Asha seemed to suppose I was untouchable and therefore hazardous in some unspoken manner.

As the afternoon wore on and I sweltered under the canopy, under the weight of jewels and heavy makeup, my fear gave way to tedium.

They brought me *naan* and *chai*. I couldn't eat. I would dearly regret that later.

By the sun, it was nearly four.
Still no one came.

Chapter Eleven
Secret Tunnels

Fear gave way to annoyance when from the edge of my veil I noted a young woman sidle up as if she did not wish to attract attention. Preeta idly arranged an ornamental pin in her sleek hair, dropping it as if by accident at my feet.

Irritably, I tucked in my toes.

"You wish to leave, Saree?" Preeta hissed, as she rose from her crouch, watching me closely with her curious, almost yellow eyes. "To escape?" She continued after checking the hareem. "I see you do. I am your friend. I wish to help. Meet me at the big fountain." She slanted her yellow eyes to a water feature across the way, fronting one of the twenty-foot walls.

"Behind the shell," she whispered. "Before they come for you. Hurry." Preeta receded in the mingle of females. "I hear them coming," she hissed, jabbing at the large scallop shell rearing up ten feet, across the vast seraglio, from which water cascaded into a reflecting pool filled with lotus. The pool's wide rim was a popular gossiping spot. Many times, I rested there fanning and planning escape. It would be even more private behind the enormous shell, I supposed, but to what purpose? *Is there a doorway leading outside?* my imp sneered.

Still, I sat frozen.

Preeta, without another glance but giving a slight shrug, moved off in a leisurely way, as if she had never halted, but heading toward the shell.

Padmavati and her "assassins" were nowhere. Women settling, their gossip now a drowsy drone as if boring even themselves, left cards and games scattered for servants to clear, among demolished sweets, languidly drifting to their quarters.

I waited overlong. *They will be here any second. Where is she?* Then I spied Preeta's tall, red-veiled head. I shot up and skirted the mass, suddenly desperate, keeping the red veil in view as a lifeline in a sea of women.

I saw Asha in passing and fiercely shook my head. *Can't worry about her now, at least until I see what Preeta offers.* I gathered my sari, kept my head down, and edged behind a row of palms in planters to the scallop shell.

****

Dusk swept up the last bit of daylight, dumping it beyond the walls, as I nipped behind the shell's cool, damp shelter smelling of lime and faint mildew. Black and green mottled the unfinished backside. Carpeted in wet moss, it was home to thumb-size toads that hopped about my feet and lizards that darted into crevices. Clammy, but not unpleasant. The air was deliciously cool. Water pipes ran from the fountain's back to the wall.

Preeta perched on one such pipe, lighting a cigarette from an ornate lighter—forbidden. I hungered for the thing. Another surprise, eyeing a litter of water-soaked stubs. It wasn't the first time she'd tarried here.

"I cannot hide here forever!" I hadn't realized how high my hopes had soared.

Preeta's unusual eyes—dark-ringed pale amber irises blackly rimmed with kohl—seemed ghostly in her olive face, but her mouth was large, sensuous, and alive. Preeta always gave me the shivers as she narrowed those yellow eyes assessing me from afar, running her tongue over full lips, or when I turned quickly to find her just staring at me.

I shivered now.

"How can you help? Are you—" I cut off my questions, nervous. Time would be better spent planning a battle of wits. I peered outside. *Am I missed?*

Preeta narrowed those cat's eyes, reassessing. "You wish to escape? To leave? I can help, *chut marike!*" Preeta spoke flatly.

She just called you an idiot, said the little voice inside me.

"Well, aren't I?" I answered imp.

Preeta rose, grinding out the rolled cigarette and showing sharp white teeth in what I assumed was a reassuring smile.

"Come—come! *Jaldi karo! Mere saath aaeeyé!*"

"Where?" I looked about with sinking heart. Preeta had gone as crazy as the rest of them.

She pointed down. All I saw was a snarl of pipe, some as thick as my waist, and crusty valves, thrusting from the shell into an opening in the wall after crossing the three-foot gap in which we stood. "I will lead you. You want to leave the palace? Yes?"

I heard commotion. Whether over me or a bad dice call, who knew?

I ducked back. In for a penny, in for a pound.

"Yes. Sure. Show me," I said, turning my mouth down in skepticism. What could it hurt? Let them search for me a few more minutes, I thought mutinously.

Preeta showed pointed teeth and crouched, prying at a small hatch through which the pipes ran. "Quickly then, my friend. You put me in danger," she accused. "We leave from here. I do often." She preened then as if licking herself and, with wiry strength, grabbed my arm, dragging me down. "*Jaldi karo!* Hurry. Someone might come!"

I caught a whiff of mildew as she yanked the hatch loose. It was old wood, with the hole for the fat pipe running through it and leaving a space of about eighteen inches to wiggle past.

I looked aghast. Preeta must have been driven mad by the seraglio; she bent and wriggled through the small opening.

If they find me missing...?
Dear God.
Do I have choice?
No.

With a glance back, as if seeing the palace grounds for the last time, I felt my heart flutter like a bird with its cage left open, then hunkered and stuck my head in the hole.

Looking back, Preeta showed white teeth again. "If the snake sleeps, the small birds may hop freely about to see their lovers." I shivered in the cool damp and glared. "What game do you play? Lovers? I have no lover." I scooted back.

"Wait!" Preeta's yellow eyes narrowed. "Don't! Yes, very dangerous for me too!"

"It's too small—I cannot possibly…"

Preeta's head disappeared, followed by her rump, and then all I saw were the soles of her feet. A hand reached back, accompanied with a muffled command: "Come, *chut marike!*"

Crawling on my expensive fragile silk sari, I wriggled through, feeling a momentary pang. The passage opened into a sort of domed tunnel of rough concrete and bricks. Preeta could stand almost full height. I needed to crouch.

"Close the door!" Preeta hissed back.

I did.

Adequate for Preeta's slim build, for me the tunnel, webbed and musty, three feet wide and perhaps two feet or so higher, half-filled with both clay and copper pipes, was a squeeze. I had to either straddle the water ducts or skirt the wall with my head at a hangman's angle.

"It is how we do it. We who have lovers." The tunnel muffled Preeta's silky laughter. "We who dare!"

"Of course, this many lonely, loveless females would find a way," I muttered, vindicated.

My spirits rose.

"But where does it go? *Jaldi karo?*" I tried.

"Outside, of course. To paradise!" That silken laugh again, packed with innuendo.

Picking up courage like a discarded garment, I grinned. "Show me!"

I was a—what had Preeta called me? A *chut marike?* I supposed I was an idiot. *Better an idiot than dead or wishing to be…* I chuckled as I thought of the maharajah's rage.

From her ornate lighter, Preeta fired a fat candle,

obviously from the kitchens. Let the devil answer.

"Preeta? But where, outside?"

"I told you! Our lovers. Hopeful I am..." She spoke in English, but irritably.

"I have no lover!" I grumbled.

"Never fear, Sa-ree! I mean this leads to *our* lovers. You, I do not know."

I scowled at Preeta's back, a bobbling shadow, one used to this crawlway, while I banged my head on a ceiling snarled with cocoons of dried insects spanning unknown decades.

Dead palmetto beetles scrunched underfoot, and glossy live ones as large as my palm scuttled overhead. I did not flinch. Somewhere, beyond memory, I had seen far worse. Wondering why the many webs, if this tunnel was so trafficked, I risked calling, "How far?"

"I myself go as far as the tiger cages, Sa-ree. The tigers' yowling masks our pleasure—my lover's and mine. Now come!" she scolded. "I do not waste time idly, you see!"

A slow dripping formed a strange soup beneath me. Detritus coated my hems. My gold slippers became sodden and useless. Gradually, though, the tunnel dried.

Passing openings dwindling in the dark like wormholes, I wondered who was the first desperate soul to travel to freedom this way, feeling a pang when rough walls caught my exquisite veil and I heard the first tear. I savagely ripped it off, along with the jeweled pins and the weighty neckpieces. After second thought, I tucked them in my sari. No sense leaving bread crumbs. The stones were priceless. I could sell or barter them.

With those expectant thoughts, I blinked, after

what seemed like endless crawling and ducking, bumping into Preeta around a hard turn, where the tunnel took on a different character. Older. Only one corroded pipe. The other snaked off down one of the side tunnels.

Preeta halted. "There. The tiger pen." She thrust the candle where a pipe connected in a T formation though another hatch.

Must be under or even in the zoo. Deadened tiger yowls and basso trumpeting sounded.

Preeta shot a bolt and wedged the hatch open. "Through there!"

The candle guttered alarmingly in a breeze smelling of sewage, cat pee, and moldy straw.

"Yes, it is smelly, is it not?" Preeta giggled softly.

"Preeta! Is it safe?"

"If one is quick, there is a place to wriggle past the tigers. I will leave you now," and she handed the candle over.

Her teeth shone in the tarnished light filtering from outside. I glimpsed dead grasses and stained cement as she waved vaguely to her left down the tunnel, hissing, "That way. Keep going. You will be nicely surprised, but if you are caught and tortured, you know nothing. Remember your friend who tried to help you!"

I heard the guttural call of tigers and a pong that suggested caged beasts. "Preeta! You are mad. Come back!"

"Shhh. Only a short way, Sar-ree!" Preeta scorned. "By the time tigers see me, I will be gone. There is a place I crawl under and be near…" She stopped. "Never mind who." She giggled and vanished in a snatch of yellow silk, it too disappearing to the louder snarl of tigers, leaving me braced for her screams.

True enough, she ran, crouched, in a ditch, with the big cats lazily fanning tails and only arousing when Preeta rolled under a fence. There was a dip where bars were embedded, too small for the beasts but large enough for Preeta to squeeze under.

Alone in the dark, I sank against the wall, fanning the candle, holding my breath as the stub guttered. Having it go out did not bear thinking about. Oh, dear God! I recalled the wormholes leading off from the main tunnel. *Probably can't find your way back in the dark,* whispered my imp.

I checked the candle, biting my lip. "Damnation! I should have demanded how far." *I wonder if she even knows,* my imp commented, with a harrumph.

Okay, I bargained, either follow Preeta, mentally judging a race against a tiger and wishing the zoo lay outside the wall—or feel your way back to the scallop shell.

The candle's light leaked no farther than my nose. Pitch blackness filled the tunnel from the zoo hatch forward.

Wait until Preeta returns from her rendezvous, the imp suggested.

I briefly wondered with whom. Just eunuchs? Could it be? They too were prisoners, of a different sort. *Oh, stop! You're just delaying things!*

Vexed with indecision, I sighed and again held my breath as the tiny flame struggled. "Besides, there were no promises Preeta would return this way!" I told myself. "I could sit here until doomsday, waiting. Move!" Bent over, I hastened in the direction Preeta had vowed would lead to freedom of the streets.

****

Twenty minutes—or an hour—later, I lost direction as the tunnel took random turns. I had tried to ignore more black mouths leading off with newer pipe connections, or the dwindling height of the candle stub as, ahead of me, the tunnel greedily swallowed my flickering light.

"Eughh!" I looked down at my wet knees. I now crawled through a quagmire with a fishy reek.

I passed under spreading rings of mildew with a slow *drip-drop*, explaining it. Ahead, black mold hung in waving curtains. "What am I under?" I breathed, searching the ceiling. For an instant, I imagined water crashing through, flooding the tunnel.

Holding my breath, shielding my candle from the wet, I swatted the sooty strands aside, at the same time feeling my hair stringed with something greasy. "Ughhhh! Wish the bloody maharajah could see me now!" I was whistling in the dark and knew it.

My knees wore holes in the fragile silk, and my veil was long lost. I began laughing in the growing dark.

"Perhaps even such as he would be off-put."

Talking to yourself now, is that it? Are we sure this exits the palace? It doesn't seem too promising at the moment. Perhaps it pops up in another tiger pen? Or worse? What exactly are we showing them, eh, my imp of doubt carped. *How to meander lost through moldy tunnels?*

"Oh, do shut up!" My breath blew out like a bellows—and so did the candle.

"Oh, no. No!" The candle flared once, went out, and something crawled across my face. I swatted my cheek, coming away with decayed vegetation, but ignored that, aware I could see my hands!

The next instant, I squinted at a beam of light spearing through a crack in the ceiling. Oh, dear Lord! So close! I touched the bright patch the size of my thumb. At least that. The swampy-ness dwindled to damp, and fustiness resumed, though the fish smell, puzzlingly, grew stronger as the tunnel slanted slightly up.

I followed the dim glow. Perversely, the ceiling lowered. When crouching became uncomfortable, I elbowed on my stomach.

Committed, now, girl. No way back, the imp nagged.

Hallelujah. Filtered light just ahead…greenish light.

I crawled faster. "It has to be outside!" I breathed. "Soon I will be free! Come hell or high water," I vowed prophetically, "I will be free!" As I neared, I realized, with a sickening feeling in the pit of my stomach, the glow came through a flimsy-looking grate hung with dried scum. Reaching out, I gripped the barrier, crying, "No!" On inspection, it appeared old. Probably brittle. I peered between segmented reeds and bamboo shoots outside, spying daylight and tops of palms.

I eyed the grate balefully. I hated it—shook it. The setting was damp. I could scratch the perimeter with my fingernails. "I'll be out in seconds." I laughed crazily, keeping the reeds and an early twilight tantalizingly in sight, I sat up, then wedged my knees behind me to lie prone, pulling and pushing at the grille, soon finding I had no real advantage and it was more secure than I first hoped.

Thirsty and hot, beating the heel of my hand against the metal more in frustration than hope, my nose detected unseen water as from a stagnant pond. I laid my head on my hand.

"The grille seems so rotten, and Lord, I'm thirsty." But the grid held fast. Scratching at the dried scum, I found each strand was braided brass in place of iron.

I checked for breaks, finding none. I pressed my cheek; squinting beyond the thicket of segmented canes that blocked my view, save for a ragged slice of sky turned ominously black. It smelt like rain. I licked my lips.

A bamboo stalk lay bleached and dead just beyond. With my fingertips, I tediously dragged it through, digging the tough broken end at the bottom where the grill was set in mortar. A poor digging tool but all I had.

After a half hour, the grille made a tiny *chuffing* as I shoved it experimentally. It did move a fraction. Just a little? Maybe. I was frustrated and hot, but the wall seemed crumbly as cheese where I had been digging at the bottom.

I changed to the right side, poking, gouging, and wriggling the woven metal until sweat dripped to join the miasma beneath me. My hands were slick. The reed kept slipping. I was aware, too, that the light was dimmer, the air heavier, and I hoped it wasn't India's infamous monsoon gearing up. Was it the season? The water level seemed inches below where I lay.

I was definitely hungry, and even thirstier. I had only nibbled at a plum before this mad undertaking a hundred years ago, too agitated to eat, before the wretched Preeta approached.

Haven't exactly planned this out, have you? You

could be having tiffin and tea and wallowing in pillows, back in the seraglio.

"Or fighting off the beast," I snarled at my irritating imp.

Blocking renegade thoughts, I squinted past the reeds before the light failed completely. I could be anywhere, even outside, as Preeta had promised, though with a sinking heart I grasped that I had only her word and frantically renewed gouging before panic drained me.

They've searched by now. I wondered about Preeta, too. *Is she back? Professing ignorance of where I might be? Or confessing her own innocence?*

"I saw Sary go behind the scallop shell…"

But then she could not use the way again.

I halted, hearing an alien sound. A tiny splash.

I waited. Dare I call? Anybody there? A worker? But I detected only a slow *drip-drop* echo behind me.

I calculated. "We walked the tunnel forty-five minutes, no more than an hour. After Preeta left, I crawled another half hour, maybe, and then I have pried this blasted grate at least an eternity—no more than three hours, all told; that would put it around seven, yet twilight for hours…"

A wave of dizziness dropped me low.

"I'll lay my head on my arm, off the mud. Just a while. It's the air. Thick and moldy…"

Just a moment…afterward, I'll…

Chapter Twelve
Primitive Beasts

I awoke with my arm numb, outstretched under my head, and one hand still gripping the grate.

Where am I? I muzzily looked about. I checked the grate. Still the same. How could I be so gullible? Yet daylight. How could that be? Is it tomorrow? The light had an early-morning feel. I moistened cracked lips. Goosebumps prickled my arms despite the clammy heat. I looked back into the dark.

"Preeta's the only one who knows I'm here."

If she didn't think you escaped!

"Be quiet!" I screamed at my imp. The sound reverberated and died.

Feeling pitchforks of hunger, thirst, and loathing, I searched the tunnel, picturing myself crawling blind for days through the dripping labyrinth, down one dead end to another, hopelessly lost.

To die down here alone? With no marker…no mourners?

"Don't be silly. Someone will hear me!"

Outside, wind rustled the segmented reeds, the sound like bones clacking against each other, accompanied now by an odd wet snuffling and burbling. I listened hard.

Pigs? The smell of pigs was inescapable, yet this odor was definitely briny.

Suddenly, I did not wish to make any noise.

Yet somehow I recognized the old Sary, whoever she was, and knew she would not give up.

Savagely, mindlessly, I renewed digging from my cramped position, alternately tugging and pushing. "Confound you! Move!" Just as I spoke with little hope, the wall beside the bottom left corner abruptly crumbled into brittle chunks. I stared at the tiny breech, too small to get my hand through.

I renewed gouging and halted.

Something low—a sound—a voice or a gargled cough. Close by. The sound wasn't quite human.

"Hello-oooo?" I tried.

A *squish-splash* answered, as if something heavy dropped into a body of water.

I prepared to call again.

The sound stuck in my throat.

From time to time, I imagined I heard a burbling, sometimes, farther off.

Then a miniature tide splashed weed-flecked water through the grille. Even parched I couldn't bring myself to test it. It had a brackish odor foul to the nose. However, the wave shoved a floating reed aside, verifying the pond was inches below the tunnel level, also affording a bigger slice of outside world. Beyond, an iridescent dragonfly flitted and sipped; farther off, a water-strider skimmed the surface.

The dragonfly rose lazily to another patch of brownish water. The dragonfly's freedom made me viciously lever the tough cane, holding my breath to ward off a soup of fish stench mixed with rotted weeds arising from the muck stirred by the loosening base.

Of a sudden, the air thickened.

I could not have cut the heaviness with an ax—between swampy-ness and the tunnel's fusty odor; while the outside heated the gumbo, I was close to swooning.

I rested, sucking in rank air like soup through a tea towel. Between slowing my breathing and turning my head, I continued digging mushy mortar, mindlessly cursing, "Like they built the bloody Taj Mahal down here!"

The grille remained unyielding.

Sucking bloodied fingers, mindlessly pulling and pushing, I thought it was hours later the grate caved outward, flattening the black-ringed canes with a lazy splash. Nothing dramatic to herald such an auspicious occasion. Suddenly I chilled with the realization that if I had not reached the tough broken reed, I'd still be…here.

Sweat dripping in my eyes, I stared out, stupefied. Wild to be free, I impulsively stuck my head out, resting my cheek on murky water. Then I wiggled my shoulders through and, by scrunching them, managed an arm through.

I didn't care what lay beyond as long as I could see city streets and people on the other side.

Half out…all but my hips…just past these last reeds… I stretched my arm as far as I could, pushing and grasping for anything solid—more reeds, floating weeds… Resting, I peered through the cane to get my bearings, and—stared straight into a crocodile's dead yellow eyes—or some godforsaken beast.

"Oh, my sweet Lord!" I breathed. I was frozen, scared to move for fear of alerting the beast, yet I was well in its glassy immovable stare. I galvanized when one eyelid slowly blinked from the bottom of its eye socket, and tried to wiggle back.

A crocodile.

Yet it wasn't.

Straight out of hell, whatever it was.

A reptile with a long sword-like snout malformed in some hideous way.

Even in shock I recognized it was nothing like crocodiles or alligators from childhood books. It still floated, unmoving, with the rise and fall of the water. Then it slowly lifted one clawed foot on stumpy, back-bended legs.

Frantically I scootched back, but my shoulder stuck. One arm, still outstretched, lay two inches from the thing's long wavy snout.

I willed myself into the tunnel, but I couldn't avoid those dead, unblinking marbles, eyes without pity, close set beside that razor-thin, wavery snout studded with needle teeth. Then the curving jaws, holding more teeth than seemed possible, lazily split wide, showing a pale pink throat.

Black slits in the glassy yellow marbles still stonily regarded me. Afraid to leave the unblinking scrutiny, I risked scanning a stonewall on the far side and making a decision which I would never have made if I'd thought about it. I thrust forward—or tried to. I had no heart to wait it out. I had no food or potable water, and I sensed the thing had the primitive patience of eons.

The trouble was that it was two feet away and the wall wasn't.

If I can just…

The thing still inspected me with its primal brain. I could feel the damp chuffing of clammy breath on my face now. Had it moved?

Prehistoric gears tediously meshed, as if the thing was asleep with its eyes open.

Then the other padded foot lifted.

"Get away!" I screamed, slapping my one arm, snatching it back as long jaws snapped an inch away from my fingers.

The creature lowered itself. Its snout sank below water. It made that odd burbling I'd heard before.

I looked for a rock, at the broken reed I still held—anything. It was worse not seeing the thing. Its long head rose again. It had drifted sideways. Then it paddled toward me on footstool legs. Moving faster, it crushed the last straggle of reed. I smelt a fishy wave and felt a splash of thick saliva on my cheek.

One-handed, I pushed hard at its snout and, with a last tear of what was my sari, scraping hips and legs, I skinned free, desperately pitching sideways at the same time; the beast swerved, snapping long scissor-like jaws, hissing, lashing a ridged, fleshy tail. *Smack!* Water flew.

Scrambling now, all legs and arms, slip-sliding on bottom slime, tangling with stalks, I ripped through reeds, splashing to mucky shallows, barely staying ahead of the monster, which was moving swiftly once it made up its mind. The croc-thing flipped a bulbous body through the water shockingly fast for its weight and short legs, hurling waves of muck, smashing more reeds in its delayed zeal to get at me.

The pond sloped up. I kept going, clawing—cane, crumbling cement, mud, broken reeds.

My feet slipped out from under me, and I landed flat, skidding back on my belly through duck wort and flattened reeds, sliding right on past the thing.

Its cold primitive eyes followed me. Sluggishly, it turned.

The pond was no more than four feet deep, yet my head plunged under murky water like liquid fog, thick with floating matter. I popped up sputtering brackish filth, lifting an arm trailing scum, brushing more on my forehead as I wiped my eyes to see.

The massive beast still ponderously spun, but it was behind me now. What a fool I was! To end up in the belly of the thing because of blind impulse...

Slip-sliding back across the marl to the edge, I knew it could swim, glide, paddle, far faster than I. Water reached mid-calf now—almost there, when the croc-thing sank, leaving a knuckle-back and two bulbous eyes before submerging in a swirl of pea soup mud a foot away.

My toes grabbed warm muck. I felt rooted, not sure which way to swerve. I was still too far from the bank. A frog plopped in. I shrieked and that unfroze me; stepping high, making an awkward bound, I landed on my side on a concrete rim. Breath gushed from my lungs. I looked back. Jaws gnashed inches from my foot.

Sensing the croc's breath *whuffing* on my toes, hearing the scritch of claws and the drag of a heavy belly close behind, I grasped green young reeds, gaining ground...

Almost there...

Out of time.

Jaws snapped, closing about my ankle.

I heard myself howl, "Nooooooo," not caring who heard me, aware of the sharp piercing of my skin to the bone, jaws gaining my calf, the insistent tug back into the water. Pain began with the trickle of hot blood. My belly backslid over the same path of broken stems until the powerful beast dragged me under.

Furiously, I clutched rotting stalks in an unequal tug of war, hearing other sleeping croc-creatures splash off banks, grunting, roaring, slapping tails. Mote-filled soup and rotting flesh floated past my eyes, entangling my arms and legs.

Oh, God, oh, God! I'm under water. Can't breathe! I am to die in this filthy water! Lord, let me drown first.

My ankle was numb, but I still sensed the inexorable tug, my belly scraping the bottom. Holding my breath, I tried to twist round, to beat at the thing. My lungs were bursting to breathe. *Those things drag victims under to enjoy later,* my evil imp whimpered.

I rejected that. Bracing against a rough bottom under the muck, I heaved backward, my lungs aching to suck in anything—water, air, it didn't matter—ripping my leg from the croc's jaws as they eased open to gain another foot of me. I felt shoulder bones pop and nails break as I pushed against a shallower bottom.

Turning, I swam, splashed, floundered, clawed my way back—back through smashed reeds, following my blood trail, following claw tracks, dragging my useless swollen leg.

I looked over my shoulder…the water was still.

I'm at the concrete rim. Somehow, I made it! I'm free.

I was blind-sided.

Just as my eyes fixed on the haven of a low stone wall and my hand outstretched, another beast, even larger, homed in from where it lay slyly in wait to one side, flattened in the stalks—a grandfather—a true crocodile, older and wiser.

Its jaws opened, snapping casually on my vulnerable arm, yanking me sideways too shocked to feel anything except pure rage.

The hoary beast thrashed me like a rag doll. It was old, missing several teeth from rubbery mottled gums. My hand slipped between the gaps. I felt furrows as teeth on either side ripped down.

Move! Move! They crawl on bellies! You do not!

Desperately, I got to one knee, dragging my other leg. My hair caught beneath—pulling it free, I tried to hobble to the wall—*I can run; I don't have to slither on my belly.*

Now or never.

Last chance.

My original enemy fought a Johnny-come-lately battle. The old croc, ignoring it and fixing its eyes on me, paddled with dignity, as if it knew the end.

Broken bamboo was all about me, dead and tough. My left hand grabbed a stalk in a death grip: I reached awkwardly back and brought it down hard on the old croc's snout.

It had no effect as the beast continued to stare with ancient eyes.

One-handed, I grabbed the far side of the wall, unaware of brown legs wading, unknown voices shouting cries, and sticks beating the water. Or of beasts feinting and snarling, breaking free to once again come for me.

Focused on the crocs, I didn't feel hands gripping under my arms or hear shouts and curses—before I suddenly realized it was humans tugging at me.

Stunned faces all around.
Hands reaching.
Excited gabble.
A cacophony of bellows and roars…
Arms pulling, scraping me across rocks.
Afterward, blessedly, dirt and grass.
I looked back, terrified.

Murky water was turning a muddy red. Was it from my blood, or…? Then a spear arced from nowhere, sinking between the sections of the old croc's plate-like armor. Confused, I finally saw the blurs of faces.

One stood out.

The cursed rajah looked on the spectacle with an unreadable expression—I detected a flicker of—what? Scorn, pity, disillusionment?

Did you suppose you would really escape? my imp crowed. I saw the same look in the rajah's eyes.

I straightened from my crouch, swatting off help, swaying defiantly before the last face I wished to see, except for the maharajah's. He was offensively immaculate, superbly dressed in white as always, this time in rough cotton, his jodhpurs offsetting nutmeg skin to perfection, his white teeth and crow black brows beneath a weird helmet I vaguely recognized.

"You've interrupted practice," he growled. Later I learned he had been on his favorite horse in the polo field adjacent to the crocodile pits.

How dare he humiliate you a second time! my imp blustered.

I straightened. I am sure my green eyes burned from a mask of mud. The rajah shook his head, taking me in, in all my muddy, bloody, scum-smeared, scratched, half-clothed glory, feet, knees, arms, and hands slimed with green, streaked with blood. Ignoring an unbearable itch from a tickle of red meandering through drying mud, I met him full on.

"I see you've paid for your folly, whatever it was." He raised a brow, poking a pool of blood sinking into the earth with his crop. "Your leg looks grave. However, I cannot tell through all that slime. Where have you been? And what were you attempting?"

He started back from my intense glare, or possibly my filthy state, recalling his last encounter.

"I wanted to escape from this godforsaken place!" I snarled.

He turned and nodded gravely. "I want to hear a defense for your unfathomably stupid actions. Later, I want to hear names."

"No one! I found the way myself." I bit my lip with the name Preeta on my tongue.

"That will be remedied. Thank you for pointing it out—so spectacularly." He waved at the broken grille.

"If that is the only way, one can keep one's women!"

"Strangely," he jeered, "you are the only one foolish enough to attempt it—or wishing to." He studied me as if inspecting a rubbish bin.

"Interesting," he drawled in his King's English, lifting a strand of hair with a riding crop. "I should hire you as circus performer. Crocodile-wrestling, bear-baiting, and death-defying acts. Is that not what you advertised? As a performer?"

He looked as if he wished to erase the last words with an impatient gesture.

Even in my muddled state, the word "performer" resonated with a queer itch I couldn't scratch.

Performer? Why does that mean something? Never mind now. I shivered, standing in India's noonday blast furnace. I blearily noted a shriveled little man, dark brown, baked by the sun, in nothing but a loincloth and stout boots. He thrust a long, hooked pole, glowered terribly at me, and grunted at the detestable rajah.

"You disturb my friend." The rajah nodded at the man in the loincloth. "He is caretaker, you see. Half *gharial* yourself, aren't you, Old Neelam?"

Old Neelam, still glaring, grunted something derogatory.

"We had to destroy his old friend. They go back."

I gathered self-possession out of thin air, along with tatters of muddy sari. Actually more mud than sari. I didn't dare to check my wounds, fearing I might be unfixable.

"Strange pet! What else can I expect? I was meant to be free of this loathsome place."

What did your kiss mean in that scullery? I wish you blasted off the earth. Leave me in my humiliation…please.

Instead, with his riding crop, he lifted a string of mucky sari.

I slapped his hand and crop away, swaying, painfully aware my wet hair, strung with unidentifiable filth, hung heavy in my face. My sari, clotted with rapidly drying mud, itched, and where it was not full of mud, it clung damply transparent. Why was this irritating man always finding me at my most loathsome and defenseless? Why must I always have hair strung with muck when in his presence?

There was quite a crowd interested in my circus act. The rajah gestured to another man on the fringes.

"Your wounds will be attended to," he said stiffly. "I trust they will not leave scars." And he waved, as if waving away my existence.

One knee buckled. Shaking off Old Neelam, who somehow got in my face uttering what I presumed were insults, defending his innocent, defenseless pets, I reeled on my good leg, pushing past, more a stumble, eyeing the rajah's pristine attire; a flicker of alarm crossed his handsome features as he backed, not wishing to turn and run, I imagined, and look weak.

"Afraid I'll muss you?" I croaked. "You didn't mind a few days ago!"

My head filled with fog—nothing to eat or drink for the last how many hours? I needed help. Why was I doing this?

"Go to bloody bleeding Hades," I mumbled instead, placing a hand covered with pond scum on his cheek, like a mother scrubbing a child's face, before he could flinch. "Do your worst," I gasped.

Onlookers sucked a breath.

The rajah waved them off, including Old Neelam, remaining stoic but obviously wishing mightily to wipe off the filth.

"Oh, much worse," he said in turn. "Much, much. It is a death warrant to even touch the maharajah without his permission, much less strike or attack him *or any royal family member.*"

"So why am I still here?" I whispered, barely standing now. "You jailed me, made me do humiliating acts, threatened me. I have no"—I fought for words—"no fear left."

The dam broke. Words came tumbling unsorted. "I don't understand where I am, why I am here!" My voice rose, cracking. "I am a cipher! There is nothing in here!" I beat my head, sensing my will melting as a mud wall in a rainstorm, awareness guttering like dead leaves. Tears drenched my face. I wanted to curl up somewhere in the sun.

"You do realize you are rather—indecent?" He asked mildly, ignoring my outburst, or perhaps it was pity for the demented. "Have your injuries attended to—and I have my polo match."

He sketched a bow and nodded to a hovering man only just arrived.

"You must go back, then, mustn't you. You have my permission!" I emphasized "my" ever so slightly. "And wipe your face."

The rajah glared back. A grin fought through a deadly scowl. Removing his absurd helmet, he laughed aloud and wiped his cheek with the bandanna knotted about his neck. He put his hands on his hips and we were the only two there in a growing crowd.

"I regret, but you do look a sight. You would make even Nirrti dance for joy." There was a murmur of appreciation, nods and chuckles all around us

At my blank stare, he explained, "The Goddess of Darkness and Destruction. One of our many Hindu deities. In this case, you." He would not stop grinning. "We have three million gods…or three, depending on which Vedic scholar one examines." He wiped his eyes, joining in the crowd's laughter.

I saw him look startled. Then he must have heard the thud as my strength of will and body finally gave its all.

****

The rajah knelt, studying Sary on the dirt, careful

not to allow pristine jodhpurs to touch the earth. Her face was too white, even for weak Northern Europeans—still she seemed unusually strong for her race.

He took in the muddied sari, the knotted hair, the pale damaged leg and arm bloodied and mixed with pond scum. One puncture appeared deep. "Poor little foreigner," he muttered.

He looked at the physician, who shrugged.

The look back was dark and filled with meaning.

Perhaps she will not die. I should not have bantered so long, but she vexes me so. Indeed, a pity to die after such folly. How can one still look so beautiful?

Waving away the physician, the rajah ignored his clean jodhpurs and picked Sary up in his arms.

She hung limp, hair and sari dripping slime on the rajah's polished boots.

****

He nodded as the rajah entered the sickroom.

"A moment."

The physician nodded again, bowing out.

Watching until he left, the rajah bent over Sary.

Something had been nagging him all through the practice match.

He'd missed the seven-minute warning bell of the second-to-last chukker. The damn ball went out of play and he hadn't even heard the umpire's whistle. To say his team looked at him oddly was an understatement.

He soured his mouth.

Yet there was an oddity he had not taken time to explore. What he suspicioned were those odd discolorations visible through Sary's clean linen shift, made thin for the climate and her raging fever. Lifting it up carefully, taking care not to look at her body, as that would be a disrespectful and a somehow shameful act akin to his brother's, he leaned close, recognizing the cicatrize of bullet scars, another old wound by her left lower rib cage—and one in the cup of her left shoulder.

Sary stirred, perhaps aware of scrutiny even in her coma, drawing up her knees, hands under her chin. The back of her shift dropped away, revealing numerous thin white scars, so pale they seemed lacy tracks, like white tattoos.

"A story there, I should not wonder," he murmured. He stroked her ankle. Even a tiny burn scar. The gharial bites might leave puncture scars too.

"What life have you led, my Sary?" he whispered.

Chapter Thirteen
Panther, Panther, Burning Bright

Raucous jungle chatter assaulted my ears. I squinted at the white hammer of sun beating the earth into heated clouds of dust. I drooped over ropes, barely conscious.

I was still feverish. Most of my wounds had healed over, but not without scarring. A week after my escape attempt—*why wait so long?*—they took me from my sickroom and hoisted me on top a bloody elephant.

Gauze, stained from unguents, still wrapped my arm and leg—why treat the condemned? I wondered dismally how I could have been so ill-advised. A rage burned inside. I watched bitterly through a fog of fever and kicked up dust as men in hunting gear, armed with expensive rifles, and a clutch of Indian women in European dress and manner rode ahead of me in far finer howdahs than mine.

At a rise, I saw another elaborately painted elephant—the maharajah's.

The day turned darker and colder for me. Nothing good could come of this day. It became more so after the elephants turned off, crashing into the jungle, discerning a faint path. I was to be executed. Why else bring me trussed like a pig to market in the midst of nowhere? Why the partygoers?

But I guessed. They probably supposed me to be a

subject of British rule. *Was I?* Leaving no awkward diplomatic trace, I thought bitterly, my body soon dissolving into wet greenness…

Oh, stop the maudlin drivel. Think!

Jungle swept the animals' broad sides as they pushed deeper in. We halted. The hunting party took it with mixed grace, forging after mahouts with baggy clothes wound between their legs, the ladies picking through in high strappy heels, until they stopped at a clearing of towering cork trees, one larger than most.

A wooden box perched in branches, like a tree house, above me.

I eyed the maharajah as he maneuvered from a palanquin to a chair/pulley arrangement. Onlookers looked too fierce not to be hiding grins as aides shoved and braced his bottom, enormous in pumpkin-colored hunting togs, and wedged him through a hole in the platform, monkeying themselves up after loading vintage matchlock muskets. One dropped a powder flask shaped like a brass fish.

The rajah, dashing in hunting gear, climbed after, while aiding one of the giggly European-looking Indian women, destroying my last composure. Though I had no hold on him, it somehow seemed betrayal.

I eyed the maharajah. His pudgy hands gripped a musket now too.

Am I some form of entertainment? Are they hunting me? How could I have believed Preeta? I cannot blame any fool but myself—fool!

Ashamed of my shred of stained sari, in which they had re-clothed me as some malicious gesture, I nevertheless hugged it as the only armor between me and the exquisite women smoking, chattering, waving lacquered nails, up in the royal viewing box, while the rajah laughed broadly, gesticulating, sharing whispered confidences. He did not spare a glance my way.

I had never felt so alone.

Two guards dragged me backward to a cork tree opposite the treehouse blind, yanked my arms apart, and shackled them to the tree behind me, while I fixed my gaze on the box. They drew the ropes tight, as if I, a bare hundred and eighteen pounds, could break tough sisal. It razored into my wrists.

The maharajah looking down expectantly.

I caught his eye. "Are you worried?" I yelled up, more of a croak. "Why not your heaviest chains? I might attack you! Do you grievous harm!" I spat, literally. Why not go out in a pathetic blaze of defiance? "Coward!"

The maharajah narrowed his eyes into pillowy slits. His wet red mouth gaped. If he heard me or understood, it wasn't certain. The rajah looked on, bemused, while a woman at his side in a fuchsia blouse sent forth a plume of smoke and slapped a bug, already bored.

She would return. I would not.

You could wriggle free if only they left you... My imp again.

I froze at snapping brush behind me—somewhere. A wet swish of fronds. A whiff of animal pong.

Handlers backed and climbed the ladder half way. Something large approached, something I could not see. I'd had enough wildlife. As I wriggled my hands, raw sisal like barbed wire cut my flesh. There was no give.

The thrashing grew louder, accompanied by a harsh *PURRRRRGgggHHHHHH...*

I will not flinch or cry out. I will not.

103

I slanted my eyes sideways, compelled to see what stalked around the tree to which I was tied.

A black shape, lithe and lethal as death, slunk past, lashing a plumy tail. It grunted, looking about, and started at seeing me. Crouching to its belly, the panther coldly viewed me through the gray-water eyes in its diamond-shaped head.

Silver eyes narrowed.

Velvety ears flattened.

The muzzle pulled back in a snarl.

Its triangular mouth, issuing phlegmy rumbles, opened to a wet red yawn. Ocher fangs curved. The panther's rear end readied to spring, tail switching like a metronome.

I tore my gaze from the beautiful deadly creature to stare stonily up at the blind.

I won't look at the beast. Won't give them pleasure.

The panther leapt.

My heart thudded erratically in my throat. I twisted from my waist, turning my head, the only movement I could manage.

The muscular, furry shape thudded into my shoulder, leaving a searing graze of claws. I felt animal breath of meat and blood, hot and dripping on my neck.

I heard its snarl of confusion behind me, almost like that of an embarrassed housecat misjudging its spring.

It scrambled up, circled, lashing its tail and growling promises, while it repositioned its claws, flexing and unflexing them, belly to the ground. *This time*, the flat deadly silver eyes promised. *This time!*

I was aware of the maharajah's squeals of encouragement, heard women's shocked horror, fake sympathy, and nervous titters. I saw the howdah driver's face. There, true empathy lay. I looked up for the rajah in last appeal; he was bent to the lovely ear of one of the spectators. I heard her chuckle low, guttural and sensual. I tore my gaze back to the panther. It was indeed lovely.

A perfect machine of nature.

Silvery gray, with darker spots.

Four-inch fangs, claws unsheathed.

It was leaping with unerring aim, red glints in its tarnished silver eyes.

All this took mere seconds.

The maharajah, pushing fatty folds wide to take in my slaughter, lips loose with excitement, nearly tipped from the box as I fixed my eyes on him. The beast angled for my neck with fangs the shade of old bone, claws curved as scimitars.

He clapped and chuckled, slurping Champagne, eating sweets, all senses glutted for his sovereign pleasure.

A gush of foulness washed my face. The panther's huge head blotted everything.

Past onrushing teeth, I saw the rajah loom behind the maharajah.

I jerked my head. The panther's fangs sank home where my neck met the shoulder. Through stinging vision I saw, high above, a blue-black rod thrust past the fat man's heaving shoulders.

A crack sent monkeys exploding from treetops and macaws shrieking complaint.

The panther's body arced as if flung.

The black wraith hung an instant before dropping with a sprawling thud at my feet.

I saw the maharajah jerk, holding his ears and swiveling to see who had committed the outrage.

With my cheek, I smeared blood trickling from my shoulder. I searched the tree. After a blurred moment, I saw the stony rajah holding a carbine across his chest.

Our eyes met.

The women's exclamations, the maharajah's enraged face, jungle babble, my pain…all faded.

A message passed between us. Mine was partially, *Why did you wait?*

The potentate hurled the rajah's handsome rifle from the blind, breaking the spell. I saw a flash of gold engraving as the stock shattered at my feet. I rubbed sisal on the bark, undoing the last of my abused, once-peach silk now hanging in rotten tatters, leaving me in filthy underclothes.

The sisal held firm. The rajah stalked by his broken rifle, leaving me where I was without looking. My lips were open to speak. I snapped them shut.

I whispered a prayer: *I am still tied, feet bound. Don't leave me here!*

Women tiptoed past in sharp-heeled shoes, casting nervous, curious glances and speeding on. One seemed to hesitate. Then, seeing there was little she could do, ducked her head and scurried after.

The maharajah lumbered past, seated in his fancy gold howdah, aided by servants. The last arms bearers passed by, too. I heard elephants thrashing jungle growth and voices receding. I was alone. I tilted my head back. Apparently, this was my end, alone and helpless even as I chafed my wrists against the bark.

****

Pungent fumes stoppered my nostrils. I squinted,

reaching greedily with my eyes for the flask of spirits hovering before me. Hands doused my shoulder with it instead. The fiery stuff ran into the deepest claw punctures. My shoulder was on fire.

"Good. No crying like a woman."

I turned to the voice with eyes that would burn ice. "Never mind that. Undo me!"

I saw his shirt hanging loose, and nipples so dark they seemed black against his burnished skin aroused me even as I hated it, in my sad circumstances, observing muscles rippling like copper coils as he struggled with my ropes. I looked away.

"Have you had enough?" he whispered, with sympathy and not censure.

"You came back," I muttered stupidly, not answering. Then—"What do you think?" I hissed at him, rubbing my wrists.

"I think you can withstand anything—and have done so—many...*too* many times, in your past."

My past? On my lips was the question—what do you know of it? Pride, obstinacy—I did not know which kept me silent. I glared at him instead.

"Can you walk?"

"Apparently, I can do anything."

He stared a full second before unbending with the grace of the panther lying at my feet. Even now, servants fixed the beast's paws about a pole to cart it off. He cut my ankles free and tossed me the flask.

"We will speak again," he threw over his shoulder as he disappeared through fronds that whipped back drops of water sparkling in the green light.

He looked back once, as if to say, *Come on!*

I tried to sort numbed limbs.

I passed bearers and a soldier, furiously conscious I must hold strips of my sari in strategic positions. I stared them down. I must walk with it bunched like a soiled bouquet in front, muttering swear words as I followed the rippling undergrowth.

Have you had enough? perseverated. *Oh, yes, and more. Oh, yes, I have had enough! I'd love to tie you to a tree. Stick you in a cell and watch… I would love…*

With these steamy notions boiling in a cauldron of hurt—ways I would like to annihilate the rajah—I resolutely pressed against the mental door at which other warmer thoughts knocked relentlessly.

****

The rajah glowered at his servants as they lit the charcoal and laid sticky honeyed tobacco in the *narghile* tray, checked the water, and handed him the stem before bowing out. He sucked the fragrant vapor and exhaled slowly, seeing a face in the perfumed steam.

He'd need to deal with the conundrum of that woman! Not with his brother, but within himself.

"Why risk my brother's wrath?" He voiced the thought to smoke as roiling as his thoughts. His brother was dangerous to all. His own status meant less than nothing. Did not their mother's brother have a minor quarrel over land rights and subsequently was found mangled, hardly recognizable, in the elephant enclosure? His brother's wife, the third one, had fallen from the parapet. No one questioned why she sat on the rim in the rain, and—more chilling—the maharajah's most recent personal physician, who had the gall to order his brother stop his gluttonous habits, was discovered stone dead with a large piece of pork stuffed

108

down his throat.

The rajah did not need to ponder what fate would befall the latest doctor, an earnest young man with modern teachings from Bengali, so far dazzled by his promotion into thinking his opinions had status.

If his brother had not the notion, this woman, Sarabande—*What sort of heathenish name is that?*—held special gifts, she would be no more than a desiccated fly in a dusty web.

Fortunately, for her, his brother was erratic as a weathercock in a *chakravat* and enjoyed long bouts of drug-induced "indisposition" in which he could pretend ill health and shirk responsibilities.

The rajah held more vapor in his lungs, letting it out slowly...

What was she to him? Should he leave her to his brother? Placate tempestuous moods and drug-induced manias until his rage ferreted out some unforgivable slight and he put her to death before he could be stopped? Would that not make him, the rajah, just as corrupt? No. His brother's brain might crumble like castor sugar in *chai*, but not his.

The rajah passed a hand over his forehead. His valet, daring to read his moods, had cheekily added a pinch of opium to the *narghile*. He detected it, grimacing a smile, and closed his eyes. Funny. Her strong beautiful face with the haunting green eyes was still there.

Chapter Fourteen
A Rajah's Rage

"The beast, the slime of the pond," the rajah pontificated, "left a festering deep in the ankle laceration. The flesh healed over, but not the blood. The wound on your shoulder, fortunately, I was foresighted enough to disinfect with spirits. A panther's claws hold all manner of resilient and poisonous contagions."

"It wasn't precisely my idea," I deadpanned.

He continued, oblivious. "We in India are learned beyond the world. My personal physician prescribed a concoction of certain molds, plus a distillation of opium called morphia."

"Molds?" I raised my brows. "As in bread?"

He glanced at me in a superior way. "Precisely."

I checked my ankle and peered at the shoulder wound, which had lost its angry puffiness.

"I suppose I should thank you, who put me in such an impossible place."

The rajah turned dark granite, his scowl at the beautiful scene outside enough to turn it to blighted winter, if that had been possible.

I studied his anthracite hair, curved nose, and luminous eyes beneath the fierce wings of his brows. The fevers had cooled, thanks to him. Not all fevers, but those harmful. Yet could these other fevers be any less?

"My brother and I are of the same blood. No one would need to know! Ever—at least not officially," he added cryptically in his pedantic English.

"Know…what? Stop the riddles. I am not in the mood, nor am I a child."

He came close, beating his chest with a fist. His arm was well muscled, I mused, and the gold cuff looked particularly well on him… What he said filtered through. "What?"

"You were to come to me!" He thumped his chest again. "To me! Not my brother! Not to the maha-ra—jah!" A barely concealed sneer was present. Against whom, I was unsure. Myself, him, or the—other.

I stared, wondering if I heard rightly.

He looked away, burnished skin now turning the shade of sumac, striding the room, hands behind his back. I would beg my general weakness made my mind weak, too, taken in by his appearance once again—perfectly groomed, in his favored cream or white satin, his fanciful beard, mustache, and fierce brows glossy as a grackle's wings…

"Only later would you approach him—*lie with him*…" The words floated into my range of hearing. "But for one time only, after—after…you…"

I turned my face to stone and waited.

"After I what?" I asked quietly.

"After you came with child. *My* seed! Instead, you did this foolhardy thing! I was the one you were to come to that night, you foolish woman, when you ended up flirting with the blasted *gharial*!"

Was he speaking any known language? I finally understood all. Ashamed, I allowed my mind to wander into forbidden territory. What would it be like to stroke that naked, warm, satiny, nutmeg skin? *What would it be like—?*

While he took a dust broom to his thoughts, I said, playing for time, "*Gharial*?"

He turned, smiling as if nothing untoward had been spoken.

"Yes. Indeed. That cousin to 'crocodiles' as you most likely call them." *If you say so.* He waved his hand negligently. On any other man, it would appear foppish.

"Call them what you will. This entire godforsaken, bloody, hell-bound place is alive with things that bite, crawl, and…"

He held up a hand. "Please. Cursing is not attractive, or womanly."

"I will bloody well curse if it bloody well pleases me! And I don't care if I am—" I curled my lip. "Womanly enough for you."

"As you see fit," he answered stiffly. "It does you no honor."

"But it damn well makes me feel better!"

I hobbled out of bed. I needed to stand, fearful he would go on explaining.

He gestured me to sit. I hobbled over, sitting balefully as a raven over a clutch of a sparrow's eggs. There were tea and cakes. I took a bite of hot buttered crumpet, wanting to cry.

"The same blood, he and I," he explained as if to a child as he poured tea. "No one would dare speak of it if they did suspect. You would"—he looked off with a face like an approaching squall line—"as I stated before, stay with him another night *only*. You wouldn't even have to…have to…" He swirled his hand.

"Another night! As I recall, I did not, the last time." I gripped the chair, white-knuckled.

"Of course, how could I forget that unfortunate encounter was not...consummated either?" He meant it as a joke, I saw, and matched it with a weak smile like watery sun peeping from a gray cloud. "You would have been rewarded munificently. An estate of your own. Money, servants, anything you wished."

"Except freedom? Perhaps my life? What if I talked?"

Jet eyes flashed. *Don't push me. This is difficult for me also,* they spoke.

"Have a care, madam. You do not grasp the razor's edge upon which you tread. My brother was enraged. He has men killed for turning their backs. It took all my persuasion to set you free—disarm him from your escape attempt—let alone allow you to live! This last act cost me and you dear. You will comply and obey—in time."

His heavy-lidded eyes were hot, black pools in which I saw myself reflected—pale, stormy-eyed, and very, very frightened. His wooing left a lot to be desired.

"O-bey!" I sparked flint back. "It has been a while since I obeyed anyone!"

"Attend carefully. You insult the maharajah; you insult the princely house of Bharatpur. Simple."

"Perhaps, if your brother weren't so gluttonous, he might summon up a healthy male heir." I could not stop. "I am certainly not interested in furthering the house of Bharatpur! Are you his lackey?"

"Fortunately for you, at present my brother is not in a—shall we say—receptive mood. He is not always able to"—he swirled his elegant hand—"to…to…? Unless…perhaps you may find out his desires and that which pleasures him most—that which makes him more…more…open to, ah, physical contact."

He would not look at me.

I gaped. I am to seduce *him?*

If I had tried to talk, words would have jammed like tangled barbwire in their compulsion to spew cuttingly.

I suspected he meant to goad me. Test me. Get back at me. We were getting far afield. He smarted at my rejection. Even now, I admitted, I allowed the possibility to creep in like the nose of a camel under the tent. Instead I asked, "Brothers? How are you ever—brothers?"

Diverted, he took a sip of tea, "Oh! Same mother! I favor her—the most beautiful woman in all India." A devastating cleft in his cheek showed. I noted he softened at the mention of his mother.

"My father found and married her after scouring every province and goat herder's village. But yes, my mother tended pigs, not goats. She far prefers her present job," he said dryly.

"My brother takes after our father, in case you were wondering."

I lowered my lashes.

"My brother is not—how do you say? Every young maiden's dream? However"—his eyes mocked—"you are not a maiden."

He had switched again.

"I didn't mean to…insult you." It sounded contrite.

In a pig's eye.

"We were—are close. My brother and I have a…"

114

He hesitated. "How do you say, a checkered history."
He looked off, seeing another time. "I protected him, as
a boy. Others tormented, tortured him, even though he
was a future raj." He gestured. "Tripping on the playing
field, the cricket bat in the stomach, secret pummeling
in the baths. All behind doors, of course. It did not help
one of his names was Aadalarasu."

At my questioning look, he explained, "King of the
Dance." He flashed white teeth. I could not help
laughing aloud.

"A poor excuse for brutality and greed." I spoke
more softly than before. "He was born your brother,
with a silver spoon. Though in his case, it must have
been an entire gold soup ladle in his mouth."

His turn to smile. I saw him press his lips. We were
becoming quite cozy. Then he had to spoil it all.

"They do not behead people in Great Britain, but I
am not certain he has such...compunction. Beheading,
or worse, is not unheard of for treason, and he decides
that which is treason. Your insult to his person, your
reckless escape, could be construed as treason in the
most lenient court. Fortunately, he has..." His
hesitation was barely there. "He has forgotten you for
the moment."

I missed the easy humor. He stood, taking a final
sip. Perhaps he too regretted it. "Enough. Take care of
your words. Net them. Guard them judiciously before
more rubbish escapes that pretty mouth of yours or you
take flights of fancy—or any other flight."

It was said with the solid clang of metal falling on
cement from a great height.

Then, with a gaze melting me to my bones, he
searched my face. "So as you don't lose that pretty

head," he said softly. "Or find yourself in the maharajah's special prison, never again to see light of day. Or turn to brittle parchment, blowing as ashes in the wind. And I would hate that," he whispered softly.

His lips were very close. He smelt of cloves and bay rum.

"Above all, never forget, Sarabande, that truth belongs to the House of Bharatpur. Our *gharials* do need to be fed. Not to mention panthers." He bit the words as wire snips clipping ten-penny nails.

I shivered inside. He had changed again. Surely, he was tormenting, joking, or trying to frighten me. However, I saw his face. Sweet Jesus. He meant it.

"Your pet lizards!" I bit off, drawing him back.

He shrugged. "Not mine. But yes. The *gharial* is rare and found only in India," he said with some pride.

"Abominations."

'True. I see how you might think that." Without a hint of a smile, he fell back in the chair, dragging fingers through long gleaming hair. I was awkwardly standing. Then he pulled me—reluctantly, I might add—to him. I had no choice but to plunk onto his lap.

I fidgeted off. He yanked me back. I was tired. I stayed. Besides, I was curious to see how much deeper he dug his well.

"What I am attempting to instill, Sary, is fear—for my sake. Drugs, his excesses. My brother attempts differing solutions. Exotic stuff. Some flown to him. Yes, are you surprised? We have an aero-plane. Concoctions from China or Africa. Shiva knows what is in them. Powdered rhinoceros horn! Monkey glands in wine! Venom from horned toads, some of which understandably makes him very ill."

"It wouldn't make a difference. You, him, or the lowest beggar in the streets—I desire none of you." At last, I pulled away, limping to the small balcony outside my sickroom, overlooking a service alley and the distant lake. The jasmine and honeysuckle perfuming the humid dusk might as well be burning rubbish. The rajah set down his refreshed teacup so hard behind me the porcelain shattered, spilling tea like thin blood.

"We aren't through here."

"With all respect," I gritted, "we are. He is unnatural. So are you. And I—I am tired."

"Yes, forgive me. You yet recover." I looked for sarcasm and found none.

I turned back. "But why me?" The thought jelled in my tired brain. "There are hundreds of willing and more desirable women in the hareem, more's the pity—more coming in every day, it seems. I am...old, compared to them. I'm—damaged."

He leaned on the parapet and cast a wry glance over the black tapestry of the lake with the sparkle of moon threading its ripples.

"Perhaps you find us ignorant, twelfth-century barbarians. Why you? For no reason other than new blood, mayhap. We are not as backward as you suppose! We study genetics and the perils of an inbred, weakened lineage. There is talk of Queen Victoria and her grandson, the Russian prince with the bleeding disease. Hemo-something. Perhaps a strong, healthy female such as you, used to work, unlike the women of the hareem, spoiled *raajkumaari,* or eager peasants parading their lovely daughters"—his mouth turned down—"before my brother would suit all Rajasthan best. What do you think?" Then he added quietly,

"Besides which, I—he—saw you." He looked away but not before I saw the set of his jaw and reddening of his cheekbones.

I spoke carefully. "There is more than that. You are not telling me all."

"No," he agreed simply. "And I may never." After a moment of silence, he went on. "So you see, as despicable as you might think me, am I not more agreeable? And you would not have had to force your way through that disgusting tunnel." From my sideways glance, I saw a smile tug at his lips.

I gripped the rail.

"I am as any man," he continued. "I wanted you for—you."

I clenched the rail harder.

"Best do as our physician says," he continued oddly.

Expecting reproof, I looked up to see him nodding at five yellow eyes of raw eggs staring back at me from a platter that a servant of the doctor's had quietly padded in with.

I looked balefully at the glistening yellow-and-white islands on a plate.

White teeth flashed as he indicated the eggs. "Best get at them."

I tossed the eggs off the parapet. I heard a yelp from below. Wonderful!

When I looked around, I was alone.

Chapter Fifteen
Poor Boy

Square bundles of steaming *shondesh*, shrimps, and other savories, but mostly sweets in tempting array. Bowls of *shrikhand*, which I knew was honeyed yoghurt, and glistening balls of *sohan papdi*, *sukhdi*, and cherry bright *gulab jamon*. Plain *laddoo*, of course, and mounds of nuts, figs, dates, oranges—and milk.

Milk?

Enough to feed a bloody orphanage, offered my imp.

I sipped sticky *chai* and tried not to wonder why I was here. Still in the robe of a patient, I caught the rajah gazing at my linen wrap, open slightly.

He frowned. "Cover yourself."

What? I looked down at my plain wrap concealing all but my neck.

"My stars! I'm practically bundled for winter! Compared with the flimsy garb I'm usually given..." Soft hesitant footsteps approached.

With a welcoming smile showing all forty or fifty of his perfect white teeth, the rajah extended a hand toward a drapery.

A frail boy of undetermined years slipped through, silently presenting himself. His lovely elfin smile flicked like a beacon on a foggy shore.

To me, the boy seemed a novice actor who hadn't

learned his lines, thrust onto the stage alone and unrehearsed, staring out at a hostile audience.

I smiled wide in welcome.

Raising a pointed chin, the child tried to straighten. My heart lurched.

He was perhaps eleven. Could be as young as eight, though, given his frail figure. Then I saw the incipient mustache valiantly growing above his thin lips. Twelve, then. I looked askance at the rajah. The boy was royal, by his raiment—gathered gold lamé ankle skirt over tight puttees on skinny legs, gilded pointed slippers, a choker, the ubiquitous pearls, even on one so young. A red-and-gold turban cupped his narrow head, topped by a royal crescent and egret spray.

I now recalled his thin ghost at the birthday party, half-hidden by the maharani.

The boy studied me with intelligence. I smiled at the small dagger in his sash. The thin face changed as he raised big sad eyes to the rajah. No, not sad but fatigued from standing and holding a head on such a tender stalk.

I flashed a question. Yours? Some semblance lay in the strong brows and deep eyes, the lad's loveliest feature.

No, not mine, he flashed back and held out his arms. "You, my fine fellow, are not too big to sit on my knee." The rajah's eyes were dark with meaning—*and you need not stand.*

The boy shook his head so vigorously I feared it would snap off, and he flung himself into the rajah's arms crying, "Too big! Too big!"

There followed a whispered chat, the boy giggling.

The rajah chucked his chin. "Not big! Now, eat, eat!"

The boy shrugged as if at a chore quickly done to please an adult, nibbled a *laddoo*, took a bite or two of savories, and pushed the food around with a finger. Even this wearied him, but he drank his goat's milk. *Good boy.*

"May I speak?"

The rajah nodded, echoed by the young princeling.

"*Namastey*," I tried shyly. "My Hindi is not good. *Kyaa aap angrézee mein baat kar saktey hain*?"

"Yes, I understand—a little English, English lady," he answered my question.

"What are you called? *Aapka naam kyaa hai*? Mine is Sarabande."

"*Meraa naam*—" He raised his chin. "Kiran of the house of…" and a long string of names. "Lady Sarabande."

I couldn't help myself. "Oh, how sweet you are, Kiran!"

"Keeran," he corrected my pronunciation. "I am a prince. My name means prince! And someday I shall rule Bharatpur and be the greatest maharajah of all…"

He drew up, as I looked over his head.

"Play time!" The rajah clapped his hands, then set the boy down and kneeled, giving him a choice of hands. The boy chose something, evidently delighting him. Slapping him on the back, but gently, the rajah watched him slowly climb the steps.

As the curtain parted, I saw a hovering female. Kiran departed with a shy backward glance.

"What a lovely child! What did you give him?"

"A wish." He glared at the splendid night view.

Shamefully hungry, waiting in the awkward

silence, I perused the sweets, dropping the *sohan papdi* when he barked, "That was the son, the only son of the house of my brother. We come from an illustrious line, back to the eighth century. We won, in battle, furlongs of fertile pastures, scores of villages, a mountain range, vast rubber, tea, and almond plantations, and a mining operation larger than one of your pitiful European countries."

"Is that right? How wonderful for you!"

"Though my brother sired fifteen daughters, none was particularly well-disposed, comely—or intelligent, though with females it is hard to say," he offhanded. "The interests of you women are so limited. Mostly sweets and adornment."

I dropped the *laddoo* I had selected and bit down so hard my teeth clicked.

"The eldest is six."

"I'm—sorry," I managed. "If this is meant to influence me, I've had sufficient of your kindness and your offenses. If I may take my leave?"

"You are riled; I believe that is the expression, though spirit is good. No, of course not."

I opened my mouth to give him a bit more of my spirit.

"However, no sons," he resumed. "No heirs. No strapping males to carry his lineage and legacy, save that shining example."

"The boy can't help it! And what of you? You are—male, a direct descendant. Why don't you wive? Plus," I snapped, "we have had this conversation!"

"Ahh." He threw his rare charming smile.

"But I am a dilettante, as mentioned, if you paid attention. Strolling the Seine from l'Arc de Triomphe to the Notre Dame, visiting Monte-Carlo, summering on Como, attending my Arabian horses at Deauville. At times I ride the cups and attend matches around the world."

"Good for you, a dilettante, no less. What an accomplishment, being absolutely useless!"

"I do see that." He wagged a finger. "You lead me deliberately off track."

"We are on a track?"

"I do love the boy."

"I see that too." I softened. "I heard of a gentlewoman who taught the King of Siam's many brood. Anna something. A widow. Perhaps she might help." I halted. "Perhaps the lad is overindulged in sweets, cossetted, or never let out to play."

"You know nothing."

"How sickly?" I finally asked.

"None have lived beyond his age. My brother has lost twenty-three sons."

"Twenty-three! Heavens, doesn't he know when to quit?" I lowered my lashes. "I'm sorry. Unseemly."

"I am used to your unseemliness." He studied me as if I were a bug in a killing jar. He turned to the lake with such intensity I thought a siren must have risen from the waters.

"What I don't see is why I am here." Meaning this room, meeting the boy.

"I merely wished you to understand. We are not completely barbaric."

"And that is why you keep me here—a prisoner?"

"We shall speak again. Do you play chess?"

"Apparently!"

"My brother loves chess."

He nodded once and strode out.
What the Sam Hill did he mean by that?

Chapter Sixteen
Checkmate

The room I entered with a sinking heart was tent-like—its billowing silk ceiling wafted gently from cooling breezes off the lake, the same body of water I had noted from other levels—a picture postcard between slender columns.

Apparently, the rajah supposed he had tugged my heartstrings into doing the maharajah's will by showing me the boy. Never had I felt so deceived.

The room was oddly absent of the malodorous reek of before, sparsely decorated, airy, modern after the overbearing opulence elsewhere.

I rushed to an ivory-and-silver telephone, picking up the receiver-mouthpiece. Yet who would I call? I replaced it and examined a cabinet shortwave radio with a multitude of dials and glass bezels.

At a sound, I whirled. Servants toted in fruit, cheeses, bread, and brandy, followed by a frosted bucket of Champagne. I was drawn toward the liquor. Somewhere, I had developed a taste for the harder stuff—a flash of a clay jug stuck in my mind.

Downing a quick glass, I found it burned like an old friend.

I poured another, pacing, peeking behind curtains, searching out exits.

I peered over the balustrade. Quite high.

Tantalizing bits of streets and dusty buildings were visible over a far wall. Sipping brandy, I wandered to a filmy curtain and pulled it aside, revealing a low table with a chess set, surrounded by pillows large enough to swallow me whole.

To sit clenched and nervous, playing against a sweating monster? I looked about, frantic. Nowhere to hide in this sterile modern place. No fruit knives.

Distracted by the board, I studied it.

Expecting minarets, elephants, and turbans, I saw tiny American Indians. *War horses are knights, while the bishops must be shamans. Teepees are castles, Indians with war bonnets are kings, and the sitting prairie dogs must be pawns.*

The queens, oddly enough, were ivory and ebony *buffalos*. I recalled from somewhere that White Buffalo Woman was an American Indian deity. "How peculiar."

Do I know how to play?

Somehow, I thought I did. Automatically selecting a chief in headdress, I was well into a fantasy game…

****

Dozing, aided by the brandy, curled deep in pillows, I dreamed warm palms stroked my nape and trailed down my back under my loose sari.

Opening my lips, I sighed, arching and curving pleasurably into the hands. The warm palms cupped the curve of my hips. My lids sprang open.

I still clutched a game piece, tensing, conjuring the fat man's peculiar odor as one whose servants never properly attended to his immense size. I hurled the chess piece blindly. It shattered on an ornate statue—a Hindu deity, it too, fragmented.

A voice between baritone and tenor poured over

me like warm honey. "You do realize it is an affront to destroy anything of value belonging to the maharajah? He or I could have you beaten with a barbed whip, trampled by elephants, or used as tiger bait tied to a tree."

"You already did that. That panther thing," I taunted back. "Wouldn't that bore you?"

His chuckle was a deep rumble.

The rajah poured champagne into two crystal brandy cups. "My bad attempt at humor. I see you already indulged. Nevertheless—as peace offering."

I reached with humiliating eagerness for the ice-frosted goblet, holding it against my cheeks, then eyed him over the rim.

How vain. The rajah was devastatingly appealing, as always, in his loose white silk caftan with simple gold embroidery about a deep slit neck. It billowed in the humid breeze off the lake. Worse for my composure, the filmy silk floated against his body, revealing all his manly attributes, plus a smooth bronzed chest. His hair, unbound, hung sleek and black as that of any pirate or Cornish brigand. He even owned a dratted dimple playing hide-and-seek in his bluish jaw, which I had never before noted. Damnation but he was handsome!

Flushing, I averted my eyes, placing the frosted cup on my neck.

Oh, how I hated him!

I sucked my palm where the game piece had bit in. He set the cut glass tumbler on the table and turned my hand over.

I jerked it away.

Ignoring me, his hand hovered over my breast

instead. He plucked a jeweled pin. "Instead, I shall take this." His fingers, warm, strong, deft, and the brush of skin between my breasts, slightly raspy, sent a subterranean quake rippling from my toes.

I waited, breathless, for what came next.

Instead, he plopped akimbo on the cushion opposite, replacing the shattered pawn with my jeweled pin and, with a wave, indicated I make opening gambit.

"But perhaps you should care to destroy more?" he murmured. "A piece of your clothing, for, say, a queen or a king? A lock of hair for a checkmate? Or perhaps a kiss for—"

"They call it strip poker back in…" I scowled.

Back in where?

The dratted door to memory swung shut just as I nearly had it. *Perhaps a piece of my memory for a king? Another touch of your hand for a…* I shook my head.

Bending my head, I blindly selected a pawn, tipping it as I placed it.

The muscular hand nudged my hand aside, placing it upright. "Are you sure that was your opening gambit?"

Concentrate on the game.

I stubbornly replaced the pawn with a sharp click.

He made his move, distracting me with a lecture on chess while I sweated my return play.

"Chess was born in India, you do realize. Revered as indication of intelligence and strategy. A set is in every Indian home. In fact, even the Mahabharata has a crucial episode involving the game."

"I have no idea what or who the Mahabharata is, nor do I particularly care," I snarled, thinking furiously. *Now, if I move the queen, there lies a multitude of traps already set, but if I take this pawn and...*

He did not enlighten me. After five minutes deliberating, lingering on pawns, removing them, muttering to myself, he sighed heavily and offered, "If you lose, you will do as I say, you realize—exactly, but I am a sporting man."

I fixed him with what I hoped was an icy green gaze from eyes like chips off a glacier. "I see no such rules in any game book." Freezing him with more green ice, I asked, "And if I win?"

I sat in silence as he frowned and made his next play, brazenly shoving a knight into battle.

No dilettante he, respecting me too much, in my estimation, with his ruthless cutthroat stratagems, the first game handily won by him, though I played with wit and feverishly recalled plays dredged from deep in my hidden mind. I used female stratagem in turn, glancing greenly through what I hoped were sultry lashes, dragging my sari down by leaning over the board, vindicated as I noted him stirring restlessly. I moistened lips, biting and plumping them, and slowly ran my tongue along the rim of my glass. Oh, I was merciless, *I hoped,* turning him to a virtual custard.

When I coolly tipped his king in triumph, he glowered and topped our champagne from the crystal bucket weeping diamond drops. The night was humid. I longed to brush the ice along bared breasts.

As the evening wore on with the clicking of chess pieces and champagne, the rajah changed tactics, relating diverting tales regarding his garage mechanic, of all things, among others. Apparently, the rajah owned more cars than Ford Motor Company.

Another tale was of a five-times-removed cousin, a

maharajah no less, who reigned over a cow pasture.

I found myself giggling, sipping too much wine. Drawn to his deftly playing tanned fingers as they moved across the board, still feeling their caress on my skin, I found it hard to concentrate, and without thinking, my "poisoned" pawn became a death knell and I had a "bad bishop" corralled by my own pawns.

"Phahhhh!" I uttered, disgusted.

The rajah smoothly tipped my queen—the White Buffalo Woman.

"From whence did you learn *Caturaṅga*?" he asked smoothly, perhaps mollifying, perhaps with complacency. I could not tell which.

"Chess, you mean? Apparently, I didn't." *But I will now.*

As the evening cooled, in my champagne-fueled state I made inventive, daring plays, contriving new gambits and making an accidental but brilliant move with my queen, backing up two rooks.

I did not notice a narrowing of his eyes as he hunched over for serious warfare. I seemed on fire, sending my army of kings, queens, knights, and pawns to scorch the checkered field of play, and in an audacious series of moves, captured his last piece with ill-advised crowing.

"Hah! I won! And handily!" I clapped my hands. "I have won! You lost!" I would have danced about the room had I been able to get up unaided. I gulped more bubbly wine instead.

The rajah glowered at the board. "You are most certainly not a lady!"

With a sweep of his arm, and a face like ancient granite, he brushed the remaining pieces off to shatter on the marble floor.

His heavy hooded eyes betrayed him. I drew back.

"A draw—to be continued," he growled and, gripping me with two powerful hands, drew me bodily across the board before I could protest, scattering wine flutes and a last few game pieces.

Possibly unconsciously seductive, my eyes glazed from monsoonal heat and the wine, I dropped my head back, arching my neck, not in surrender but languor. Through half-closed eyes, I recognized his heavy gaze feverish with want, that naked thirst that comes with men and women, as his large hands strongly sculpted my back and my bottom naked under the silk, gripping me bone against bone, breasts mashed against his chest, as he ground my body into his, thrusting me back into the cushions and kissing me thoroughly and hard.

I protested weakly between kisses as we came up for air, but my body did not.

Was not this what I had wished for since he first stepped into the room? Since that time in the scullery?

His heartbeat and breath quickened. I felt his lips brushing my skin, ripping my sari with his teeth, cupping the swelling of my sex beneath with one hand. He bent his head to my breasts. I felt faint with longing. Ripping my silks aside, I dragged at his caftan in turn.

Then the imp shouted an alarm. *This will not end well. You will lose your own self in this dangerous game—this battle of wills!*

There is no battle of wills, I screamed at the imp. *Leave me alone.* Then I thought, in the last sane moment, *what am I doing? I am not some back-alley trull he can have at will!*

Pushing the rajah off with shreds of resolve, I

stiffly gathered myself, awkwardly pulling my sari straight, brushing damp hair from my lips and trying to get my breathing under control.

"I thought you were saving me for your brother," I said as coolly as five flutes of champagne and a tot or two of brandy allowed.

Digging your grave deeper, Sary girl? my imp sneered.

"Does it seem like it?" the rajah snarled. His eyes bore into mine.

I stared at his lips. His mouth so close…

"Make up your mind!" I snapped—*Oh, please.*

His grasp loosened. I fell backward even as I longed to burrow closer. I jumped up, no easy task, found my flute was empty, hitched over, and gulped chilled wine from the jeroboam on the sideboard. Then I railed, "I am here against my will. You will not tell me anything, but you give me bizarre reasons. You assume, sir, I am someone I am sure I am not. I wish to leave!"

"Are you certain you should be doing that, when you are so recently recovered?" He eyed the jeroboam with alarm. Perhaps he thought I would defend myself with it.

"I've drunk stronger, more manly stuff than this, and I do not need anyone like you telling me what is good for me!" I sneered, taking another hefty swig. *Oh, I was making a lovely impression.* Did I want Dutch courage, or was I wishing for oblivion? On the other hand, was I striving to breach my own defenses? I would never know.

The rajah jumped up, strode over, and with a controlled sweep of his hand, just stopping from a blow, barked, "You bore me! Get out of my sight!"

Our stance, toe to toe, would have set a forest ablaze.

I welcomed the fire. His wrath made me strong. "You are no better than your brother! You only suppose you are." The look on his face would have stopped a Brahma bull.

"Perhaps you invite the comparison, madam! That can yet be arranged."

I stood as any bare-knuckle fighter in a garbage-filled alley until his eyes blazed black fire—like the touch of ice can burn—and then, the rains, threatening all evening, came as if to quench our mutual fire, not a second too soon. I yearned to find out just how far I could have pushed him.

Against batons of lightning and thunderous rolls, the rains played staccato music on the marble terrace. No wind, only the solid drumming of a tropical deluge.

We looked out, startled as if just awakening, then at each other with sultry, heat-crazed eyes.

He reached for me.

I ran into his embrace. My head fit neatly under his chin. Our hearts beat miniature earthquakes, breaths mingling as our mouths neared, hesitantly, lips brushing past and returning, his lingering where my lips curled in at the corners. We were the eye of a storm, while heat lightning lit the sky. The rajah eyed the couch with crazed longing, yet unexpectedly set me aside. At the sudden release, I drunkenly swayed.

"The choice must be freely given," he called below the thunderous music of the storm. "I do not beg. I do not steal that which is not mine. However, I cannot wait much longer than—than a burning wick on a barrel of explosives. But for now…you may go." He spoke harshly. "Go, damn it! Leave while you can!"

I half-fell on the chaise, hiding my face in a cascade of hair, feverish from a hunger I could not name. *I did not want to feel this way.* "Make up your mind!" I snapped.

I picked up my tattered dignity and fled in confusion.

Muttered Hindi curses followed me.

Chapter Seventeen
Addiction

After a turbulent rest filled with scorching green eyes and storm-frizzed clouds of hair, the rajah was shaken awake by a servant. "My Lord, come quick! It is his supreme highness!"

The rajah frowned, torn from his dream-tossed sojourn with Sary. "What is it," he snapped, "that you should disturb my rest?" *Shiva! He sounded waspish as his exalted brother!* He brushed his long hair back from his face. "Yes, yes, I'm coming."

The rajah gazed down at his brother. Rain still pounded a marble balcony outside. In the tumult, his brother did not stir.

The maharajah's new physician washed his hands, literally and figuratively.

"I cannot rouse him, your excellency. He has been rather—overindulgent of late. I tried to warn him of excesses and all that it entails. His heart—his..."

"Drugs!" His brother's breathing was stertorous, like a cart with square wheels. White drool foamed from his mouth. Sticky paraphernalia, on the gilded table beside the massive man who resembled a beached and very sick whale, told the latest part of the tale. He picked up a syringe, dropped it with distaste, and poked a messy scattering of gray tablets.

"Oh, my, yes, I fear so! Yet I must obey him. You

appreciate that, your excellency."

The rajah waved him off.

The look the physician threw him suggested, *That is easy for you.* "An overdose, my lord. A race between overeating, drinking, and drugs…to the very edge of the abyss."

The rajah made a disgusted, "Tchaa!"

"It would be my neck in the gallows like his last caregiver!" the doctor blurted.

The rajah gestured again, impatient, *Go on.*

"His excellency experiments on his own. I had nothing to do with this! I prescribe purges, unsweetened tea, clean water, and raw vegetables without sauces, but…"

"You surgeons go overboard. My brother cannot fall from such a great height to settle for rabbit food and water! Give him a middle ground, at least." Not that his brother ever took things by halves. Why was he even trying?

Showing heat, the physician decried, "I beg your forbearance, my lord. He must dig himself from a great hole before he starts even the rabbit food!"

"What this time?" The rajah sighed. "Was it mushrooms?" He picked up the syringe again. 'What is this?"

The physician shrugged. "Some. Before, I had supposed his only drugs were gluttony, drink, and a few soporifics—cannabis, light doses of the poppy. But…" The physician's gaze swept the bed, disgusted. "For the last year, I fear, others supply him from foreign parts via the aero-plane service."

He pressed fingers to his mouth in covetous awe. "Exotic barks, sweat from frogs, insects even! When I arrive, I see the most fearful concoctions—the residue—"

The rajah began to say, "Yes, I know all that—" Startled by a sudden movement under the coverlets, supposing his brother roused, he saw instead the tousled head of a frightened boy peeking from the covers.

He strode closer, yanking the covers. "What is this?"

To his astonishment, the head of a girl also—twelve years of age, perhaps, looking no better, poked out too. She watched the two, warily.

"These are children! Half-drugged children!"

"Oh, dear—oh, my! I neglected to tell you. I—I thought you knew...were tolerant..." The physician read the look on the rajah's face and corrected his assumption that all potentates were corrupt. The stony look told him different.

The physician thrust belatedly past the rajah. "Shoo! Shoo!" He waved at the children. "His excellency uses them as bed warmers—he says."

The rajah's grimacing look would have shattered glass. "Bed warmers? The sun is high! This is India!" He flung open the draperies that kept the room in fetid golden twilight. "Get them out of here!"

To the children, he roared, "Go! Hide yourselves! Disguise yourselves. Mark yourselves, but do not come back. No! Don't wait for your clothes!"

"Yes, but..." the boy whimpered. "He will have me beaten." Just then, the maharajah stirred himself, blinking in outrage at the light.

With a panicky look, the girl hopped from the bed, falling onto the floor, then dragged the boy away, urging, "Come, Jaya!"

Grim-faced, the rajah turned back to the table, fingered the hypodermic, noted a residue of brown syrup in a brass spoon, smelt crumbles of tan grit, and rolled a scatter of dull green capsules in his palm like bullets. More telling were the tracked lines of brownish powder on a pair of the boy's small-clothes. He looked at his brother, sickened.

"Take them to a safe place," he warned the doctor.

Abruptly, the maharajah muttered, "Lea' me 'lone," and dropped back into an open-mouthed snore.

"Is he safe?" The rajah asked, blank-faced.

The look told the physician his interest was too small to register.

"His breathing calms."

"Swell!"

"Yes. Just your loving presence…"

At the rajah's warning look, the man abandoned that thought. "He does need a purging."

"I shall not be around for that," the rajah answered dryly. "But leave us now."

****

The rajah contemplated the gray, corpulent face. It was like old lard left in the sun. Trying to drum up pity—or even some compassion—recalling the plump, rosy-cheeked brother who had been hedonistic, true, yet always laughing at himself, with his belly-busters in the pool, chuckling when his arrows hit all but the targets…

When had that changed?

When he reached twelve or so…a young man's passage, be he king or beggar, into adulthood. Maidens flashing almond eyes looked up through lashes not at the heir to the throne but at the rajah instead, even though he was but a twig of ten.

That's when his brother's laughs became twisted and mean tricks a palliative. Drinking, and stuffing himself with sweets, made him even more repugnant to all within his sorry sphere.

The rajah smoothed his brother's sweaty, sparse hair. This time, though, recalling the boy and girl, something clicked like a clock stuck at an hour, and suddenly meshed smoothly past the sticking point.

"You did this to yourself, my brother," the rajah whispered. "More's the pity."

He gave a final look at the sodden heap on the bed. Then, with a mighty sweep of his arm, brushed the "medicines" and the boy's small-clothes onto the floor and stalked out.

"We begin a new game, my exalted brother! Now I make the rules!"

Chapter Eighteen
Caves of Ali Baba

"Come, come! Make ready!" Padmavati scolded. I recognized what that meant when her coven bore in caskets, mirrors, brushes, and perfumes. I could not believe this was happening again. Not after that night. I had not seen the rajah since. I turned myself into a wooden doll with frozen hinges, enduring the prolonged beautifying ritual. Numbed when they came for me, I was desperate and determined this time. In the folds of my sari, I had secreted six-inch hairpins.

I had not seen the rajah since the chess incident. He was finished with me. *On to his next conquest,* I thought bitterly.

I gripped the pins, praying I would have the courage to use them.

We crossed a bridge over a pond awash with lily pads in an area I had not been before. They left me in sculpted gardens, alone. Stunned, I watched the eunuchs melting into the dark, like bad actors leaving a stage.

I looked up in the sudden freedom. The moon was a melon rind and just as orange. Beyond the tarnished glow, the garden dissolved into misshapen contours. I revolved in place, looking about.

What now?

A trick?

My sari, per usual, was thin silk, yet I shuddered in the heat of the night, waiting for the maharajah to lumber from the massive topiaries. My ears, attuned, heard a whisper of cloth.

I tensed to hide among the dark shapes.

A brush of footfalls through short grass.

A faint aroma reached me—honeysuckle and jasmine mixed with something pungent and earthy—and the rajah, his face in shadow, emerged like a shimmering shade and waited silently for me. He held out a hand.

The other hand gripped a gnarled pitch torch, unlit, of rags, reeds, and—by the odor—creosote.

He waved the torch. "I could use one of those novelty electrical torches, but this is more appropriate and, perhaps, more reliable. Come."

I stared numbly at keys bunched at his waist. A tarnished ring as big as an embroidery hoop held one as long as my hand and as thick as a rifle barrel. The others rattled on a smaller ring, differing by bits of colored string.

My heart stopped—resumed. Why keys?

"Come." The rajah without another word forged over a path of crushed shells gleaming as though magical.

I caught sight of my sandaled, hennaed feet flashing beneath me, gauzy veils fluttering behind like dragonfly's wings. He was, as usual, in cream satin, this time only in breeches ending at the knees, displaying everything he had as well as a taut backside flexing muscularly as he strode ahead. I watched his broad naked back tapering to a neat waist, his black unbound hair flying behind like a young boy's. It wasn't often I watched him unawares. He was indeed beautiful, yet I must not lose sight of where I was. I tried to take note.

****

We were farther even than the zoo—animal yowling was fainter, shrubbery dustier and untrimmed, weeds higher. Dead fronds littered the ground. No more white crushed shells or mosaic-floored follies here, as I skidded past forlorn, waterless fountains to keep up and, after that, nothing but weedy rampant growth, alive with insects, which the creosote kept at bay. *What is this all about?* my imp fretted.

Though the palace grounds were sprawling, I sensed we neared an end.

I looked back. The palace was a pale toy on a slight rise between the trees.

"Stop! Wait!" I gasped, spitting out a bit of palm leaf.

But the rajah disappeared into a deeper jungle of palms and ferns. He seemed in a tearing rush, now. Fronds scraped my face, dragged at my silks, and tangled my feet as I stumbled after him.

He pulled me through a last straggle, stopping abruptly. I could see nothing beyond a sudden mound blotting the dark sky—a hillock covered in coarse grasses. "We are here. There is a more direct way, but…" He did not finish that thought.

I checked my surroundings and slapped at mosquitoes. "Here? Where?"

The rajah withdrew an ornate lighter from skintight breeches in answer, torching the bundle of faggots. Creosote sent sooty spirals upward.

The rajah's face took on a wicked, sensual mold, the flickers of light casting his eyes into unreadable shadow as he rummaged the key ring.

Keys? *A key?* But where to put it? What to unlock?

I studied the odd green hill looming before me, a plain green dome of grasses and weeds hidden until now behind the vegetation.

He brushed hands over the coarse grasses covering the unnaturally smooth mound, muttering, "It's here somewhere," and by digging through dead patches, revealed stained concrete covered by the skim of dirt and weeds. Then he inserted the key as large as my fist into a slab of metal corroded green and studded with welds and crude hammered designs, absurdly set in the wall of grass.

It looked centuries old.

The sound of the key in the lock shattered the night air.

Crickets ceased.

A bat fluttered off in the dark.

The rajah wrenched the massive door, which squealed like a cat with its tail trod upon.

Air, curiously dry and odorless for India, rushed out.

As he stepped into the dusty gloom, holding the torch, I instinctively stepped back.

"Come, *prya*."

I looked behind me into the dark. It was the far side of the moon. Inside was no better—stygian dark. *The dark of a crypt,* my imp suggested.

"No!" I pulled back.

"*Mere saath aaeeyé*." He spoke soothingly. I translated his words haltingly as, "Come. Don't be afraid."

But I was.

"See? I will light this." He waved the faggot at a sconce on the wall.

"What is this? Why—?"

Why have you not spoken to me? You were angry when last we met. It is dark and disturbing way out here. Now you wish me to go in there?

Oblivious to my hesitation, he used the torch to light a flame in the metal sconce. Looking back at the bug-filled night, I ducked just past the doorway into the domelike cave or room that followed the contours of the grassy hill. *If I keep behind him, he cannot trap me.*

Reservedly, I stepped farther in.

Now his back was to the massive door open to freedom. One way or another, he had gotten behind me.

I could claw a century and never get out of here. No one would hear, not even if any soul ever did venture to this godforsaken end of the grounds.

I braced to run, croaking instead, "Leave the door ajar," staring with longing to the beckoning, bug-filled night.

He laughed, showing his fine white teeth. "Ah! But I cannot do that, little one," and drew the door shut with grinding force.

"I—I hate being closed in," I tried, desperately tugging the door, all pretense gone.

He laughed and disappeared as I still regarded it, spinning to find him fooling with another door. It was nothing fancy—wood, crude welds raised like scar tissue, bolts and padlocks. The key from the smaller ring now sounded as if the cat were having a wrestling match with a saw, as tumblers clawed open with a sharp screeching.

This portal, five inches thick, solid monkey wood

with nail heads the size of dessert plates, swung lightly on pivots as if well oiled.

Dignity intact, I passed beyond, knees only slightly knocking. It was too much like the tunnel I had so lately traveled. "Hard to breathe. This air is dead. Sorry, cannot…"

He grabbed my hand, bringing me about.

"*Mere dil ka pyaar.* I've frightened you." His smile could melt slag.

Indeed.

I understood "pyaar"—"love of my heart," or close enough.

"But what is this ridiculous place?" I demanded.

His answer was to lock the door from inside.

****

I sensed this passage was far older, perhaps centuries, crumbling brick under whitewashed walls, bemused by the frieze of fanciful, faded animals and birds, flickering as if animated as the rajah rushed us by.

As the passage curved deeper, doors, older and riddled with wormholes, now studded the passageway along one side. The outer edge followed the contours of the hillock.

I checked for grills or slots indicating human occupancy. There were none.

He halted before one door, scratching a plaque, dark with age, and muttering, "This is it."

As he unlocked it with one of the tagged keys and reached inside, lighting another lantern, I scanned engraved symbols on the door—Hindi, but old.

I followed hesitantly into a room bathed in golden light as thick as honey. Sucking a breath, I squinted against the wavering glow.

Gradually my sight adjusted, after he lowered the wick—this one shaded, thank God, or we would have been blinded by the glittering mounds, bars stamped with exotic symbols, heaped in tottering piles surrounding drunken barrels of coins, all dumped among pyramids of tangled oddments. Shimmering, gleaming, and glittering, points of light sparkling off walls clear to the rounded ceiling and over-tipping in messy, glistening avalanches.

"It is like sunshine washing over us…" Eyeing the unstable piles, letting my hands play in the light, I needed to trod oddments and scuff litters of coins to enter farther. The dazzle quivered until I could not tell if my vision was flawed or the golden hoard shifted subtly, flowing from one stack to another.

He kicked a stack of coins over. "All this is my brother's," he said with a rueful disgust. "I liked to play with it from time to time, when I was but a lad and could steal away the keys. I nearly scared auntieji Madhuri to her death when no one knew where I'd got to."

"You mean—Madhuri was your amah?"

He nodded.

"A pretty dazzling sandbox!"

"It's been a while," he said, bashfully for him, plunging his hand into a pile. A piker at three feet, letting African rands, Dutch guilders, American eagles—some rough coins were older, with crude crosses and figures of eight—fall in discordant clatter.

Tripping, I sat hard on a tangled mound of chains and medallions, a ransom in solid gold baubles, earrings, pendants, diadems, and arm cuffs. Not plate or brass but pure gold, feeling a light touch of envy.

He supposes this excess will impress.

Of course, I'm not impressed.

Certainly not.

I owned gold once.

I squinched my brows together, puzzling this new information that came from nowhere.

I owned gold? Not just a little, but a lot!

I was still lost in thought, trying to recapture the memory, when he unceremoniously yanked me up. "Time wasting!" He laughed like a boy, and I forgot my one clear moment.

"*Mere saath aaeeyé.* Come!" he said when I lagged, still staring at the gold, striving to recall why that pile of glitter was a key to the past.

****

Color seeped out from the next cell like a London fog, if fog were pink.

My skin bloomed a rose-red blush, for the room was a rainbow, if scarlet was the mother-color. Boxes and barrels of the maharajah's birthday bounty—blood red, garnet, pink, carnelian, fire-red crimson, lavender. Dull, smooth, or polished cabochons like fat little pillows—oblong, square, round, sparkling with facets.

"The latest haul," he said heavily.

"Indeed!" I dryly eyed the excess. "So this is where it ends up. Buried!" My feet trod stones, rubies all, rolling under my step. Hot reflected light pinked my pale flesh. My body soaked up feverish hues as if the room were on fire and not my blood.

"May we go now…?" I whispered.

"Not quite yet."

"I've seen enough!" I added pointedly.

He watched me, stoic, yet something indefinable stirred in his eyes. Curiosity overcame my unease.

Grudgingly, I allowed him to lead me farther on.

A soft glow radiated from the next cave-like room as if it captured moonlight, and I entered a grotto this time filled with tributaries of pearls rolling and clicking about my feet. At the disturbance, an avalanche spilled rattling out the doorway. Pearls—oblong, angular, lumpy, or perfect spheres like small lustrous planets—clacked smoothly against each other as I picked my way carefully through.

I scooped handfuls: some black as ebony, sober grays, lavenders shading to deep purple, pale green, mabe pearls like lustrous blisters, and seed pearls…pink pearls and…

I sighed. A fairyland shimmering in the mellow glow of the lantern. So sad never to see the light.

"It's beautiful! Indescribable."

"Yes." He nodded, pleased.

In the torch's flare, shimmering moonlight from the mass of pearls washed over us. Angrily I brushed desire away like a stray, dangerous dog. Instead, I forced myself to glance coolly about, though I longed to throw myself into that lovely mound of pearls and feel them shifting, chill and smooth, beneath me, to bury myself in them—let them trickle through my fingers…

Don't be silly!

The rajah as usual looked through me as if I were a pane of clearest glass.

I glared back.

"More?" He nodded at the corridor.

What could be more? "If you must."

The pearly moonglow extinguished as the light

receded from the room, and I slammed against his back, his muscles rippling beneath warm pecan skin like steel coils. The tips of my fingers tingled, imagining running them down that deep cleft of spine. He halted slightly, and I felt a quiver before he strode on.

Sucking a breath, I murmured, *"Kshama kee-jeeae,"* not registering I spoke in Hindi—"Excuse me."

We were far under the mound now, halting before another oxidized plaque with more ancient Hindi writing.

Chapter Nineteen
Green Passion, Emerald Lust

Even after the excesses of the last cave-like rooms, I glided unprepared into an underwater realm of a shimmering sea. Dazzled by the bottle-green effervescence of what seemed like endless oceans—the phosphorous lime of spring grasses, green as translucent as May apples, even the velvet green of deep forest pools—washed in waves over us.

Verdant luminosity surrounded me, invaded me, coloring my vision...

I whirled, enraptured. As before, barrels and mounds, caskets, heaps, and pillows of loose stones cluttered the chamber.

Emeralds!

The whole cavern awash with them!

I imagined climbing those verdant swells of shifting sparkle, and slip-sliding back in a musical heap. How pleasurable! Swimming these chill green seas...

Over there, as an afterthought, a pile of duller, uncut stones rested. And here, in another heap, iridescent polished cabochons, ridges and waves of faceted effervescence—shimmering, dazzling, flashing.

I kicked past a sparkling mound to discover to my astonishment a low table and plump velvet cushions—green, of course.

The table was set with jade cut-glass decanters and

gold plates studded with sea-bright stones.

I was reckless with a feared-forever-lost sensation of youth.

"Won't you dine with me?"

"I am already drunk on riches, and have feasted on jewels."

Oh! How simpering! my imp chided.

As if I beheld such enchantment every day, I sank before the priceless plates, the tempting pastries, savories, small roasted fowl, sweets, and fruits ripe to bursting. Cut glass buckets of white wine reflecting green glints dripped icy condensation. What magic made this happen? I had heard no servants. Roast game fowls were steaming. The breads, crisp outside, soft on the inside. This was what it was like to own almost unlimited power. I refused to allow the thought in.

We sweetened our mouths with wine and honeyed *sakar-loung pani* with the bite of cloves, tart lemon *nimbu pani*, and candied ginger…*prolonging anticipation of the inevitable?*

The rajah sucked a ripe mango from its hard smooth seed. Sticky gold ran down satiny chest muscles. I trembled, longing to run my tongue over that glowing skin, lick its sweetness up to the pulse throbbing in the hollow of his neck, and end at the rajah's mouth, sweet with mango…

I tore my gaze away, certain my face flamed. *What am I thinking?*

You know. My imp smirked.

I brushed the imp aside; feeling as sensual as Delilah with her scissors, I threw my head back, gazing at him invitingly, or so I supposed.

****

He could only drink her in, her pale hair coiled high, her supple flesh as underwater-green as any sea creature, the pink tongue licking wine from a moist and inviting mouth, her body lushly revealed beneath diaphanous silk—but most of all, those ensnaring sea-green eyes.

With difficulty, he tore his gaze away...

Too soon, too soon.

****

Dreamily, I contemplated the luminous grotto. How would these smooth sea pebbles feel rising in chill green waves over my body?

As if reading my mind, the rajah chuckled. "You are a—how you say it? A mer-woman?"

"A mer-maid?" I grinned happily. *Though hardly a maid!*

"You are my—my Varuni, under the sea."

"Va-runi? And just who is this—Va-runi?" I flirted.

"Wife of Varuna, Lord of the Seas, celestial oceans, and the underworld." His expression seemed to say, *Doesn't every one know that?* "Lord Varuna would be envious of me now."

He lowered his head, melting me with his hooded gaze. "And I would see all of you..."

"All?" I shivered, not from cold.

"Primarily, to see if you own two legs...or an iridescent tail." He grinned his charming, lopsided smile.

I owned two hungers now, with both raging through me. Since I was not certain of one, I would let one hunger feed the other.

Wine and food made me languorous, yet blood

coursed my veins, warming my thighs and belly. To answer my first hunger, I sank into green clouds of pillows, lifting my arms in invitation. It was the wine, I told myself later.

His eyes spoke volumes as he sank beside me. Crunching emeralds made a musical clatter beneath us. Then he withdrew an ornate knife.

My eyes widened. I flinched aside. He merely cut the knot on my sari. Filmy veils drifted as lazily as butterfly wings over the stones, leaving me clothed only in verdant light.

Chill emeralds yielded. We sank into shifting masses that went slip-sliding away, crunching, tinkling, reconforming, until there was a comfortable niche— cool and delicious against my heated skin.

I helped him, tearing at the knotted cord at his waist, slipping my hands beneath the band and down long, cool, hard thighs; my hands, trapped between us, eventually felt the epicenter of greater heat, greater hardness, and sensed his body quivering with ravenous need as his hands explored me hungrily in turn. The rajah roughly dragged off the rest of his raiment until he was as free as I. We held and stroked each other, exploring, until our bodies, overriding desires, took over our minds and any reservations we had fled.

He cupped long, brown, articulate hands about my face, kissing me lingeringly, nipping my lower lip, brushing my eyelids and tonguing my ears. Keeping my own hands from straying, he held them securely above my head with one strong broad hand and, working down, nuzzled my breasts and brushed lips over my belly, bruising it with lusty kisses. When he finally entered, I groaned with a lust of my own, as if he had waited until the last possible moment or he would die. Or I would.

Still he delayed, until our combined union was the crashing fury of two thunderheads igniting the storm within us with primitive intensity and our bodies flickered silhouettes against the walls as lightning struck repeatedly, and electricity coursed our bodies.

****

We lay gasping, murmuring nonsense and gazing in wonder and yes—love. At least at that moment in time.

"Has it ever been like this for you?" I longed to ask, afraid he would ask in turn. I had no answer.

I whispered instead, "We can't leave yet…" *Unless it is to leave forever…*

The rajah whispered raggedly. "Never. Yet only Lord Vishnu knows when we may have this time again, little mermaid. Events change like a sword standing on end and just as dangerous. Plus"—he kissed me—"his excellency attends his treasure house infrequently, true—the only time he exerts himself is when he is…able." He shrugged. "Yet there are spies and eavesdroppers everywhere, currying favor from the one they fear most. We are not safe."

"And today?"

"Today I have it on good authority that he is captain of his bed. He has the grippe, as they say in France. Flags at half mast, the nation in mourning." He grinned sardonically. "We are safe, little one."

Haunted by the bloated specter, I clung to him.

He cupped my chin. "I am unafraid, yet I cannot put you in more peril."

"I am greedy too," I whispered huskily. "I weary of

being fearful. I want to live, if even just for now." I reached for wine, warming now. I'm afraid I drank from the bottle, my throat raw from lusty breathing. Laughing, he did too. We lounged there, passing the huge bottle back and forth, like two hooligans chuckling at nothing and continuing to drink, watching each other over the bottleneck, already tasting the next sweetness to come...

The slippery wine felt good trickling down. Our next kisses were wet and sweet. Pushing me into cushions, he trailed winey kisses down my neck to my breasts, lingering there, covering them with sticky sweetness; he licked and sucked sweet warm wine off my nipples.

I shuddered, lifting my face to thrust my tongue into his mouth. We stayed locked, exploring, touching, gripping shoulders and waists and buttocks, as if wishing to grasp every part and make us one, filling every curve, bone, hip, or knee into a matching hollow, until bodies seamlessly melded.

Then, in a fit of shyness, I burrowed into the stones so glacial, so smooth, relishing the sensation of translucent pebbles, the crashing and tinkling of discordant music, while this strikingly erotic male lifted handfuls, trickling emeralds over my shoulders, spilling them down the cleft of my pale breasts, his muscles rippling strongly in the warm flickering light. My flesh was cream satin against his polished bronze—a beguiling contrast and the only color against the verdant glow washing over us in a weightless tide.

Murmuring Hindi, he dribbled stones down my taut belly until they fell into the crevice of my thighs, lost in a pale silk tangle.

Selecting a small emerald where it fell in the dip of my navel, he ran soft lips down, down, delicately plucking more stones—a flick of the tongue here, a nip there—from where they secreted themselves.

I moaned and twisted, trying to reach him as he held me back with one sinewy arm.

"Stop. Tickling!" I gasped, gripping his black mane to stop his search for more elusive emeralds in my most secret parts before I exploded.

He raised his handsome tousled head, regarding me with eyes shadowed by long glossy lashes, eyes hot, black, and drugged with desire.

More? Shall I stop? They spoke.

His long naked copper body, warmed with cinnamon oils and slick with sheen, was now above me, propped on both arms.

Oh, yes, do not stop! Ohhhh, yes—now, please.

When I would fly to the domed roof and circle the room screaming my pleasure, he had no mercy.

Yes, yes, yes, please…spare me begging. Grind my bones…kiss my breasts…do things.

We rolled off the cushions. Myriad facets felt like small pinpricks. I wriggled to find a comfortable hollow…then forgot any tenderness as the tiny sharp jabs stimulated and heightened my pleasure. I had never felt so abandoned. *Oh, yes, closer still—invade me like a ravaging army…*

Wrapping my arms tightly about his lean, muscular waist, I was buried in him…and him in me.

With a flash of teeth like a grimace, he rolled me on top and held me up at arm's length.

I saw my tumble of pale hair drop heavily, shielding our faces.

In the bower of my hair and breathing in the scent of our recent pleasure, musky and perfumed, I couldn't hold back a shy grin matching his, feeling as wanton as a baud, yet aware he had made our first union special and we should not waste it.

He raised me higher, sliding me forward with the strength of muscled arms, plying his tongue, sliding down to my belly, tickling my navel, while I, giggling, breathless, fought to be let down.

"Stop!" I begged.

He stopped. "No?" he asked.

"Y—yessss! But…"

I answered by wriggling down, drawing my knees up and, before I could tumble off, pressing down on his hardening center…gasping, "Ahhhhh!"

He grinned up at me, conceited, the burgeoning growth immensely hard now and unbelievably large. I wondered briefly if I was supposed to be this lustful? *Am I supposed to be this abandoned?*

Easy! You act like a back alley strumpet, my imp insinuated.

I quashed my imp, lying full length across the rajah's chest and kissing him with renewed ardor, tongue to tongue.

My reservations did not last. Sensing a blissfully familiar escalating pressure, I rode him—he matching my rhythm, trying to take over—but I held him back with the flat of my palm, and so we swam, rolling in the green seas of our underwater grotto, awash with wave after wave of desire…

I was out of my mind…urging him, floating and twisting, plunging and lifting above the green stones, until our bodies soared to the ceiling with ecstasy and a fiery explosion erupted deep in my secret self.

Satiated and exhausted, the tide receded, washing us at last to the shore of sanity…or relative sanity.

****

Later I pondered if we had both gone mad, not from forbearance but from the uncertainty of the future.

I would never be the same.

Sated, throbbing, and pleasantly exhausted, we eventually found contentment in entwined fingers and the touch of shoulders. The rajah whispered against my hair, "Do you know why I wanted this?"

"No, not quite," I whispered inadequately.

"It is beautiful. No?"

I nodded numbly.

"I wanted"—he waved a hand—"something to please you. You've had little that is pleasant here," he murmured through my hair.

You can say that again.

"The first time I saw you, your eyes so filled with green fire they would turn these stones into dull pebbles of no consequence. I knew my brother's riches could never compete, nor would I wish them to."

"This was a challenge?" I rose on one elbow.

"I spoke clumsily. Yet a lifetime of looking into your eyes gives all the emeralds I could ever wish for. I no longer care what my brother wills."

I giggled.

His turn to glare.

I waved him off, stuffing a knuckle in my mouth to keep from laughing. "No matter," I sputtered. "You speak at times as if reading from *Jane Eyre*."

"Jane—Eyre?" He raised those fierce wings of brows again. I smiled up at his exasperation, his annoyance at being found lacking in any way.

"Never mind. I love it when you speak that way. Don't stop."

He looked at me so gravely I wanted to laugh again but quickly sobered at his next words.

"You are my wife now, my little foreigner." He spoke as if it were an ordinary comment, like how salty or sweet a dish.

"Wife…?"

"I am your lord and protector. No one will ever harm you," he stated in his best pedantic style. "Let him have all of this. All Rajasthan—all India. I have you."

****

I woke aware of cooler, wetter air, his strong arms cupped under my knees and shoulders, my head bouncing on his chest under his chin; I stared up at the muzzy moonlit sky. A wet moon.

"May we come back, ever?" I whispered against his neck.

"I will move the mountains to make it so."

Reluctant to break the spell, I rushed on. "Might I have another wish…?"

"Anything, *pyara*."

"I wish to leave the palace. If even for a day," I whispered into the hollow of his strong neck.

His grip tensed.

"With you!"

"You are beloved as a wife now, Sarabande." He spoke in liquid Hindi, then, changed to his stilted English. "I can deny you little. But think you that I cannot protect you?"

"It isn't that, my—my *love*." The word seemed so new on my lips. "This is my place now. I—I feel it so."

And truthfully I meant it then. I considered carefully. "Yet I am not real. I need to see people," I explained inadequately. "Real people. I need outside these walls."

The rajah looked down at me oddly. "If it means so much," he answered shortly, "we will see…"

I was miserable. I had spoiled it all. He would avoid me now, so as to avoid these conflicts. Yet I had a right. I could not turn myself into a doll to be dressed, cosseted, and taken out of the box every so often.

And grow fat and indolent? my imp suggested.

Chapter Twenty
Uncontrollable Tide

"*Pri-ya…*" The rajah put his finger on my chest.
"*Pri-ye…*" My love pointed to himself.
I parroted, pursing my lip, of which the rajah took full advantage. A good time later, I asked, "But what does it mean? You've never told me…" I laughed, swatting him with one of the multitude of pillows.
"It means 'sweetheart.' Now say after me, *Mera pyara…*"
"*Mera pyara*," I echoed.
"My love…or if you like, *mere dila ka pyara…*"
I raised my brow.
"Love of my heart." My rajah folded both hands dramatically over his own. I hid a smile.
"You have many ways of speaking it," I murmured low, stroking where he loved to be touched. He shivered and stayed my hand.
"You are a strumpet—a witch, *a kali*. You make me forget my priestly upbringing." He grinned impiously.
I looked from beneath my lashes. "Say me more." I relished how he spoke—the tenor resonance of formal toff English. He could recite a book on laying brick and still I would listen, like a rapturous schoolgirl.
However, my rajah had been distant, or so I imagined, after our idyll in the treasury crypt and my

apparently ill-timed demands.

Next morning he had gone. Busy with affairs of state, I told myself, or his prize horses, or perhaps he left the palace altogether. Yet his leaving put me at odds, restless and always looking over my shoulder.

We had been overly polite upon return to his rooms that night. He read my mood. I did not sleep but lounged on the parapet overlooking a lake as deep and black as my thoughts.

I must have fitfully slept. In the morning, an old servant, stiffly formal and openly disdainful, told me with some relish, "His highness left early. I do not query where he goes, memsahib, or what business commands his attentions." *Clearly not you* was implied.

I had the sulky notion to return to the seraglio but could not make myself. I would have liked to have Asha with me, however. Virtually ignoring her in my captivation with the rajah, I did not deserve her friendship now, she who had shown me charity.

The rajah seemed suitably chastened when I next saw him, even shy.

"Madam, I presume you are well," he uttered formally. Then we rushed to each other's arms with graceless abandon as we bumped noses and missed lips in our eagerness to make amends.

"I am not used to announcing my leave-taking," he said grudgingly. "It is new to me, and unusual for a—"

"For a male to need to, here in India?" I raised my brow.

"Precisely."

"Then I shall not care."

****

We grew reckless, even flaunting our relationship

before spies and staff alike.

My rajah assured me, "My servants are loyal. Isn't that right, Anupam?"

I blushed that first time, sinking slowly under the covers.

Anupam, the rajah's aide de camp and best friend, had arrived as usual, cheerfully whistling. Anupam smiled, man to man. "So right, my lord!"

Throwing open shutters, plunking chilled *chai* and rice cooked in milk and fruit, *kheer*, and generally making himself at home, even sitting on the edge of our bed, he chattered on about the day, kitchen gossip, the maharajah's disposition—homicidal, drugged, or just his natural suspicious nature—and whereabouts. Serious fare along with the *chai*. It forewarned if the maharajah was on a rampage or safe in "his cups." Until we are not...

I looked forward to this gossip of the day—like having with breakfast a juicy gazette that one did not need to open.

Still I pressed. "Why, my love? You seem to be doing more and more *away* these days."

The rajah grew silent, clenching his jaw. "I do not wish to speak of it. Let us say my dear brother grows more—irresponsible." Moreover, he would not elucidate, no matter how delicately I picked at the subject.

Either way, my rajah often needed to take over the reins, leaving me much alone.

****

It was one of those days we were abed feeding each other dates, *chai*, *paneer* with *naan*, peaches bursting with juice, or green melon, and wallowing on finest linen scented with jasmine, tuberose, and lily. Outside of a troubling fogginess regarding my past, I could not recall living any other way. I rather liked being a de facto princess.

"Oh, stop, silly!" I toed the interesting bulge in his linens. "Stop tormenting me"—I looked up beneath my lashes—"with speeches." For he had been reliving a talk he'd had with a stuffy German manufacturer of hunting rifles, a subject not dear to my heart.

He began loosening the bedclothes twisted around me, rolled me onto my tummy, and commenced the slow journey of kisses down my back. "So then, I proceeded to ask of him naturally, the quality and caliber of his ammunition, the accessibility and…"

"Oh, do stop." I giggled as he showed me the quality and accessibility of his ammunition.

Later, we lay drowsy and satiated, with the scent of love heavy in the air.

"Must get up, insatiable wench." He slapped my rear. "I have duties."

"In-satiable! My, we are learning big words," I cooed.

"I can teach more than big words." The rajah kissed my ear, then sat up and groaned, thrusting a hand through long black hair.

"*Pyaar*," I tried in Hindi, "what troubles you?"

"My brother—is ill again. I meet dignitaries—these from Holland. Something delicate. Treaties, in case of war. Possible loans." He smiled over his shoulder. "It is time I lifted something besides you. And I must attend to the maharani," he tossed out negligently.

At my quick look, he continued. "She is brought low. She needs friends, love. If not me, then…?" He left the question dangling.

"No friends!" I raised a jealous brow. "With all her ladies in the seraglio?"

He bit his lip.

"The maharani is very beautiful." I said clumsily.

"Indeed, the most lovely in the country, and with the fairest disposition," he agreed, oblivious.

"You are a trial." Unreasonably jealous, I teased him again with my toe, hoping to divert him. He snatched my foot and tickled the tender instep. I writhed, breathless.

"Trial, am I? I will show you the full wrath and power of your master." He held me, arms above my head, and pressing me deep into the feathers, kissed me thoroughly. Tasting the last juices of the peach, I wrapped my legs to bind him more tightly—he lifted my hips to affix me tighter still; our ardor took over, mindless, fevered, and breathless as usual, with lips bruised and bodies delightfully used.

Still gasping, the rajah tossed me over. I rolled back, pulling my long hair out from under. It was different now, though. I sulked. I was being appeased. I examined him with a raised brow and pushed out my lower lip as he fitted on the red sash and gaudy badge of rank, with the aid of Anupam, to meet the ambassador from Holland—and also, it seemed, the Secretary of Defense from France.

"Later, the dinner of state, my lord?" Anupam asked.

"Oh!" My eyes widened. I jumped up, holding the silk sheets before me.

"Should I wear something more—dignified?" I plopped back and lifted a leg behind Anupam, letting my sheet float back. "A state dinner with maybe four hundred of your visiting cousins and the French Defense Minister… Is he handsome?"

"Of course! He resembles me."

"Sounds dull indeed!"

"Sary, love." He watched me in the pier glass. "I thought you understood. You will not be seen—not be attending this time." He bent to kiss my nape. I swerved aside.

I kept my expression pleasant. Was this a change I should worry about? I had grown too complacent, too assured.

I despised the face-covering veil, yet occasionally I sat, the subject of curiosity, in the balcony, with select ladies of the seraglio. The dinners were glamorous, candlelit and glittering. I longed to be by his side. Occasionally the maharani made an appearance. I hoped this was due to her heightened influence and not his interest.

The rajah, with dark dangerous eyes, said when I mentioned it, "I am no longer concerned over what my brother might think, yet why stir the pot? Who knows what might float to the top. Besides, the maharani implied her husband might be making an effort this evening." He grimaced.

"I'd feel like a fun-time girl trotted out at a men's smoker, at any rate!" I fumed.

Well, aren't you? goaded my imp, who had been, thankfully, silent these past weeks. *Neither wife nor recognized, I would say. More like a handy trull.* My imp apparently was making up for lost time.

"You said something, love?"

"No bother." I bit savagely into a persimmon,

spitting the seeds like a hoyden.

He raised his brow.

"Yet there is your brother's birthday. There is precedent for that!"

I grew silent as it struck me I had been within these confines for almost a year. He threw me a cool glance.

"Have they run out of precious stones with which to gift him? Lead weights might be suitable." I said as heavily as the subject, happy to see his mouth twitch.

He sighed and turned to admire himself, straightening the back of his tunic. "Please don't vex yourself, love."

He held out his arms to allow Anupam to fasten bracelets, bent his neck for the choker of pearls, and finally let him fit on the turban before the man sailed out with a knowing expression.

"Sary, *pyara*. If you sit discreetly with the other women, behind a heavier *ghoon ghat*, at the end, perhaps you may look on."

"Look on!" I shouted, warring between selecting the heaviest candlestick to whack him over the head or shoving him off the parapet. I began weeping instead.

"What else may I give you?" He cupped my cheek with long brown fingers. "Anything you desire."

"Don't appease me! You broke your promise! I wish to leave. I told you!" I flashed my eyes at him, hating my wheedling, carping tone yet suddenly wild to leave the stultifying palace, this small confining village. It was before the maharajah's birthday when I was reborn in this alien place, the last I knew of the world outside.

The desire became a need so strong I could not breathe.

He removed his hand.

"Just a day," I amended. "I am"—I searched for words—"losing myself." *And that before I am found.*

"Indeed, I did promise. You shall have it." Yet it was as if he meant, "You will be sorry."

"And another…"

He lowered his brow, nailing me with his dark eyes, and picked up his ceremonial saber. "An-other?"

'It will keep."

"As you will." He spoke distantly, wincing a stiff smile, his mind already on the evening and the Dutch ambassador. *And the maharani?*

I was learning Hindi and a smattering of Urdu, and attempted strumming simple melodies on a stringed instrument called a sitar.

Yet I ended the evening by hanging over the parapet and staring out at the far distant city under the stars.

Chapter Twenty-One
Unbridled Passion

"Oh, how pretty. A true sweetheart!" I babbled, giddy as I stroked the mare's glossy neck. Soft silver gray. Velvet nose. Large silvery eyes under ladylike lashes. I looked up at the rajah, ecstatic. Starlings flitted and rummaged straw in the rambling stables. The smell was heaven. Warm animals, hay, sunshine, and dust…and freedom!

"Approve?"

My face said it all.

"Now," he asked, hand hanging onto the bridle, "what is this other task you have set before me?"

I toed the ground. "It is silly. Since you have not offered it." I suddenly felt shy and hated that.

He held the reins out of reach. "I must have this boon before we go thither," he jested.

"Thither? Is that a word?"

He shrugged, as if to say, *With you English-speaking creatures, who knows?*

I blew a ringlet off my forehead. "After all this time—you know my name, yet…I do not know…yours. I…think of you only as 'the rajah,' you see. No one ever calls you by your given name. The one your mother might have called you," I finished lamely. "I thought, since we were going off together like this—" I waved my hand, exasperated. "Oh, never mind!"

He smiled, bemused, suddenly interested in a starling's flight to the rafters. "My mother named me after one of her favorite books," he said gravely as he cupped his hand for my foot.

"How odd. Not a family name or—?"

I placed my foot in his hand and lifted myself with ease of familiarity over the saddle. A fact I filed away. I sat astride. *I saw myself racing like the wind. Away from someone, someone riding hell-bent for leather, bullets whipping past. The crack of a rifle. The saddle between my legs, the pommel banging into me as the horse galloped off kilter in its mad race…*

He brought me back.

"What?" I stared at him confused.

"Quasimodo, from Victor Hugo. *The Hunchback of Notre Dame*. Quasi, for short."

I yanked the reins from his hand. "Please!"

"It is at least a yard long. I prefer the first of them—Ram." He pronounced it Rawm. "Or Rami." He shrugged elegant shoulders.

"Ram." I tested it on my tongue. "It suits you— Ram. But has it a meaning? Ram?"

He mumbled something, adjusting my stirrups.

"What? I didn't hear that."

He mumbled something else.

"Say it!" I wheedled. "What does it mean?"

"It means…oh, god—or god-like, I suppose." His ears turned red. "Now, can we be off?"

I held back a giggle. God-like.

****

His stallion, gleaming black and bad-tempered, suited Ram with his billowing gypsy silk shirt and hair whipping like a black flag.

Leaving the last archway, we entered Bharatpur's dusty, packed streets. I grabbed the pommel and twisted to look back at the immense golden pile blotting the skyline. No wonder I could not find my way. We had slipped out an obscure side entrance behind the royal stables, all but lost in vine.

My first impression of the sprawling city was—too loud, too open, too dirty. City odors fought—sewage, frying food, incense—those of bodies. Crowds mauled us, ignorant of his status, in a tide of hawking messy commerce. Beggars brushed our horses. Children stood in the way to slow us while nimble fingers tugged at saddlebags. Ram, apparently foresighted, sprinkled them liberally with *annas*, half rupees and *pices*.

"Cheeky little buggers." He grunted cheerfully.

The rajah could have been a wealthy corn merchant as we wended south through Bharatpur slums next to walled mansions, which became farther apart until, passing fields, we approached a wilderness. Entering under a rusting scrolled arch, we cantered into a world where egrets stalked, swans drifted, birds chattered crazed overhead, and unseen things slithered.

"A hunting reserve," the rajah explained. A curious mix of swamp, greenswards, and arid islands, the reserve was seemingly untouched.

For an instant, the urge to dig my docile mare in the ribs and fly like a hot breeze to further freedom—here, or back there in the winding streets—was nigh overpowering.

True freedom.

"The reserve has no real end," Ram was saying as if reading my mind.

Still, as we passed under the arch, I raised from my

saddle and looked behind me at the retreating city, when Ram was not looking.

****

Ram hobbled our mounts at a sun-rippled clearing ringed with lotus, scrub willow, and thickets of honeysuckle and blackberries. The air was cool and moist, with the essence of moss.

Feeling my aching backside and tender parts, I dismounted, throwing myself down on springy tufts of moss laced with tiny yellow flowers, and gazed through a funnel of branches.

Sun dusted leaves of lime lace, spattering us with gilt as Rami sprawled beside me, chewing on a red clover. The palace was far behind. Anything could happen. We prolonged our feast of bread, cheese, olives, cold chicken, dates, and oranges, sipping a sweet red wine that coated our lips and tongues with wildness, fueling the banquet to come, where we could taste each other, mouths spiced with wine and garlic.

Heat blossomed like a red flower as the day grew on. Ram's shirt and my silks stuck. Sweat slicked our bodies. Still we lingered, enjoying the sun-spattered relative coolness and mossy wet fragrance.

While horses grazed on fern, we eyed each other through heat-glazed eyes. "Hot..." I breathed as an outdrawn breath.

The rajah—Ram—plucked at my riding shirt. Airy fingers of breeze dried sweat, leaving a delicate chill. I shuddered, closing my eyes, in unconscious seduction, dropping my head back as he wriggled off my jodhpurs.

Our flesh was slippery. We lay there relishing the tickle of grass and the playful breeze brushing our skin, delaying the unspoken.

He without ceremony pressed me into the springy moss, murmuring, "Sary—Sary, my *rājpatnī*, my sweet wife, my beloved," and more incoherent words of love and naked passion. I didn't care what they were.

Despite the languid breeze, our bodies slicked against each other, my full breasts slipping against his chest's springy black silk; sleek as a mermaid, I shot from his grasp, only to swim back, gripping his long black mane and thrusting my tongue deep, meeting his, as if we wanted to consume each other.

He held each wrist as efficiently as manacles. Our mouths slipped off each other, his hands slid down my arms, he licked the cleft between my breasts, tongued my neck, nipping my chin and finally my mouth, which he used fully. Then I felt the full weight of his wet, sinewy body. Feeling familiar strength against my belly, I reached between—I didn't have to reach far! He was slick there too. I laughed deep in my throat as my hands kept slipping no matter how hard or big he became.

"Shhh, shhh. *Mere dil ka pyara.* Love of my heart. Now, allow me to pleasure you." He stayed my hands with difficulty. They had a mind of their own.

Ram explored me, diving fingers and caressing my warm damp floss. "Don't wait!" I demanded. My breathing was hard and harsh, burning my throat. He resisted, an agonizing moment in which I thought I would die if he did not continue. Then, crying out in delighted surprise, I allowed him to do his will, for his will was strong, and he was adept at the pleasures he performed. I needed to do nothing but drift in an erotic dreamscape for what seemed timeless hours. When I attempted to answer him with my own rhythm, whispering coarsely while biting his ear, he rode on, and I surrendered, wailing instead to the lacy branches above us, "Don't stop…"

"Never," he rumbled thickly. "I want to devour you while I can…but am I hurting?" I answered by binding my legs tightly around his narrow waist and purring, unblushing, ferociously returning his bruising kisses.

As if forbearance that even an angel would repeal came to an end, he, a magnificent stallion straining at the gate, at last let go the reins, and his weight took me with such grinding force, such thorough abandonment and power, I was overwhelmed—at first.

Then I matched him, tasting the salt of his shoulders with my teeth sliding across his slick hot skin. Felt his muscles bulging and rippling, with each thrust deeper as if demons drove him under passion's dark spell, until at last we cantered together to a gasping halt. We lay stunned and sated, watching the sun's passage turn the green lace over our heads to honeyed orange.

Our horses nibbled sweet grasses, in no more hurry to return than we two lovers; the day faltered as if reluctant to let go its honeyed kiss of the sun. I brushed a thumb over his full swollen lips—a spot of blood, like a ruby, welled where I had bitten him.

We had entered a new realm.

We both recognized it: I more than wife, he more than husband, destined to feel the need and the loss if absent from each other's company for more than an hour—intuiting a restlessness that would follow us all our days…

Or however many we had left.

****

We bathed in a pool, black and chill as onyx, cooling our fevers and reflecting the young moon—leaving wine bottles, baskets, and picnic cloths where they lay. I looked back from my horse with a sad smile—a memorial of sorts.

As we rode into city outskirts, I tried to hide a restlessness. I watched throngs going about normal life, closing shops, lighting lanterns, the hot grease of suppers cooking, mothers calling children, and I felt a renewed hunger. This was the real world. What was I playing at?

The outing turned the palace into a mere stage setting, unreal and shabby in places, if one looked closely enough. I closed my eyes to keep from bolting. I gripped the reins. "I wish we need not return. I wish we were them." I nodded at hawkers and night customers milling the market, women admiring bright silks and cottons, a man frying fish on a roadside stand. "I wish we lived in a small house, and..."

He too studied the street bustle and shook his head. "Suicidal folly," he said shortly. "Blood ties run thin where pride and a throne are at stake. For all his sloth, my brother holds unlimited power and riches, if not the effort involved." He cast a rueful glance my way. "He would hound us to the ends of the world. He treats his spies and assassins well, if little else. For now, he pretends you are nonexistent; on the rare times he regains his wits, or rouses from his latest opium dream, imagined injuries roar back with creative vengeance."

We rode on through crowded streets.

"But why? He is a monster. Surely they know he could turn on them."

"The same love of our necks we all hold. Sentries,

palace guards, even the army, all remain loyal," he said with a bitterness I had not seen before. "No one wants to die on his bloody altar waiting out the inevitable. Besides, it is rolling a boulder uphill to change thousands of years of tradition." He looked at me with self-mocking irony.

"No—" I looked about—the same fear infecting me, and whispered, "Have they not even…tried…?"

"Assassinating him? I will overlook that. He is my brother! However…" He looked off, brooding. "Indeed. That is why the *gharial* pits—and the tigers. That is why the blind in the jungle. He threw a three-day orgy to watch the slaughter of a would-be assassin, a demented beggar, the last time, six months ago. Much as Roman emperors, some members of the elite, and the generals, are drawn to long-drawn-out executions. They seem to have developed a taste for it."

I stroked my gray's mane, thinking furiously.

"If we have no future, why not release me and let me take my chances? And you are as much a prisoner as I am."

It was perverse, and I knew it. Both of us shied from discussions of the past or future, or where I came from. Neither mentioned the oddity of my forgetfulness. At times, I wondered why. I had not dropped out of the sky like a Hindu deity, after all.

The set of his jaw always stopped me when I ventured close to the mystery—something in his face, even pity, when he covertly watched me.

He tugged at my pommel. People milled around us; we were an island unto ourselves. Anger jarred a latent sensation of the hot-blooded woman I must have been.

"But there is more!" I demanded, clutching his own

reins. He looked at me, furious. I would not be deterred. "I know there is. I feel it!"

"This was a mistake!" His eyes flashed beneath thick expressive brows, and I mourned the willful assassination of our recent passion.

To punctuate, Rami cantered ahead. Irritably, I raced after, nearly running down a crippled woman. After apologies and backward glances to see if she was being helped, I caught up.

"We would be happy anywhere...I would! If I never see another jewel or eat another rich dessert, I will be content. I am not afraid! And you would not need to cover your brother's mistakes. Surely someplace..."

He looked at me with that pity I'd come to loathe. "Don't ask again." Then in a softer tone, "Nowhere is safe, *mera pyara*. And I love India. She is my other mistress. I cannot leave her to him."

The rest of the ride back was silent, each of us in our own world, yet some of the magic lingered.

Change was coming, though, like a tiny ripple in the ocean creates a monsoon half a world away.

Not a ripple to be seen, but monsoons were coming, both real and in our private worlds. Perhaps we should have sucked every bit of joy from that day.

Chapter Twenty-Two
Monsoons

Our idyll lasted through seasonal rains flooding streets, dampening walls, slicking marble, and invading the palace in sultry wetness.

Like children, Rami and I stood on the privacy of our parapet under warm volleys that turned our hair into weighty curtains and our clothes as sheer as onionskin, until, laughing, we stripped, reveling in the deluge engulfing us like a waterfall.

"Haven't done this since I was a lad!" Ram yelled through rain hammering the slick marble with silver nails. Mercury skirts danced about my bare legs. Wet hair flung silver tinsel. When I lifted my face to the invisible skies, the rajah kissed my wet mouth, and rain as warm as blood mingled with our tongues and lips and teeth.

Hands slicked over buttocks and chests, clasped necks, gripped shoulders. He kissed my streaming wet nipples until my knees gave out. In one quick swoop, the rajah carried me inside. I clung to the doorway.

"No! Here. Let's love each other in the rain." Without a word, Rami carried me back out into the cloudburst; slip-sliding, we landed in a heap. Warm drumming rain drowned our words. Lips clinging, we let torrents sluice off us, silvering our steaming bodies. He pulled cushions from the settee as increasing gales of water threatened to drown us. Laughing at the sky, we admitted defeat and scrambled under the overhanging balcony. He impatiently braced me against a wall and there, shielded by a cascade plummeting off the roof tiles, we made love, with the spray clouding us in silvery mist, he murmuring through the wet tangled hair plastering my face.

"Now I know you are a mermaid! You are Circe. My only addiction, as dangerous as my brother's."

"And you mine."

****

How could anything go wrong?

Yet our Eden was reaching a crisis so sharp it could turn on the blade of a guard's scimitar.

How could any serpent destroy this?

Yet it was serpents—very real serpents—that were the catalyst for events neither the rajah nor I could have foreseen.

Chapter Twenty-Three
Elephant Walk

The end began on an outing, one grudgingly given, I might add. The monsoon's enforced imprisonment finally wore at us. It was like breathing through a damp tea towel. The business was a marauding tiger, the hunt delayed due to the rains.

The days had turned starched blue and the sun into a cauldron. Still I reveled in the dry heat, high on the back of the usual elephant for such undertakings, this time traveling alongside a wide, sluggish, brown river. "They are perfect and beautiful as they are!" I protested. "It is their nature to kill—what, livestock?"

"I have no yearning to drape myself in hot smelly pelts and parade about on review." Rami grinned, waving at the retinue in open trucks ahead, bristling with rifles. "If that is your concern."

"Do you really need them all?" I scoffed, trusting we would be together somewhere, not on the back of another piebald elephant tearing into the jungle with a tribe of bloodthirsty, armed males. I shuddered in the heat, remembering the last such time.

The rajah threw me a warning look, and I subsided as we turned for the village in question. With each thump of a mighty foot, the earth shook and saplings bent, leaving a leafy wake. The skies were hot and yellow now, through trees evaporating moisture into a soupy fog; the jungle turned acid green, and birds wheeled in torpid currents.

"This is all his, is it not?" I asked, to break the awkward spell and slapping a mosquito as large as a dragonfly supping on my salty skin.

"He grows sicker, more…ungovernable. I must do more, I must be prepared." He swatted a broadleaf. "Yet"—he smiled at me—"by that time the maharani may have another son, or he will name the young prince."

"Or the sky could fall," I answered in kind and brushed a damp curl off my neck.

The mood passed. "Oh! Look!" I pointed at scolding monkeys making daredevil leaps. My mood darkened again as I recalled the purpose of this outing, the possible death of a magnificent Bengal tiger.

The rajah read my thoughts.

"But we aren't killing it, are we?"

"Is it their nature also to dine on children?" he asked quietly. At my look of dismay, he said, "This particular beast developed a passion for human flesh. Young human flesh. Several children have been dragged off, as seen by witnesses. One father found the poor child's chewed bones. A girl of three. This one's a stalker and pure killer. If my brother won't investigate, I must."

I was chastened and mortified. "Children! How can a tiger attack children? Where are their parents?"

I brooded a moment. "Tell the villagers they should be more careful."

"Yes, I shall do that," he answered dryly.

"Why don't they look after their children?" I cried. He waved at the open jungle. "Children run freely here.

Do you see walls?"

"Of course not," I muttered. Ragged villagers now gravely lined our path.

"Tricky, too right." Rami scowled beneath fierce brows. "I wish they would stop that bloody bowing! My brother needs little excuse to threaten unspecified treason, if there is a hint I overstep."

"You walk a thin rope."

"Razor wire, more aptly. One of the chaps up there is a spy." He nodded at the truck of armed bearers.

And I do not make it easier.

I felt the villagers' anguish when, after setting fresh meat lures and waiting, we failed to trap the beast or see any sign. With promises of returning with more scouts, we left the ramshackle village along the riverbank for another spot the trackers excitedly led us to.

A mile later, the rajah nodded at water buffalo stomping muddy holes in a far bank. "See that motion in the canes? The fellow's stalking them."

I glimpsed tawny yellow and black rippling the bulrushes across the brown river, near shaggy buffalos hitched to a water wheel. "Yoked! The poor beasts are fair game!"

He motioned. His men raised carbines. The distance was too far, I thought, and then shots peppered the bank from rifles and shotguns both. I could see puffs of dust. Even a pot shot from a pistol. The canes across the way thrashed and stilled.

The rajah held up a hand—Stop. The men waded the murky river and, shouting happily, held up the tiger's head. Hauling the body above their heads, they recrossed the river and fixed it to a truck bed.

Exultant, we turned to head back.

We re-entered the narrow jungle road. Neither Rami nor I saw the sinuous rope hanging from a tree until the motion, a yellowish flash, caught the edge of my vision.

"Rami!" A thick loop of scales swung a foot from my face. I noted, as I turned, one man smiling secretly, but spellbound, I took no notice...

Black squares decorated the hanging length, dropping down, down, seamlessly coiling and recoiling.

The elephant placidly jolted aside and plodded on.

I rose from the cramped space, as we left the snake behind, scraping my knee.

"Okay! Laugh—fool!" I cried. Somewhere below, I heard another man's low chuckle.

"Ah, Sary. That is an *ajgar*, that is all."

"All!" I twisted my mouth, eyeing the undulating rope looping to another tree. "It's following us!"

"They don't bite. They may crush you to death and afterward eat you, of course." He snorted like the despicable male he was.

"Fine! If I am really fortunate, I might find one in my bed one night!"

More annoyed than puzzled, I saw the guard suppress another knowing smile. Apparently, I was the source of endless humor.

"It is what you call a python," my unthinking male continued. "Grows twenty or so feet and can swallow a water buffalo if allowed."

"I wouldn't know!" I swallowed a sharp remark as Ram droned on about how colorful, fascinating, deadly, brilliant, intelligent, and bloody downright delightful snakes are, apparently ever since Adam and Eve's infamous cajoler.

I balefully scrutinized the jungle.

"Now the *daboia*," the infuriating man continued, "common in Punjab and Bengal, is most aggressive. The deadliest of reptiles. Most certainly. The *daboia* delivers maximum venom, unlike species with a dry bite. Invariably…"

"How fascinating. You don't say," I snapped.

It was not his joking manner making me tedious. *Something is wrong.* My primitive brain center had been set a-jangle. I decided to ignore him.

"India even has snakes with tails like monkeys that grasp, or let them fly from treetop to treetop to drop down on…"

I drew my hands inside the howdah, checking trees.

"However, I find the bamboo viper and the sea krait, oh, very nice—the sea krait, black with brilliant blue stripes, while the viper is green, like a beetle—but the ugliest fellow…" He chuckled. "The ugliest is the hump-nosed pit viper."

He continued chortling at my disgust—typical male the world over—while I tried to drown him out with thoughts of pitching him from the howdah.

"But for sheer evil"—he sobered—"King Cobra. Enormous!" He spread muscled arms wide. "A snake who feeds on other snakes. They rear three feet if aroused, though I find…"

"Enough!"

"Oh, but *mera pyara*," he teased, "I haven't listed all our reptiles. There is the *naja naja*, the most famous. The spectacled cobra flares its hood, hypnotizes one, and causes instant attacks of the heart if…"

"I said, enough!"

"Are you ill, *priya*?"

"Of course not." I looked away. "Takes more than a few silly snakes—just—tedious is all!"

"I take it you would not fancy my dear brother's snake collection, then." The cleft in his jaw deepened.

I flashed him a horrified look.

"Yes, that domed building behind the animal enclosure. Dear brother owns species from—"

"All your bloody buildings are domed! Don't jest."

"I was—how you say—"

"Teasing?"

"Yes, teasing. I forget I am nearly twenty-two years of age now."

Twenty-two! Younger than I! Suddenly I felt cranky, old, and tiresome.

"Yes, only teasing."

"That…that thing was rather remarkable. However, your brother… What…what does he do with…?"

"Let's leave it that he has inventive ways, as I mentioned, of dealing with thieves, spies, and those harmful to the empire, or those he *supposes* harmful, or simply for whim or boredom."

His face darkened, and he shrugged his broad shoulders as if to say, *Who kens?* "See, we are well past. The snake has not climbed in with us. I will never tease you again. Feel free to get back at me"—the cleft in his jaw deepened—"when I least suspect it."

"Never fear." I laughed, still seeing legions of reptiles dropping from trees and rapidly crawling after us.

"Yet I would love to tease you—a little?"

He had the familiar question in his hooded secretive eyes and wicked lingering smile.

I read his ardor and felt myself respond unwillingly as he touched me, for I still wanted to be angry with him. It did not matter. Even if our elbows brushed, I felt a tremor entering my bones—no matter we were atop a jogging elephant.

"How?" I widened my eyes with the innocence of a schoolgirl.

Ram drew the side curtains, murmuring, "This is how. We have a mile back to the palace, and transportation is agreeably slow."

It did not take long for Ram to convince me that the back of an elephant in a curtained howdah was the most pleasurable place on earth in which to become intimate.

The gentle lumbering aided our lovemaking, rising and falling to the heated rhythm of our passion. The sun turned the shades molten gold. Resting my forehead against his, I rode the rajah face to face, he holding my bottom and kissing every reachable part of me. I felt the urge to giggle over each lurch and jolt subsiding as our ardor grew.

Eyes closed, uttering a breathless shudder, I dropped my head onto his broad, slick shoulder. Gradually we cooled—difficult in our sultry bower— and, laughing, attempted to make ourselves presentable to the rational world, clothing our sticky bodies as we jostled in the small space.

The rajah whispered before raising the side curtains, "Ask me anything, my love. I will move that mountain an inch nearer, if it pleases you."

"I need nothing." I meant it at the time.

I detected the elephant had changed its tempo and its feet struck broad bricks in place of dirt…

We returned.

Chapter Twenty-Four
Bitter as a Serpent's Kiss

I floated in the bathing pool, dreaming of yesterday, alone except for Asha—friend, servant, or spy, and most likely, unwittingly, all three. If Asha minded her status, her small monkey-face revealed nothing as we splashed each other and happily gossiped away.

Apparently, Preeta had been caught *in flagrante delicto* with the elephant tender's boy, Kamala.

Or so Asha told me in halting English, a skill she was thankfully learning far above my Hindi.

I hid a smile. *The elephant tender's boy!* So that was Preeta's lover. Complacently, I lifted one leg, examining my toes, idly watching my figure shimmering like a mermaid's, reflecting smugly that it was a shame Rami could not see me now.

Oh! You are insufferable! Vain and irritating as those pea-headed peacocks, mewling love calls outside! scolded my imp.

I had to agree, returning to Asha's tittle-tattle.

My mouth gaped satisfactorily at what she revealed in the next item of gossip.

"Yes!" Asha clapped tiny hands, sending bubbles flying. "It is indeed true, this thing, Sar-ee! Preeta was selected as night companion to the maharajah! And now, she grows the belly! The maharajah is to have a son, perhaps. Preeta will be much high!"

She drew a mock regret face, impishly shrugging.

I smiled, putting two and two together. *Of course, the elephant tender's lad.* I could figure it out as well as any suspicious person. Apparently, Asha was not so discerning, or judgmental.

"Asha," I queried mildly, "did Preeta ask to go to the maharajah? Before she 'got the belly'…or after? Or did he summon her?"

"I do not know this thing. Why do you ask, Sa-ree?" Innocence shone in her eyes.

I smacked the water, vexed at myself. Why worry? I could just see Preeta parading around with her ever-growing belly filled with the elephant tender's offspring and no one the wiser. The pressure was gone. All would be well. Asha chuckled with me, and we began a splashing war. Scented water flew.

I hesitated, lifting a hand for silence.

I thought I heard an alien sound above our noise.

A slight burrrrrrrrr-ing—riiiipping of tearing silk.

I shrugged and held my head back, still mulling over Asha's news. She was pouring rinse water over my hair when she raised her head—and the pleasurable time was forever shattered with one taut scream.

****

Asha's shriek cut off as I looked up at the bulging tent-like ceiling—the rose silk canopy over our bathing pool was writhing, alive with something, until the fragile silk split wide and torrents of snakes of all sizes and colors—a tangled knot of snakes—tumbled down, irately slithering, twining, thrashing about each other, furiously hissing as they plummeted and plopped heavily into the bath.

The instant the wriggling mass splashed down—a small one landing on my head and slithering down my neck before coiling rapidly off under water...*Where was it?*—I shrieked, floundered, and tried to scramble out. The steamy, scented bath boiled with activity.

"Asha, run!" She seemed frozen, still gaping in terror at the ceiling.

I leapt out in an awkward vault. Asha, open-mouthed, still crouched in the water with snakes swimming all about her, too frightened to scream...

Snakes! Fat black snakes, crawling over my legs.

I slipped, half lying on the floor. I looked up. Snakes, still dropping over the ripped sides of the canopy, flopping onto soapy, oily marble, angry, confused, their primeval brains striking at anything moving.

I scrambled to my feet, keeping the reptiles—thin, thick, long, sinuous—in view. Asha, moving jerkily, managed to get out of the pool. Our splashing and the reptiles still plopping down started a tidal wave of sudsy, oily water turning the floor into a swamp as Asha slipped and dragged me down with her.

We held on to each other, trying to keep to our feet. I kept going back to Preeta—Preeta's face, her reassurance, the way she popped up to lead me to the tunnel and left me in the dark to die.

Snakes. My mind flashed to the rajah.

I saw his face, too, as he pointed them out with certain pride.

"The maharajah, my dear brother, keeps them as pets."

Then Asha found her mouth and courage at the same time, yelling for help, while we stood, an island in a sea of reptiles. I looked over. The bath was yet alive with gleaming snakes slithering out, flickering slim black tongues.

My feet went out from under me while my mind boiled over with suspicion. I landed in a knot of snakes amassing in the middle of the floor. Yawning cottony throats wide in agitation, some sank backward-facing fangs deep into other snakes as I scooted gingerly past them.

Asha tried to skirt around and reach me. I scanned the acre of floor still swarming and alive as the last agitated snakes dropped down. The cascade had thinned; now only a few fell as afterthoughts and bobbed placidly in the bath water.

"Sary!" Asha screamed, but in a different tone. Immediate. Urgent. Hurt.

I darted a look. A slim, deadly black thing clung to her arm. Asha back-peddled, swatting at it.

"Asha! Don't wave your arm!"

Asha flailed the reptile against a dresser. It recoiled once, falling off with a broken-back look. Asha huddled in a corner, holding her arm, whimpering, eyeing the advancing tide as they slithered for concealment.

"Asha, hold still. I'm coming!" I looked about, helpless, playing hopscotch. One minute the floor was clear in a spot, then vanishing under the knot of reptiles as they rippled my way the next in an unending pattern. Which were deadliest? What did Ram say? My mind shrieked, "Think!"

I leapt. Swerving close to my foot, while I watched, was the deadly green Bamboo viper—I was sure.

Oh, dear God! And that black slim thing behind

me—a pit viper, certainly.

All but the beautiful, repulsive King Cobra…

Move—move! my imp shouted, but I was spellbound, eyeing the slim brown snake humping over my foot, feeling a slight pressure and smooth cool belly. The innocuous-looking thing was the deadliest. I kicked wildly, spinning it off into the steamy air.

Asha, examining her arm, was now wailing softly.

"Sar-ree, why?" Her arm swelled as I watched.

Almost there.

"Asha, tie something around your arm. Tight! Please, Asha, do it now!" In my concern for her, I forgot to check the floor—moreover, my mind was churning with suspicion.

All those snakes…a sick jest from a sick man, or genuine assassination? Had Rami grown tired of the troubles I must cause him?

He would not—even in jest.

But perhaps, besides his brother, he too is ill!

He bragged about all these only yesterday.

Ill, like his brother… my imp whimpered. *Too much a coincidence…* No, it was the maharajah!

And so, as I waded to Asha, my mind stumbled over itself, trying to make sense of the incomprehensible: A flicker of a guard's evil smile, the one on the tiger hunt. Rami, my beloved Rami's admiration of the reptiles. And Preeta and the elephant tender's boy—she knew the zoo.

All this flashed before me as I slid my way over to where Asha lay still, her arm ugly, swollen. From the corner of my eye, I spotted a eunuch's broad back and the sole of one calloused foot as he pounded off.

"Help! Help! *Bacnā! Sahāytā karnā!* Hey!" I cried

to him. "*Bacnā!*—help!'"

Instead, I heard a scraping sound and a round wicker basket tumbled in from the direction the feet had vanished, and as if summoned, an immense king cobra spilled out. It coiled massively, rearing three feet high, undulating side to side and watching with cold yellow-green eyes from a flat spade head, its spotted hood flared wide.

While I watched, frozen, a cold sensation ringed my neck. I realized some snake's tail had slithered about my neck from behind, like a cold metal choker, while the cobra's flaring hood, flickering tongue, and merciless eyes two inches from my nose had kept me in thrall.

I wrenched my eyes away from it and looked about. The muscular tail of a python I had not seen before continued undulating thick coils obscenely down about my chest, tightening as it took over more of my body in its single-minded zeal to squeeze the life out of me.

I futilely clawed the strong, rippling muscles; I could not draw a breath. With each exhale, the coils clasped tighter. I looked desperately about. I finger-tipped a brass side table that until now had held oils and sponges. Spots before my eyes enlarged. I was airless. Only my fingers clutching the metal leg had any sensation beyond my starving lungs. More in reflex than by conscious thought, I whipped the table sideways and back in a clumsy action, tearing at my shoulder and elbow. Awkward, but it did the job.

The table hit the cobra's head, only grazing it but still enough to anger and distract it, while the python behind me loosened its grip for a moment before rippling and squeezing harder in reflex, gaining an even tighter hold.

Through a haze, I saw the jumble of other snakes undulate swiftly around me as if as anxious to escape as I. Several looped about my leg and crawled over my feet even as I clawed at the strong muscle binding me, down to my hips now. My nails kept sliding off the slick, rubbery skin.

I barely felt the sharp needle in my foot where a small viper sank its fangs.

A swishing roared in my ears, along with singing blood—and there was old Padmavati, swinging the sharp-legged brass table first at the cobra like a cricket batter, then at the python. I heard a splintering sound like breaking toothpicks. She back-swung the table at one head and then the other. In her small island of space, Padmavati dropped the table and dug in her pocket. With one hand, she gripped behind the flaring cobra hood and plunged a wickedly sharp fruit knife deep into its neck. The snake spasmed once—twice— and slithered down into a heavy heap.

Immediately she began sawing at the python, still circling me from neck to hip, while the snake's body lashed strongly about us, its grasp gradually loosening. When she had finally overcome it, it lay looking like nothing but a pile of thick cut rope. Clawing my throat and sucking in air, I stumbled out of the ring of coils. Padmavati kicked other snakes away and, twirling like a dervish, smashed down on the cobra's head until it lay still. I pointed wordlessly to Asha.

The king cobra and the python were vanquished, but the other snakes were not.

Padmavati, using skinny but wiry arms, dragged

me off, all the while kicking at furiously striking reptiles that hit only Padmavati's heavy swirling cotton sari.

"*Bacnā! Sahāytā karnā!*" She yelled out.

Eunuchs poured in at her basso command. Where had they cowered until now?

My sight returned. Sinuous shapes wriggled up walls and into corners.

Padmavati, stern-faced, sought out Asha.

****

"Brother, good to see you—so well."

Summoned, the rajah looked around. True, he had not seen his brother so alert in months. Bright-eyed, clean shaven, not still in stained night robes but smartly dressed for the day. Would wonders never cease?

His brother smirked as of old, however. "Is it? Or are you perplexed, perhaps? Dismayed? Perhaps you thought the throne was at hand and all you had to do was wait?"

"Brother, as I have assured you on many occasions, I have little desire for the duties and trappings the throne entails." The rajah sighed inwardly. *Even though I have performed those duties.* "I am puzzled, Brother. What has changed?"

"Ah! But that did not stop you. You and your *chinaal* were plotting all along. You overstepped while I was—ill. They are shouting from the rooftops how brave, strong, and clever you are. They made idols of you. Why, you are practically a god. You!" He named the tiger-plagued village, although he got the name wrong.

It was on the rajah's tongue to say somebody had to. He narrowly eyed his brother while pouring a whiskey.

"It will be a long while, in any case." His brother snapped fingers. In place of a sharp crack, a thubbing sound ensued, but enough to summon someone the rajah only vaguely recognized.

Prita? *Preeta?*

Preeta emerged, sailing proudly into view with her slightly burgeoning belly thrust forward like a figurehead on the prow of a ship, from around the bed curtains. She stood preening, hands across her belly as if protecting a religious icon. Her self-satisfied glitter took his breath away.

The maharajah held out his pudgy hand. She took it, smiling triumphantly at the rajah over his head.

"One time was all it took, no matter your slander!" At the maharajah's words, the rajah caught Preeta's contradict-me-if-you-dare stare. "Brother, your days might be numbered, as well as those of my dear, loyal, faithful, simpering wife. Oh, yes, I failed to mention, I have already seen to your *chinaal*…even as we speak. It was my love's idea." He pawed at Preeta's hand.

The rajah did not fail to see the unease or perhaps disgust flash across Preeta's face. He narrowed his eyes, already backing to the archway.

His brother's two slits glittered malice. The rajah wanted to wipe that look off his face with a fire ax.

Preeta, still clutching his hand, smoothed her belly.

"Let us say she is welcoming new pets in her bath." The maharajah giggled. "Pets that crawl on their bellies!" He smirked up at Preeta.

The rajah's face turned to ash beneath the walnut skin. Snakes! He strode from the room, and once out of sight ran, and the sound of his brother's gurgling laughter followed him.

****

"Don't *Pyara* me!" I hurled at him as legions of women around the world had since speech was invented. "Snakes in my bath! Not exceptionally original! Did you dream it up yesterday, when we were...when—we...?" I halted, losing my thoughts, venom, though I did not know it, raced to my heart. I stared stupidly at my veins as if I could see the poison, and old Padmavati kept tugging at me, urging me to do something.

The rajah had come running toward me, shouting something that reverberated strangely in my head.

"You are all mad in this backward land, keeping women in prison...then...then killing them..." My ears seemed stuffed with cotton, my own words far away. Rami would not stay still, and Padmavati was still pulling me, and my chest felt tied with iron bands.

Still I stood, weaving, striving to speak, but I could not get the words out. My throat closed.

I saw Rami brushing Padmavati aside, one hand out, the other on the hilt of his dirk. My eyes widened.

I backed into Padmavati.

"Sarabande! Enough!"

I looked down, bewildered. Then I saw what he saw—the punctures, and my ankle swelling like an eggplant.

The rajah dropped me to the floor. Padmavati held me down while he grabbed my foot and made slicing marks, vigorously sucking and calling out between spitting.

My leg seemed on fire.

"Asha..." I think I said...

Chapter Twenty-Five
Torrid Zones

His hand hovered an inch from her body. The woman he prized above all was too hot to touch. She thrashed, mumbling nonsense—something about a mountain and gold and Africa and diamonds…and names as if carved in rock, or written in blood or shooting stars….names called repeatedly, but he could not make out.

One exquisite white leg lay propped, puffed and angry about the ankle. Red streaks crawled up the calf. Two punctures resembled dying purple blossoms.

His own guards flanked the door. His own physician tended her.

He turned with a face grim as a tombstone.

Chapter Twenty-Six
Unveiled

The rajah thrust aside sentries, striding to the vast bed, roaring, "No more will I ignore your bungling, sick attempts at outright murder! You will cease now!"

"Or what?" The maharajah cast a sneering glance his way. His new status of impending fatherhood lent him a new confidence, his brother saw. It would do him no good. "You dare? You dare lecture me? Tell me what to do? Now my line is secure for generations to come! Preeta is lusty and strong, not like the weak-as-milk female you irrationally prize." Spraying crumbs and plum-paste, the maharajah dropped his chunk of sticky pastry, eyeing it with regret. "You forget who you are—the younger brother! A nobody! The realm no longer needs you."

"Cowardly! Underhanded! Evil! Childish!" The rajah hissed the words. "Even for repulsive wretches such as you."

The rajah reeled from the mixture of odors emanating from the maharajah's mouth. "No! Don't look for comfort in your disgusting sweets!" With one hand, he swept the tray from the bed, trailing *chai*, jam, fish paste, and gravy in its wake. "Even as a boy it was no secret you had few chums, even when threatened or bribed by parents to be with you. You stole, cheated, hid things, and played these same gutless tricks, crueler, cruder, and even less justifiable over the years. This is the twentieth century, Brother!"

He faltered briefly, aware he himself had managed to overlook his brother's escalating excesses because he could not be bothered. Was not he at fault too, always playing the dilettante favorite?

He subsided, watching his brother's mouth open and close, his brother's body puffing up like a noxious fungus, and purple in the bargain. Could he be having a stroke? He studied him clinically. No, it wasn't to be, unfortunately. Something lodged in his throat. He coughed and spat; a chunk of pastry flew across the room.

"Are you through insulting me?" the maharajah whined. "It is my divine right to do as I please. No matter what century."

The maharajah smugly plopped another lump of Turkish delight, found sticking to the coverlet, into his maw. "She means that much to you?" He sniffed. "That you would go against your brother again?"

"No! Humanity means that much."

"How lofty!" The maharajah's hand strayed for another sweet. "You learn that in Oxford?"

"No, right here in blessed Mother India! We are better than that."

The maharajah's tiny eyes were slits full of calculation. "I like the old ways better," he finally said. "You liked me better when we were boys."

The rajah stared stonily back.

His brother pulled in his belly, raising a chin as far as a neck resembling an inner tube would allow and ticking off-on-off-on sticky fingers…

"She spurned the royal house not once but twice.

She attacked me. The whore, the *chinaal* and you are traitors. I could have you beheaded along with your— *whore.* I did not know about the snakes until after it was done," he admitted, looking regretful.

"And what, thenceforth? You might actually have to govern. Mollify foreign officials you insult daily. Lay down uprisings. Oh, you do not know about the poor's bloody resistance to your yearly bleeding of rupees! Or, should I say, *rubies?* Moreover, you would have to appease the British Empire, while ignoring the growing popularity of a young hothead named Gandhi. In other words, rule, Brother, rule!"

"You'd never leave. You love India." He whined.

"I would leave to save this piece of India. Outside of India, I could appeal to the British Empire." *Could he? He did not know, but it was effective.*

"I forbid you to abscond! I forbid you to take that whore with you! I can arrest her as a spy and imprison you and your *chinaal* in the deepest part of the palace, never to see light again—unless it is the day you die!" He spied Preeta in the doorway. "In fact, I will!"

The maharajah, showing vindictiveness like bird-droppings in a pudding, narrowed his eyes in triumph. It appeared the notion simmering like a pot of poison for years had finally found the pot stirrer.

****

The physician gave what antidotes were on hand. Usually one built immunities in India. I had not that advantage. Fortunately, Old Neelam, who also tended the reptiles, kept private stocks of anti-venom. However, the zoo tender was busy capturing all the misplaced reptiles, which took up precious time while I lay in the midst of dying. And of course, by that time, they did not know which viper had bitten me.

The dying hour gave me back. Fever peaked, leaving me pale as cheese, and drenched as if in my own private monsoon, but releasing the last poisons.

When I opened them, my eyes were clear as stilled water, as was my crazed mind.

"Preeta. She meant me to die."

"Yes, Preeta. Your Preeta has planned many things."

He told me of Preeta's elevated position, with a light sardonic wit, hiding his fear. I smiled but held my tongue regarding the involvement of the elephant tender's boy. There had been too much malice and bloodshed already. Let the maharajah be cuckolded. "Now we are free," I said simply.

The rajah grinned, showing all his beautiful white teeth. "*Pyara.* You raced in just as you were when you fled the bath."

A change of subject hid behind his lighthearted banter. I knew him too well. "Rami? What are you saying?"

"Starkers, you were!"

"I scarce cared, at the moment." I spoke calmly. "What is it, Rami? What is troubling you?"

Suddenly I was afraid. Unreasonably afraid. A fear made up of primitive instincts for survival made my insides quake. Something unspeakable was to happen. I knew it.

His handsome face turned grim, and I sat because my knees no longer supported me. "If you will forgive me, I waited until now, but I have unfinished business." I had no hint that he had gone directly to the maharajah and that a crisis was not to be denied, after a lifetime of rivalry, covetousness, and hate came to a head. A bursting carbuncle, filled with murderous poison. That was the last lighthearted moment we were gifted.

We should have fled while we could.

****

They threw me into another dark place from my sickbed. I heard moans, muffled, as through stone. Still weak from poisons, I thought they were my own, initially. Then a rustling. Close by, it was. The thing, the unknown being, was in the cell with me, for I recognized the place, but it was not the same one as before. This was larger. I could tell from the echoes of my breathing and the clammy, stirring air. The space had a cavernous hollow feel, and no window. But I knew.

I had little resistance when the palace guards, not the gentle giants, morose as they were, yanked me from my cot and hustled me away in my sweaty bedclothes.

I shrank, banging my shoulder into a clammy wall. Moisture runneled down, wetting my arm. I jumped from the chill. My body could not respond to hot or cold properly, and simple wetness seemed frigid or hot, in contrast to the oily heat of the cell.

"Sarabande!" I heard a rough voice croak out in the dark.

I screamed silently. I would give no quarter, swinging out blindly but feebly.

"I never meant this—" The voice rasped as if the owner's neck had been strangled. "He is beyond insane. I should not have…"

"Rami!" We clung to each other. He kissed my face in the dark, clumsy but passionate. I felt him wince. "Rami. What did they do to you?"

"Hardly matters, does it, my poor Sary?" he rasped. We sat against the stone, clasping each other and whispering.

"It finally happened." His bitterness flooded the dark like acrid wine. "My fault, mine entirely. I pressed him. I never thought he had the—the balls of a lame donkey, to act against me. My friends, and I have many, would rise up, but they don't know! He did it cleverly. By now, he has spread the word I am on a diplomatic mission. Later he will say thieves in wicked foreign parts or some such tale, attacked me, or I am suffering from *yaksma*—as you say, consumption—taking the cure in the Alps," he muttered as if I were not present. "And finally, regretfully, he will announce my death. No one will dare question it. You, my darling one, I do not know."

"Will your allies believe such nonsense?"

I felt him shrug. "By that time, it will be a *fait accompli*. Why risk it? If they still live."

"But where are we? Exactly." For a moment I hoped we were somewhere outside the palace grounds.

"An older prison not used much anymore. Except for the forgotten. The long-timers. I have not been out here in years, to my regret. Well, old girl"—he turned to me in the near dark—"I am making up for neglect now. We will disappear. Sary, love."

Don't be so truthful, I wanted to scream.

I pressed my hand over his mouth. "Shhh. We will find a way. You and I." More bravado than reason cowered behind those words.

He held me in the felted light until I grew impatient. Apparently, he supposed he needed to comfort me, in place of finding a way out.

"Please, Rami." I got up and began pacing to get my strength back. I thought of redoubtable Padmavati, and brave little Asha, thankfully recovered. Yet what could they do? Even if they had an inkling of where we were.

I strained to see something. As my sight adjusted, or the day shifted outside, wan light seeped through a grille in the door where I had clung so desperately when they threw me in.

The door was old, wooden, and dry. I still mindlessly clutched a sliver in my hand that had splintered off as I hung onto it. Thick on one end, raggedly sharp on the other. A useless weapon. My hand hurt from gripping it.

"Rami, it will be lighter soon."

"I do realize that," he said with a hint of exasperation.

"We will find a way, if we have to claw with our fingernails." Yet this was stone, not the crumbly brick as before.

He barked a laugh and paced, thinking deep thoughts, no doubt, as was I. I still clutched my useless trinket, the splinter of wood. What would that do? Stab the guard? Scratch our way out? Feeling along the wall, I attempted to wedge it between two stones. The tip promptly snapped off. I tossed it angrily toward the door.

"Perhaps his mood will change once the child arrives," I said. *If we live that long.*

The rajah dashed those thoughts.

"Preeta is dead, you know." His words hung in the dark like extinguished candle soot.

I felt my blood drain. My face must have glowed

white in the dim light. "Dead! How? It is not her time! The maharajah would never—"

"He did," he said simply.

I wondered what that portended, if even Preeta was not safe. The rajah's eyes glinted in the dark.

"She lost the child. I heard it before the guards dragged me off. Gossip had it the maharani herself had something to do with it. Preeta was in her care. She was very ill, before…"

"Oh, Rami, no!" I exclaimed, thinking the maharani was in danger.

"My brother was enraged, hurling blame at Preeta for all manner of crimes. Not eating and…"

"I know. Morning sickness." Poor Preeta.

"Indeed. Or she stayed too long in the sun…then, that she hid in the dark—that she willed the baby dead, when she complained overmuch. It did not matter. He had Preeta dragged out and destroyed. The maharani said the whole palace could hear her screams. He would have at any rate, if she had lost the babe on her own. I cannot believe the maharani had evil in her heart."

I was not so sure but said nothing. I could hardly blame the maharani. She was saving her own skin too. I still saw Preeta's face, in the tunnel, secretive, gloating. "She meant to leave me there," I said slowly. "She supposed I was a rival. If only she knew! She did not think I could free myself the way I did. Thanks to a hunk of dead bamboo!" I shook my head, still taking it in. "Preeta supposed I'd crawl the maze, blind, until I died of thirst, or of whatever was down there. No one would ever know."

"He threw her in the tiger's cage." Rami's words were dry as rust. Dry as old bone.

"Tiger's cage!" My thoughts flew back to Preeta's boasts. Had the maharajah heard the truth?

"The—the elephant tender's boy. How—is he?" I ventured. Rami must think I had gone soft in the head.

"The elephant tender's lad. Well—I suppose. Why ask? Have not we enough to think on?"

I smiled in the dimness. So the maharajah had heard nothing. It was all coincidence that Preeta met her end in a cage of tigers. I closed my eyes to keep from seeing the tigers tear into her. Poor Preeta. I could hold no malice.

"And the maharani?"

"Well too, but reticent, keeping to her quarters. Not under siege, but she has put up her own discreet guards."

We wasted time. I suspected the maharajah did not intend for us to languish. "Let's see what is here, then. I suspect she cannot help us."

He nodded. "When it is lighter."

"Now, Rami! We must try!" This was all new to him, I could tell. After a life of privilege, he still could not believe anything was happening to him in this manner.

"At dawn, when it is lighter, we will try." His voice slurred. I realized I was exhausted too.

I shook my head no, till my hair flew in my face. "Must be a loose stone somewhere!" *To what, another cell?* my imp roused his ugly head.

I stubbornly fumbled along the wall, striving to hook my fingers in any crevice, aware Rami stirred himself and, moving in the other direction, scraped and pounded walls for weak spots.

When he reached the door, I went to help. Maybe

the door was rotted or weak. We felt along side, but the hinges were outside, and the rest seemed built for eternity. We slid down the door, leaning against each other, each with our own thoughts and rejected schemes.

****

We jumped up to the sound of scuffling feet and muffled groaning, as if many hands lifted a hefty burden, followed by a thud on packed dirt, followed by gargled curses, more grunts, and rasped breathing.

"I know that sound. He's come to gloat." He did not need to tell me who. We rose, facing the door, holding hands with our backs straight. The door swung. Stuck like a bung in a whiskey barrel, stood the maharajah.

He strode in, or what he thought was a princely stride, more an agitated waddle, surveying us, his hands like puffy unbaked bread on wobbly hips. He did not look dangerous. I could not take him seriously. Rami squeezed my hand in warning.

The maharajah wrinkled his nose and waved back a phalanx of guards—easy to be brave, I thought, with those thugs. Holding up a kerchief, he beckoned a guard with a faggot and fit it in a sconce I had overlooked. The metal was old rusty lace. No weapon there, even had we found it.

In the glare I took a stumble back. Even my stalwart prince twitched. Behind the supreme ruler, a terrifying sight emerged from the gloom. At first, the giant seemed dressed in a costume. I heard Rami's intake of breath.

Nervous laughter welled. Rami tightened his grip again in warning. "Courage, dear little *rājpatnī*," he whispered, even though I felt him tremble.

Little wife. I gazed boldly at the behemoth, though my insides quaked.

Bare feet, from the dirt up. Tight puttees wrapped spread, tree-like calves, a short robe with a drooping sash, topped by a square boulder-like head. He was immobile as stone, too, all but the pebble eyes, glittering like a dog eyeing raw meat.

I noticed more, with an alarm I tried to conceal. A noose hung carelessly about the bull neck, but the oddest, most ominous feature was his padded-leather vest and arm pads studded with five-inch spikes. The same wicked barbs bristled from wide shoulder pads. The metal thorns even spiked a cantilevered cap extending over long drooping ears, and his massive fist gripped a broad, gleaming scimitar—the other held a small round shield, innocuous among his other murderous regalia.

So this was it. The end of Rami and me...or perhaps only me, for Rami was of royal blood, after all. I would have courage. I would not tremble. I would meet death celebrating the recent past, my other hidden life might be revealed only on the other side. A small reason to rejoice, but a comfort and shield for what was to come.

But, oh! I wished to live.

I risked a look at Rami. As any brave man, he was suitably expressionless. I bit my mouth and gripped his hand tighter, speaking many things in that gesture. Love, regret, fear...but not acceptance. I heard words through a haze and tried to focus.

"Forgive my interrupting your cozy—" The maharajah swept the insalubruious space. Still holding a dainty kerchief before his nose, he minced, "I would like"—his belly shook as he giggled, waving a hand at the massive figure hulking behind him—"to introduce your executioner. This handsome fellow is quite efficient—when he is not drinking."

He turned to the behemoth. "Are you drunk now?" And named him, though I did not hear it.

The giant gave a slight sway, a tightening of the mouth. My face grew as numb as my thoughts. Execution! Now? So soon? I dared not look at Rami.

Instead, I watched the maharajah closely for any meaning. My hand in Rami's grew slippery. Would he mean the giant to—*do it here*? I faltered. My gaze swept to the curved sword at his side.

No! Not now! A little time! Let us think. Plead. But no. Never would Rami beg. Perhaps persuade…if we had time. My brave resolve seemed to have evaporated.

I saw the maharajah's pupils were all black. I knew what that meant. He could not be reasoned with.

The studded creature shifted as if readying himself—a dog straining on a spiked leash.

Rami tightened his fist—*courage, love*—and then moved slightly in front of me, muscles tensing as if to do battle. What could he do? Get slaughtered? Affording me a few more precious seconds—minutes—hours, in which to reflect on my own death while sorrowing his?

We would go together, God willing. The armored giant shuffled forward, pressing the maharajah's back. Armor! Against us! I surveyed his studded vest with such contempt that even he could read it.

I scarcely heard the maharajah's next words.

"In benevolence and consideration for our once-close kinship"—he wiped tears from his eyes—"I am allowing you one more night"—the fat man chuckled. wheezing when he regained his breath—"to reflect, pray, or whatever else your feelings run to."

He leered. His small black eyes swept the dismal cell. "Do you fancy your love nest—your bower for your last night? I only wished you to be prepared, giving you the courtesy of time to dwell on your fate upon the morrow," he oozed.

"This woman is nothing to you," Rami said. "I am the one you despise. Let her go in peace. Take me on—yourself, if you dare, if you do not fear to do so." He ended bitterly, "You always let others do your bloody chores."

Oh, Rami, do not annoy him further.

"Fear!" The maharajah narrowed his eyes to slits. "Seems your strength is in words, not deeds. It is you in prison, not me. I was not blinded by a female. Fear! Look about you. See you not these walls? Impregnable! And when all is prepared, I invited a few—favored guests to your, ah, rather inventive execution."

He chuckled again and turned to invite his guards to join him. They dutifully responded.

"Here is the guest list, and a copy of the invitation." He waved a sheet of vellum. "They will be quite amused and entertained. It is getting more difficult to shock them."

He shoved the paper back into his pocket and gestured to the giant. "Come, come, we must not waste their last precious hours together—alone."

However, Rami shot an arrow. "You mean your depraved, sadistic, lunatic sycophants who laugh behind your back? Those special guests?"

The maharajah, sweating and losing steam, wavered at that last volley, backing into the doorpost. A slave wiped his forehead. He backhanded him and dug in his voluminous robe, thrusting out the thick vellum sheet, which I now noted was inked in black calligraphy, with red wax seals like drops of blood.

"Say what you may. The guest list!" He thrust it in Rami's face. "This might kill the hours." He sniggered again like a hideous boy killing flies. "Until that time you are led out to greet them."

Then, not sure what to do with it, he flung it at Rami, who had not reached out to accept it.

And that was the maharajah's undoing.

"You will find familiar names," he continued, oblivious. "Some old friends, who will be surprised, astonished even, to find themselves following you into *Naraka* to meet *Yama* as eternal guests of the God of Death."

He laughed soundlessly at his own joke, then switched to English, shifting his bird-dropping eyes upon me, and said, "Where sinners are tormented after death. But we need not wait with either of you. Oh, yes, you shall certainly experience the torments of death before you die."

He wobbled again. No doubt it was one of the rare times he was forced to stand for any length of time. To keep pride intact, he swept out. Actually, he lurched backward into the arms of the bearers. The clutch of guards and the huge creature with the spikes lumbered after. His retainers rushed to support him to a litter before they dragged the door closed. Did I detect a smirk on the giant's face?

I'd like to think so.

Instantly, the cell seemed cleaner, fresher, if not filled with hope. After the cricket chirp of locks and many feet thudding off with the wheezy sound of the maharajah's efforts, Rami and I avoided each other's eyes, each deep in thought.

Again, laughter welled up behind my fortress wall of clenched teeth. Hysterical laughter.

We both began a low humming, as if trying to smother amusement. Soon the chuckling became uncontrollable, tears rolling down our faces. We could not breathe. We finally eyed each other, stifling our loss of restraint.

"Frightened?"

I nodded numbly. "Yes—no." I shook my head. "I cannot believe this is—real. It is all so—"

"Theatrical? Yes, that. Yet he is serious. He must do something to prop up his pride. He has nothing to lose, except us."

He eyed the cell like a fox ferreting out a mouse, squinting and prodding hidden corners we already had scoured a dozen times.

We talked the night through…sharing memories, laughing over frivolous things, even our meeting in Madhuri's kitchen. We yet eyed walls and talked of escape. We avoided what might come at dawn.

The air lightened with the passing of rain, filtering from God knew where. I roved dully over an abandoned tin plate and caught the pale blotch of vellum in the corner getting wet.

I ignored it, looking with despair over rough stone and the door with its tiny solid grille. Was this it? Our last hours? Here? But Rami was with me. I wished he were not.

Suddenly I began giggling, scrambling up as I stared at the discarded vellum the maharajah dismissively had tossed at us. Rami jerked around from digging near where he thought the outer hinge might be set. "Sary?"

With a savage whoop, I picked up the piece, waving it like a stiff flag.

Rami frowned as if I had gone daft. As I had. Daft with hope. Recalling the wood splinter, I tracked the floor for the only other light scrap in our grim space. "This is it, Rami! This will do it!"

"Throw it away. We don't need to read it."

He made to snatch it from me, but I held it behind me, searching frantically for the jagged wood splintered from the door when they forced me in. Had they kicked it out? Picked it up?

"Oh, no, no…Rami! Where is it?"

"Sary, end this."

"But Rami! This will"—I lowered my voice—"get us out of here. We can escape," I added, in case he did not understand. At the moment, he watched as if I were mad as the hatter's wife.

I ignored that, for just then I spied it, shoved behind the door all the time. I landed on the insignificant splinter, holding it up like a sacred relic. I even danced.

Rami studied me with pity.

"But don't you see?" I waggled the splinter before his nose. "I will show you!" Rami cocked his head. After listening, he shook it, bemused, shrugging. "Could do."

"Could do? In a pig's eye." I crouched by the door,

gripping the vellum.

"You said you—read this, somewhere?" As if reading were an alien concept left for silly girls, he took the usual stand of the male claim to superiority over any suggestion brought by a female, which must be taken with a condescending grain of salt.

Humor her was all over his face.

"I did. Somewhere. I remember! Doyle. Arthur-something. One of his stories. Oh, never mind!" I shook my head, impatient. "First, create a diversion."

"A diversion?" He sighed. "Ohh, Sary. You make me smile and forget our…troubles, but it will not do, my dearest heart."

Oooh! Insufferable!

"We must get serious. We do not know when…" He looked at the door.

"We die? When his thugees return? Oh, Rami!" I tugged his shirt, pleading with my eyes. "Will you just do it? We have to try!"

"Yes, but be quick."

So I can attempt a manly thing. He cast an impatient, worried glance at the door. "If they come…?"

"Go—go!" I tossed him the tin plate and shoved him to the far wall. Sighing deeply, he stood there clutching the hefty tin plate, looking foolish.

"You know," I hissed. "Bang it!" I motioned frantically.

Looking embarrassed, he tapped the plate against the stone. Whether it led to another cell or outside, I could not tell, or if it made a difference. Our plan depended on the guard—his sense of hearing, or duty, or both. Nevertheless, it was our only chance.

Rami thought that wall faced outside. I hoped so.

I motioned, *BANG IT!*

He did, making up for his reluctance and giving the stone wall a great whacking—back and forth, back and forth, *clang, bam, bam! Tang, ting boom, clang*—! A cacophony of sound that echoed and bounced inside our cell and off the stone.

The plate slipped from his hands, skipping across the floor with a heavy metallic clatter. He resumed, but not before we heard circular shuffling, as if a body turned in place, then boots rushing off…then a door banged somewhere.

Good! Outside!

Instantly I shoved the vellum under the door.

I had crinkled it.

It stuck.

I shoved harder.

'Damn!" The vellum wedged like an accordion. The space below the door was uneven, though. Angry at my haste, I dragged it back, smoothed it, and slid it down toward the frame. I was all thumbs. I heard feet approach. Frantically I waved to Rami. He renewed banging. The feet hesitated outside. Air rushed beneath our door. He was outside again.

Perspiring, I shoved the vellum through, skimming it until I positioned it under the keyhole. Next, I jammed, poked, and prodded the jagged splinter in the hole, praying it would fit.

A bit broke off, jamming it. I poked harder, holding my breath until I heard the tiny rustle as the fragment fell inside. I peered in. The way was blocked. Surely that was the key. I worked the rest of the splinter—still no resistance, but then it stuck, or hit something solid. Gently, I pushed and wiggled.

As I had the splinter all the way in, my fingers barely cleared the hole. I could push no farther. I hit it with the heel of my hand, rewarded by an iron *clunk* thudding outside.

I winced. The thud came a second time, musical this time. Off the vellum? No, thank God, because the sheet was heavier when I tugged at it. I jerked it and then, breathing slowly, gently teased it through the gap. It stuck at the jamb.

"Oh! Damnation!"

"Easy, Sary," I heard. The rajah saw what I was attempting.

Sweat made my hands slippery. The crude key was too thick for the crack between the jamb and door. There was only one spot near the post—where it had been kicked over centuries, most likely—worn away by a full inch, leaving a mouse-sized gap. I cursed the dim light for not allowing me to spot it before.

I slid the vellum to the gap. Again it caught. I was aware of Rami anxiously watching over my shoulder. I thrust my little finger through, catching the filigreed head of the key, clamping down with teeth-gritting punishment on the tip of my finger.

It scraped through, and I had it in my hand—all three inches of beautiful battered iron—just as I heard the guard clomping around outside. *Dear God, please do not have him notice the key is gone.* It was as dim out there. Probably he would not. Why should he?

We listened.

I heard the man make water against the wall, and stretch, I could hear the crack of his bones, and groans. I smelt strong tobacco. He was in no hurry to return to this dismal place. Perhaps the new day beckoned him too. I held the key out to Rami as if it were a newborn child.

It was. The infant of hope.

The rajah gave me a quick hug that smashed the wind out of my lungs.

****

The maharajah's eyes opened as far as they could, pushing at jowly cheeks, and his plump lips, gaping with stupefaction and fear, dribbled saliva and half-masticated figs upon a stained coverlet.

He struggled to his knees as he stared at Rami and me. His face, pale as goat cheese, flooded red, like a pitcher filling with wine. "You!" He started to croak an alarm and fall out of the bed.

Rami snarled, "Stay! Don't say one word!"

The maharajah's corpulent body wobbled, but he got no farther than one foot thrust from the covers. When he opened his mouth to call, Rami stuffed into it a gob of whatever was on the brass tray within the maharajah's reach, clamping his hand over the whole resultant mess.

Rami wanted to suffocate him, it appeared. I stayed his hand. "Don't kill him, Rami!" Rami looked at me, unfocused, as if he did not know me. His brother would destroy us with a wave of his hand. Yet I did not wish the stain of mortal sin coloring our days. And we would not have lasted past his first thug of a sentry. Only Rami's position, fragile as it was, had gotten us as far as we were.

The maharajah was wild-eyed over Rami's fist, turning the shade of a muscatel grape. I watched, appalled, as Rami made to pinch his blob of a nose shut, then pinched his mouth open instead and ruthlessly hooked fingers in to drag out clots of food.

The maharajah coughed, moaned, and tried to drag away like an enormous rat. Rami yanked him back by the neck of his caftan, nearly strangling him.

There was no question of my not being there, as we made our bold way. We were beyond fear and reason, a unit without a plan. As we had raced from the prison, we approached the palace openly, leaving our jailer no worse off than a lump on the head and locked in his own cell. I hoped someone found him. In time.

The maharani then rushed in, staying Rami's hand and offering her husband water. Blinking tears, he looked grateful, then spitefully grunted, "You took your time!"

She stared at her husband and spat, "I do not care! I merely want to avoid *suttee*. You are not worth it!"

What is suttee? I looked questioningly at Rami and saw him grimace. Whatever it was, it was not pleasant. Before I could ask, she dashed the water in his face, spat, and swept out.

"Where are my guards?" the maharajah whined. "Where is everyone? I will have you executed immediately. That is what happens when one is lenient with assassins!"

"I suspect they are out rounding up escaped animals. Oh, we let them out. In addition, they will be attending to several fires within the compound…small, true, but they will be busy for a while. Time, dear brother, for us to have a chat. You know, a brotherly confab. To negotiate better terms, if you will."

"It won't last forever!" His brother waved his hands, apoplectic.

219

"Oh, but Brother, I have supporters too, it seems. No one has rushed to your aid. It could be you chained as an animal…"

Not only did no one hinder us, but I had caught fleeting smiles as we raced through the grounds, rampaging our way, filled with blood lust and settling scores. No one—not sentries, sycophants, eunuchs, or servants—tried to stay us in the face of Rami's approaching wrath.

"I only wished to frighten you," Rami's brother bleated as he pressed against the headboard, gaze darting about for escape, his outrage weaker, less convincing. He gulped piteously, rubbing his neck. "You have no idea how exhausting it is to be me. I don't wish to be the maharajah. It was thrust upon me. Don't hurt me!"

"Be careful what you wish for, exalted brother." Rami savagely ripped the silk sheet aside. "Nights are long and dark, and you, dear brother, have many sources from which your food is gathered and prepared. And not all your women or even all your soldiers appreciate your skills—or your favors," Rami ended silkily, reminding me of a sleek panther cornering a mouse.

"You still threaten me," the maharajah whined.

"Wrong. Most threaten you."

The maharajah struggled to the edge of the vast bed, looking over Rami's shoulder and croaking, "Help me, you fool!"

I whipped around. I glimpsed a bodyguard, eyes crusty with sleep, who ducked from sight.

Rami narrowed his eyes at his brother's pole-axed face. *See? That is your future. Tread easy!*

Rami was not quite right.

Sentries still loyal, for whatever reasons, belatedly boiled up corridors. Rami, still popular, waved them off as, undecided, they surrounded us. "A brotherly spat, you know how it is?" And, winked at his brother, red in the face and opening and closing his mouth. He never could make hard decisions without a month of waffling, only cruel and impulsive ones, Rami confided later.

Indeed that was the case now. His face took on a constipated look, as his mind waded through options, as murky and insalubrious as a cesspit. Risk rebellion and mortifying expulsion? Rami cut a more princely swath, and was a man anyone would much rather follow. The maharajah appeared weak and exposed, squatting naked in his bed, while my Rami stood strong, handsome, and dangerous in the doorway.

No, the choice must seem clear to most. We took the gamble and won, for now.

Rami quietly took my hand and urged me away.

****

After we delicately melted into the labyrinth, I was unsure, after the first exultation, what was to happen. "I went too far. There will be a bloodbath to pay for our sins." His mouth curled. "His wives and innocent guards. He will call them traitors. I should have taken him prisoner."

Rami was not his brother, however. As he had stated before, traditions ran bone and blood deep in India, and most changes were thought to be cataclysmic if not world-ending.

He prophesied rightly. It seemed no matter how he tamped down on the maharajah, his brother still owned those twisted in the same way.

Mysterious deaths occurred in the seraglio and among sentries. Even old Madhuri of the kitchens was a victim. However, her demise could have been because of age. We never knew. Rami grieved openly and bravely at her hasty funeral pyre.

The maharajah showed a public benevolent face. He left the palace in an unheard-of gesture, showering rupees, holding festivals and puppet shows, and doling out grain allowances. His generals, guard captains, even head eunuchs were beneficiaries of precious jewels, early retirements, and country estates.

Chapter Twenty-Seven
Vivāha

Gradually the blood purge ended as the maharajah became bored, complacent, or distracted. In his final madness, he ordered a statue of Preeta placed in a shrine-like garden, giving her goddess-like status, and declaring a festival in her honor.

"My brother supposes deification may soothe any demons that might plagued him."

Or so Rami supposed.

"It is time." Rami took my hand. "My little *rājpatnī.* My wife, my queen. We will make our own reward, and I can keep you safe by my side, forever."

"Oh, Rami," I cried in despair, "you only want to poke the hornet's nest." A young man's folly, I told myself, not admitting his youth and passion.

Yet his words stunned. They seemed etched in stone, a prison of a differing sort. Was I just a thorn in his brother's side? Was passion enough? Why could I not throw caution to the winds, as had he? Was I growing brittle and old before time, losing the sweet juices of youth? My breath caught in sudden panic. I wasn't sure how old I was. Surely in my twenties.

"I cannot be wed, Rami. We cannot!" I blurted instead.

"I do whatever I wish, and I wish to wed!" He drew himself up.

How easily offended men are! I could not sort out the sudden alarm, only—the wrongness of his proposal.

"You sound like your brother!" I evaded, shrinking from the look he threw me.

"Come, come, *mere dil ka pyaar*, do not deny me. We shall be properly wed, as you Brits say, in full pomp and circumstance." *Am I a Brit? Or is that a chance riposte?* I did not feel any kinship to being a Brit. My rajah had burst in, announcing our wedding plans as if it were an event discussed and endlessly mulled over.

My mind raced to my heart's rapid tattoo as I faltered to what must have seemed a perplexing and insulting degree.

The rajah had looked upon me kindly, as if I were a child. "Yes, my love, it is a shock, is it not? Yet you must find me agreeable, yes?"

I did not know why my outburst. I needed Rami, didn't I, with every pore, with every look, with every touch? I walked an untamed wilderness, with no star chart of the past or the future.

I was a nothing, neither slave nor wife, worker nor part of the hareem sisterhood. Other than sweet Asha, I had no friends. I fit nowhere, clinging to Rami's love as a net of safety.

Those flashing eyes narrowed. "There are myriad reasons we should not, only one that we should. And, that is all consuming. Is it not?" He asked with a hint of ice.

"Cannot we go on—" I gestured. *As we are?* Yet latent pricks of joy bubbled, as intoxicating as Champagne.

In the end, I looked through lashes, placing my

hands on Rami's broad shoulders. "Of course, Rami. It is all so—"

"Overwhelming? Yes, for me also!" His grin lit the room. "You will be a *rani*!"

A rani? A princess? Me?

Lifting me high above his head, he strode about, leaving me breathless as I gazed down, searching his face. Rami's hawkish features seemed boyish and younger than his twenty-two years. I had to keep reminding myself that I was older than he. I still felt fifteen. I just could not recall it.

Then I heard the fatal words:

"The Holi festival…"

Words that would haunt me to the grave.

"Holi is almost upon us. Bharatpur's great bonfires and colors will celebrate our *vivāha*, also!" I was yet dazed. He had called me his little *rājpatnī*, little wife-queen, often enough. A lovely endearment, but what was *vivāha?*

"Our wedding, of course. Our *vivāha!*"

Perhaps this was my destiny, yet I could not pluck that niggling feeling, like a splinter one cannot find, that all was not right but was in fact very, very wrong.

****

I recognized the Holi festival, through Asha. A messy, exuberant celebration, welcoming spring by drenching friends, most of whom welcomed the gouts of eye-hurting colors—cobalt, magenta, ocher, reds, oranges, and purples. All Bharatpur lit massive bonfires and set off fireworks that colored the sky, too.

"Let us leave here. Why cannot we—just go?"

His face darkened.

"Out there." My arm swept, taking in the whole

world and nearly knocking him aside. "Not come back."

"We've had this discussion."

I stopped short of saying, *You love India more than me!* in womanly fashion, realizing in time that it was beneath me.

In the end, it was not we two lovers who did the leaving.

****

The maharajah died.

The physician announced to the world that the maharajah had expired from tainted fish, a heart attack, or an apoplexy of the brain. The theories were accepted. Readily.

After a period of mourning, with all the ceremony of state due a supreme ruler with a bushel basket of titles, the maharani announced she would enter an *ashram*, a sanctuary for widows to last out their days among other women in the same state, ostensibly so as not to be a burden on their families.

It sounded hideous and dull. Thankfully, I was ignorant of a much worse fate that could have befallen her.

In this case, the maharani seemed safe enough, taking a large endowment, including her enormous stockpiling of jewels—a paltry amount compared with her deceased husband's hoard, buried inside the mound—servants, rich clothing, and musicians, one of whom was extremely handsome and only a few years younger than she, to an ashram high in the mountains of the Aravalli Range to the south of Bharatpur.

An affable place, even luxurious, for women of higher class, Asha confided.

"You need not leave. You are my sister too!" Rami protested, to my green-eyed suspicions. "You have friends—your apartments. Who will help me run the government?"

I gave Rami a stare of shock, furiously thinking. *Maharajah!*

I gawped at this lovely creature leaving us with oodles more grace, dignity, and majestic beauty than I could ever aspire to. Of course, it was unseemly. *Preposterous,* huffed my imp.

A maharani! Me? What an absurd thought! I suddenly felt I had hay in my hair and mud between my toes.

My mind stumbled over facts I had ignored. The maharajah had named no successor, and there was no other claimant besides his sweet son, whom the maharani insisted on taking with her, and an elderly uncle of the maharajah's father. I supposed now Rami would choose someone more suitable as his consort, never mind his "you're my *rājpatnī*" vow.

I sighed, picking up the maharani's next comments.

"The world is a big place." She slanted her knowing sloe eyes at us and grinned with unexpected wickedness. "Perhaps I might stray far from what is expected of me." Her serene highness's eyes twinkled then, and she actually winked.

Perhaps it was the chilled wine on an exceptionally torrid day that allowed her veils to slip. Perhaps she wished to reveal her own guile and skills, after years of subjugation. I never knew.

"I must say this thing to you." She watched Rami but spoke in English for my benefit also. "Did I ever tell you…?"

Her eyes took on a look deep within their black depths, as if a pond reflected stars.

"My village was renowned. Oh, yes. Travelers came from all parts of India, for all sorts of"—she smiled—"remedies. My mother was a most adept practitioner. She taught me arcane resolutions—secret herbal infusions and tonics for all manner of suffering, tribulations, and"—she hesitated—"complications."

She sighed contentedly and arching her long neck drained her flute, running a pink tongue across her upper lip and narrowing startling green-blue eyes, reminding me of a Persian cat.

"I never forgot them." With that, she withdrew. The next day she was gone.

****

"Cannot we leave too? Please, Rami." I envied her chance to see the world, once again feeling the walls enclosing me.

An old squall brewed between us.

"No one would know who we—"

"I cannot leave Bharatpur!" His face turned into a thundercloud and lightning flashed from his eyes.

"Me or your country?" I said as lightly as a falling concrete block.

The stormy look abated. "A maharani by my side, the most enchanting, beautiful, charitable…"

"Maharani! Me? But I—" My laughter was false even to my ears, as if I only just envisaged it. "I cannot possibly be. Even if—"

He kissed me. It sounded as if he then said, "*App merijidagi, meridhadkane aur season main hain…aap hi mere sab kuch hain ji!*" Way too long for me to translate, and with such passion. I understood the meaning, however deciphering "princess," "heart," and "queen." *I was the queen of his heart.*

I played for time. "I need to learn Hindi, my prince, or should I say king, or maharajah-darling." My heart thumped, and my thoughts were like chasing cats.

I wanted the rajah, Rami, with all my soul…but the role of maharani?

I was in no way suited, by either temperament or background as far as I knew. I could be the long-lost, wrong-side-of-the-sheets daughter of some hanged scoundrel. Or wanted by the law. Why else would I be here, if not in hiding? Why not Queen of the May?

This was his world steeped in this stultifying atmosphere, ritual, and culture since childhood. I was the possibly embarrassing unknown.

Chapter Twenty-Eight
Purdah Most Foul

Rami eschewed ceremony, taking over the reins of governing without fanfare.

My mind strayed, in the long hours apart, to dark thoughts of wondering why I could not escape, now the maharajah's heavy sword no longer hung over my head. What kept me here? *Besides the man himself?* my impious imp suggested.

The seraglio's curiosity grew as eunuchs carrying a palanquin passed them by. It stopped by me. Priests had decided I was to return to the seraglio before the *vivāha*—and thence to the rajah's compound after a suitable time. I was on a runaway train hurtling down a hill.

With his new status, my Rami became maddeningly traditional, at least by day. Nights were a different story.

Asha gave me a tiny wave. "I will send for you," I whispered.

I brushed by the head eunuch waiting by the lowered seat, suggesting he was about to lift me bodily onto it.

"I can walk!"

"No, no, *mem-sahib*! *Doli—doli!*" He pointed at the shaky contraption on two poles. "It is custom. The gods in their wisdom decreed *purdah* for those"—the head eunuch coughed, regarding me as if he emptied a rattrap—"of elevated degree."

"Oh, all right, but this is silly."

He indicated I should kneel on the platform and cover with a *ghoon ghat* as thick as felt, head to toe, coarse and stifling.

Clumsily, I climbed onto the low, shifting platform, gripping the sides. Perched on my knees on the elaborate *doli*, swaying like a boat on high seas, I made my procession.

Purdah!

I kenned what *purdah* was but had assumed the custom was ancient history.

Yet you've been in purdah in the hareem, where females hide from men lest you enflame them beyond all reason, my imp scorned.

I fumed beneath the stifling tent, peering balefully through the coarse weave until jolting to a halt at the rajah's lush courtyard, surrounded by a suite of lofty rooms. I glimpsed Rami's own new opulent quarters, befitting his rank, glimpsed through a broad archway.

Bowing, the eunuchs lowered the *doli* and backed.

I whirled. Rami made the mistake of striding to me with a cheese-eating grin, hands out in welcome.

"Sarabande, beloved! At last! Come, my—"

I lost no time hurling a copper pan of fresh petals at him. It had been lying about sweetening the air; blossoms fluttered about us. I admit to nerves. I did not care.

"*Purdah!* I will not be in *purdah*! It—it is old-fashioned! And suffocating! It is a prison of another sort. I am my own woman and will not—"

"Sarabande." He spoke soothingly—as if to a

horse. "You are always throwing things. It is meant as special protection, an honor for a woman of highest value."

"Honor? A canary in a cage! A slave has more freedom. You will not keep me here, isolated, on a stupid pedestal. I prefer the seraglio! At least there…"

Why was I so hysterical? I had no intention of following the custom.

Visibly I calmed.

"Sary. I have no wish to imprison you. That would be against all my desires."

"Then why this, this—?" I gestured at the *ghoon ghat* as if it were a dead rat.

"I did not think how you might see it, my dearest heart. Now—may we begin again?"

He beheld me with his sleepy hooded eyes. "I had very different plans for tonight."

I did not pull away.

"Rami," I warned. "I will prowl at will, see whom I wish whenever I wish, and leave this royal prison whenever I feel the need." I allowed myself to be bent back, convinced by Rami's languorous and thorough kisses that turned both our knees to jelly, that he agreed.

Later, from our vast plush bed—a bed as large as a small island, where one could set up housekeeping—we came to an accord.

Neither of us could have foretold how our joyous wedding celebration would end, moreover with such disaster, though I had more premonition than had he…

Chapter Twenty-Nine
Wedding of Fire

Sumptuously gowned in silks—as a *dulhan*, recalling my early days in the seraglio. Every inch weighted with gold, hennaed, bejeweled, veiled, diademed, and bangled to within an inch of my life. The rajah bestowed an emerald the size of a quail's egg, now hanging level with my eyebrows.

I surveyed my loaded-down reflection in the copper mirror.

I do look rather magnificent!

Like a princess? sneered my imp. I wasn't sure I hated that notion at all.

"You are to be a *rani*! And soon maharani!" Asha's eyes were round with awe. The news spread like a green-eyed plague throughout the seraglio. "Shall we not be friends, then?"

"I am no better than you, no matter what I am called." I wondered when the sumptuous dress, the gems, and being addressed as "princess" or "maharani" would become second nature, leave alone *first* nature...

Yet, to my shame, these fancies crept in the back door. No more fear. The world at my feet. Exotic splendors. Travelling in opulent style. Feted and admired—forever, with the most striking man in the universe by my side.

My bewildered image frowned back as I gazed at

myself in all my wedding finery. What was wrong with this image? Why did my foot not fit in that particular glass slipper?

Quit being a goose! Of course you deserve it.

Admiring myself for the last time—*yes, this is the last!*—I saluted my image and left to meet my prince, my love, my Rami.

No more looking back.

****

I paced regally, as befitted a queen—or at least so I supposed—up to my Rami waiting on a balustrade, overlooking Bharatpur that moonstruck night. A man of exotic eastern flavor whom all my senses found most pleasing.

"On Holi, people make huge *Holika* bonfires and sing and dance!" Asha had spread her slender arms wide, exclaiming, while I prepared.

True. All Bharatpur exploded with high spirits. Everywhere shining faces, flashing teeth, swirling mobs, while brilliant powders tinted the air with rainbow clouds of mist, music played from all quarters, and celebrants chanted.

The pearly moon shimmered off Rami's ivory satin tunic and tight breeches, complimenting his burnished walnut skin and molten black eyes. As a salute to his youth, he let his long black gypsy hair hang free as he stalked wordlessly to meet me, hands out, his mysterious hooded eyes expressionless and his mouth set in stone.

Detecting the barely controlled emotions beneath, my last doubts evaporated like the brilliant clouds of mist tinting Bharatpur's night sky.

Now I faced my most handsome, passionate

companion-to-be, pleasuring my mind, my body, and my very soul and offering, after these few promises and prayers, an undreamed-of life.

And me, soon to be treasured, wealthy beyond words, feted by crowned heads and worshiped by Indian society. *At least Rajasthan's.* My imp snickered.

I glanced over, hearing a subtle cough from the waiting priests.

Troubled, I glanced over my shoulder at the mob below. What could go wrong? The arrival of uninvited wedding guests, hinting at the horrors to come?

What could go wrong?

****

The Vedic *yajna*, the ritual, began. Soon to be Her Royal Highness the Maharani Sarabande—or whatever name was dropped on my head—I heard the buzz of the ritual only through a baffle of laughter, music, and chaotic thoughts darting about me like large night moths.

Most prophetic—yet how could I know?—the primary witness of a Hindu wedding was the fire deity, *Agni*. Yes, the fire god Agni was much in attendance that night, a jealous god watching over all, in all his blazing, vindictive, destructive glory.

Innocent of all this, I found my world forever changed as, beyond the priest, massive joyous crowds lit yet another enormous bonfire. Dazzling, earsplitting sound and fury kindled the sky amidst thunderous blasts from fireworks. Colors danced across faces, turning Rami's ivory satin to rainbow hues.

At the same time, the mob lit a massive bundle of Catherine wheels and roman candles. Then...

A stack of shooting-star fireworks tipped onto an

igniter. Cartons of firecrackers detonated, in chain reaction, followed by more shooting stars, Catherine wheels, and strings of crackers. The indigo sky exploded into orange, turning incandescent white-hot fury, with the force and blast of a volcano, as if the god Agni bestowed his most generous angry gift upon Rami and myself.

The beating white-hot heart blossomed into a poisonous, hellish, sulfurous yellow, vanquishing the velvety sky, the distant crowd, and all of my senses.

My ears vibrated with shock waves, and simultaneously my memory returned with the full force of Agni's vengeance.

Chapter Thirty
Agni's Vengeance

My howl was that of a wounded animal. Memories burned deep caught fire, as if smoldering coals ignited, setting my heart and head ablaze.

I remembered.

Staring into the hellish sky, I remembered all.

I cried out, "Jude!" with all the anguish of pent-up bewilderment and pain.

I looked wildly about, turning and turning again, winding my wedding finery about me like a shroud. "Tommy! Tommy! Where are you?" The last I could recall was as he approached an enormous bonfire… *No, that wasn't right.* My mind still refused to open that last door, but my hand was on the knob and I was pulling hard.

Walls of flame met each spin. Panic-stricken celebrants screaming, colliding, as rockets and pyrotechnics continued exploding and ashes from burning stalls and buildings rained down on our heads.

I lifted my arm to shield my face, shrieking as my veil caught fire…fire… *As it had before.*

Rami yanked off my veil, lifted me in my wedding finery, and carried me off as I beat at him, struggling to be let down.

"Let me go! I need to find them!"

"I know, Sary, beloved…"

Chapter Thirty-One
Suttee

The suttee…where widows burned to untimely death.

The suttee, where widows young or old flung themselves on or bound themselves to husbands in hoary tradition—or because of coercion or perverted love…

That was my last terrifying moment before my memories walled off, but now the walls came tumbling down…

That unleashed fury at our wedding matched perfectly the horrors of the suttee.

That other great fire, blackening my mind, heart, and soul, scorching my memory clean…until now.

I saw…

Jude's dear, puckish face.

And Tommy's Irish good looks and charming grin.

Immobile as stone, ashes smearing my face, I could smell my singed hair, just as before.

Still in wedding finery, the gruesome scenes played in my head.

"There was a fire that other time," I whispered.

"Yes." Rami agreed sadly.

But the fire was the answer…I must hang on to that.

****

"Good port from our British protectors. Better than tea." Rami handed me a beaker with enough to knock out a horse, but gall would have been no less bitter.

"Do I need to be restored?" I whispered huskily, my gaze traveling his face like an explorer over unknown territory. "My name is Sarabande. Sarabande Swinford! I was born in Indiana. I'm a farmer's wife," I blurted with a sense of wonder, then beat my forehead in irritation. "That isn't right! He—he died. I traveled with—with my brother to a gold mining camp. It was in California." I faltered. "Big Bear, it was. It was in the mountains—but that was long ago, and…"

Rami watched me. "You wish to know more, *mera pyara?*" he asked me, sadly and oh, so carefully.

"Yes," I whispered between dry lips.

"There was a man, Sarabande. The bravest I have ever seen. I do not have his acquaintance. Yet this man rushed in, as you say, 'Where angels fear to tread.' "

"Thomas. You speak of…my Tommy." His name died in a whisper as ebony night enfolded me, and stars blinked out as if a ghost appeared. A man I knew and loved. Slender, fine-boned, strikingly handsome as only the Black Irish can be. My…almost husband, for I had never consented to marriage, me, forever playing the tease, the contrary, the independent.

"Yes, Thomas. I noted the name on your banner." Rami smiled almost wistfully.

I saw it all. Tommy. Beloved Tommy. Brave little Jude.

The colorful jolly parade of Rolls Royce motor cars, performers…and me atop that elephant…

"Tommy was an actor—he owned a traveling theater company. That is how we met. He toured Big

Bear…and…"

"Continue. You must."

"*Sut—tee!*" I managed, twisting my face in disgust and horror. My hair flew about my head, stinging my eyes as I tried to shake the image loose. Even the word *suttee* scorched my throat.

Hot. Hellish. Vile.

Sut—teeeeeeee! Like a snake's evil hiss.

"It was barbaric! Suttee belongs in the dark ages with the bloody Inquisition! Burning a woman alive—burying her…with her dead husband! Or drowning her!"

"The custom is indeed horrible…"

"Horrible! Indeed!" I had nailed up the past, but those walls burned down in the chaos of the Holi festival.

"When Tommy and I first heard of that—that *practice*, we thought it was a hideous myth to intrigue credulous tourists—the practice of burying a widow along with her husband…alive, or drowning the unfortunate creature, whose only sin was that of being an awkward widow."

It had almost made the thought of suttee seem a blessing, quick and searing…

Until we beheld one…

"I saw one of your God-blasted suttees!" I slanted eyes at Rami so scathingly he winced, as if my words physically cut.

"Please!" I held up my hand. "Let me finish, or I never shall."

The glare, the heat, the ghastly nightmare images—all horrifically true…

"There were massive flames then, too, raging two

stories high from a tower of faggots so scorching hot it blistered my face from a half a block away."

I looked at Rami, unseeing. "It was a glorious day in India, not sweltering, for one used to the cold." I smiled, wistful. "Our entourage was elegant. The troupe traveled in Rolls Royces—in style."

"Indeed. Go on." I knew him. He wished to lead me away from the horrors. I was willing—for the time. Happier reminiscence rushed in that I would not deny. "Yes. Twenty Rolls Royces—trucks, vans, buses, cabriolets, and passenger coupes in the brightest colors, especially kitted in every rainbow shade." I could not help crowing. "Brass gleamed so it hurt the eyes."

I saw a series of pictures parading before me.

"We spanned southern India and then decided to travel north to here. I was on the lead elephant. I remember its ankle bells jangling as it thumped along. And the flies! Lord!" I smiled again. "Trucks of props, and costumes, the cooks' car, and a dressing van, one for me and Tommy. My son, Jude, had his own caravan—though he was only six."

I swallowed hard and looked away. I did not want to ask. Not yet. I was picking my way.

"Dormitory vans for crew and cast, plus quarters for Malcolm." I smiled fondly at the memory. "Malcolm was only three and a half feet tall, but a lion." My mouth stretched wide at the happy recollection. "Plus, his red-haired wife and three daughters, with one on the way. Rose, Lilly, and Tulip."

I went silent again. *What had happened to them all?*

Rami sat quietly.

As if he already knew.

I left it for now. How could I ask that for which the answer might plunge me into despair?

"Abandoning heavy velvets in favor of Indian dress, we performed *The Taming of the Shrew* and *A Midsummer Night's Dream* in saris and sandals instead." I chuckled at the memory that could have been forever lost.

"I attended *The Taming of the Shrew* in Stratford-upon-Avon," Rami could not help boasting.

"Indeed?" I said politely, wincing at a fragment of another recollection. Where had we performed before, in the cold…the wet, the rain? Oh, yes. England! Mismatched pieces grudgingly fit into place, some forced and others I feared never found.

England. Misty greens, chill fogs, cozy fires and teas…Also, a humiliating bout with a con artist who stole the fortune I had gouged out in cold dank gold mines in far-off Big Bear. Tommy, back there in that hostile mining camp, armed with nothing but a scared expression and a bandolier of ammo but rushing to my aid.

"Where did you go, Sarabande?" The rajah broke in softly. "Take me with you."

I shook my head and forged on.

"We gave a command performance for the maharajah that night. *A Midsummer Night's Dream.*"

Rami nodded assent.

"Terribly thrilled and puffed up to be invited to the palace!" My face showed I was anything but.

"Yes. My brother took great notice of you. And of your son," he finished heavily. "The maharajah was besotted. Scarce a man did not send roses from his heart. My dear brother stalked you about the stage as if he wanted to suck the marrow from your bones."

I shuddered.

"I overheard orders for your abduction, long before he saw your son in that last act. But the boy! All he could see from then on were the lusty sons you would bear—besides the other benefits he would enjoy." An unaccustomed sepia flush was evident under his polished nut-brown skin. "Yes, how do you say it? I put both feet in the stew up to my chin."

I bit back a grin at his malapropism, no matter my unease.

"I wanted no part, Sary. I was disgusted. That a prince of our noble state would need lower himself to an abduction. I heard guards would rush the stage to arrest you on made-up charges. Sedition. Religious heresy, the troupe jailed for rabblerousing, or Lord Shiva knows what! Not beyond him to have all but you and your lad put to the sword, to the last man and child. Even your son was not safe. My brother already viewed your splendid boy as an unneeded rival, if he could beget an heir on you. That was my brother's sick, poisonous mind in a sea shell."

"Nutshell," I murmured automatically.

"All eyes were on you. You captured every male in the house. When you made your bows, you announced, oh, so proudly, 'My son Jude played the part of Puck extremely well, don't you think? It is his first adult role, though my son is only six!' Do you remember?"

"Yes."

"And that was your undoing, *mere dil ka pyaar.*"

Don't call me "love of my heart"! I cannot bear it.

"I saw my brother's eyes open wide. Greedy for your son. The health, vigor, and lusty strength of your lad compared to his own poor boy. Your remarkable son looked at least ten years of age, with the beginning of mannish muscles. All my brother saw was the impressive man he would become, that his own son would never be."

Again my past invaded me. Jude, the result of an attack by E'vret, a sweet, childlike giant, years ago in those same rough mountains of Big Bear, that depraved California gold-mining outpost.

By some alchemy, the attack resulted in Jude, perfect, bright, and beautiful, defying all odds. Jude. My faultless, darling son. My green eyes and intellect—my attacker's muscles, height, curly hair, and sweet underlying disposition, no matter Ev'ret's criminal lapse to please his sick boss, who ordered the attack.

"I killed him," I said simply.

"Killed?" Rami raised a black wing of brow.

"Yes." I looked Rami full on. "Jude's…father was the bodyguard of a mad man…he was"—I hesitated—"not simple, just trusting, child-like."

I shut my eyes. "I killed them both before they could murder me." Aware Rami gazed at me with new eyes, I did not care. So I was not the woman, faint of heart, he supposed.

"So. He wanted my boy." I looked at Rami coldly. "What has he done with him?" I jumped up, prepared to tear the palace apart.

"No, my love. We—I do not have him. Please."

My eyes must have turned the stormy green of the sea when squalls threaten the horizon. A storm was definitely brewing. I sorted words, like picking glass from the bottom of my foot.

"We blundered, that day of the suttee, after that last

performance, into a narrow passage."

And straight into a blazing orange hell.

"The way was blocked. We had to back out. Not easy with so many of us—the crowds and stalls. And of course the"—I choked—"confusion at the other end. We thought it was unrest against British rule or some such riot, and we were perilously close to what I thought a bonfire, an uprising." My eyes darkened. "Only it was not. Unable to back up, we were shoved right to the ragged end of the mob. It was still dangerously high, yet men were feeding the blaze. When the flames lowered, other men—and women, too—tossed coconut shells onto the fire that roared in a whirlwind of smoke, as black as evil…

"My elephant became restive. Then I saw the girl on the pyre—so young, so lovely, in a plain white flapping sari whipped by gusts from the fire as she tried to scramble higher up the faggots, as if the logs were stair steps. Then smoke curling around the side hid her. When it thinned, I saw her crawling sideways where the wood hadn't caught yet."

"Shhh, shhh, *priya.*"

I was not about to be soothed. "I saw fire and smoke enveloping spectators, who leaped back amid hoots and laughter. Cinders burned pinpricks in my arms."

I looked up at Rami. "If cinders were so fiercely hot, I thought, what must it be like for her?"

It was turning dark. How searing-bright the flames were, up close. Spicy acrid smoke battled the night air. Black clouds shifting, furling up to the moon, revealed…

I shuddered, swallowed hard, and went on.

"Hands prodded the poor soul back up. They thrust burning faggots and sticks at her as she tried to climb down, or—or to leap from the top.

" 'Stop!' I yelled, but my voice was lost. I wondered if this was some hideous execution, because women shook their fists too, even as the poor thing looked for other ways. I saw the tail of her sari, pulled loose, catch and spark."

"You do not need to speak of it more. A hideous practice!"

I stared at him, unrelenting. "But I have no choice, Rami. It is all a part!"

He tried to hold me then. I brushed him off.

"Her blazing sari looked like a comet. She jumped off the far side, away from grabbing hands and sticks…and she ran…she ran like the devil!" I recalled her shriek.

"I heard a scream. I screamed too. They prodded the woman back to the bonfire, their faces burning with excitement. The mob and even our elephant mahout cried, 'Suttee! It is a suttee! We are most fortunate!' I remember my mahout's turban. A ridiculous thing, all gaudy, with big paste jewels, bobbing in pleasure. He had guided us to this by accident—even so; his face was filled with anticipation. He kept saying, '*Tamasha.*' I watched the mob urging her to go higher. What is '*tamasha.*'?"

"It was," the rajah murmured sadly, "*tamasha.* Their entertainment." He snarled, "As I said, I do not approve!"

I ignored him.

"Our mahout argued. 'Her husband is dead!' he shouted. 'She has no use. She has money shared by the

246

family and priests. She is giving herself to join her husband in death. A good pious thing, memsahib!' "

The rajah nodded gravely.

"He went on and on about how this sainted woman would be a deity. 'You have seen the many shrines along the roadside,' he told me, 'each devoted to a new saint.'

"I wanted to shove him off the elephant. 'Difficult to enjoy being a saint, if one is dead,' I yelled at him. Then I screamed above the crowd, 'Save her— someone!' It was a long way to the ground, and the elephant was pacing. Then I looked for Tommy, behind me somewhere in our train of cars—to see, I suppose, if he could help. All this time she was screaming atop the pyre. I couldn't find him, so I climbed down the rigging and beat my way through the mob.

" 'Stop, memsahib!' I heard the mahout. He shook his fist, with a face I had never before seen. 'She was wishing this!' he yelled. 'She has fasted and cleansed! Look, even now, she goes willingly!' He climbed down and followed me as I forced my way through.

" 'It looks as if she is forced into being willing!' I yelled back.

"He held my wrist and snarled when he caught up, 'A momentary thing, memsahib. She will not feel it...after a while.'

"I stared up then at the uncontrolled pyre, white as the sun at the center, with flickering orange tongues eating the velvety sky. I snapped, 'Have you tried it?'

"His face turned dark. 'It is not a man thing.' Then I saw Tommy near us, weaving through the crowd. Our mahout, divining his intentions, grabbed him, saying, 'Don't! It is forbidden!'

" 'What? Come on, my good man! We can save her!' But the mahout and the mob chanted, 'She wants to be chaste. A sati!' I can hear them now— *'Sati! Sati! Sati!'* Men tossed more coconuts on the fire. I watched the woman prodded, with long poles, farther up toward her husband, a white bundle with flowers on his chest, while our mahout wrestled Tommy. He kept repeating, 'She will be esteemed. Worshipped. Shrines made to her. What life will she have otherwise? She is elevated, sahib—remote, untouchable. It is very popular here, a thing done in Rajasthan, and in all Bengal and India.'

"As if trying to make it right!" I glared at Rami. "He went on and on... 'You see the stones and monuments to these chaste ones? Hundreds every day. Why should this woman be different?' he said. 'Besides, she will not be a burden to her family.'

"When I looked again, the widow, perched near the white bundle now circled by flames, beat at her hair and ripped off her veil."

Rami interrupted. "Sarabande, my love. Please. No more. A hideous, odious practice I do not for one instant believe in. I abhor it. Abhor. Is that a word?"

I nodded absently.

"The custom is centuries old, true—fueled by greed, religion, part venerated tradition and part practical, as they see it, if one does not wish to support the widow. Very hard to wipe out, rich or poor. They do it secretly, but some, even royals, quite openly and proudly. Some women fight for the right to immolate themselves..."

"And that makes it convenient and right?"

"No! When I—*if* I am made maharajah, I will halt this barbaric practice. You have my vow."

I closed my eyes. I knew if I wanted to find out about Tommy and my baby boy, I must follow this to the end.

"Tommy finally tore away," I said. "I screamed, 'Stop. Don't do it!' But he approached the pyre with his arm wrapped in rags before his face. He was like a mythic warrior—a Viking or a Roman soldier could have been no more brave. Even our roustabouts, who were not afraid of anything, held back.

"The crowd still pressed with threats and grabbing hands. I lost him. They swallowed me too—I can still smell garlic, spices, sweat, and oils. I can feel body heat, sweat, and throbbing excitement. I looked up where they pointed.

"At the top, the woman had managed to ease to the back side. I could see the flap of her white sari and just make out the top of Tommy's head as he started to climb. It looked so rickety! Part of the pyre was crumbling to ash.

" 'Tommy!' I screamed. I pushed my way closer. I overheard an angry man say, '*Soower ki bachi!*' and he spat. 'Son of a pig,' my mahout translated right behind me.

"Then—the fire, the…the body, shifted. Some of the logs rolled, and Tommy leapt off. The crowd gasped and cheered. I heard a priest shouting as Tommy looked for another way around.

" 'Sati is the highest expression of wifely devotion to a dead husband!' The crowd took up the chant."

Rami spoke up then, smiling grimly. "I can imagine. It purges sins, releases her from birth and rebirth, and ensures salvation for her husband and seven generations to come."

Rami appeared to half believe it. Venerated tradition died fighting, I saw.

I twisted my mouth, flashing an angry glance. "The priest kept ranting, 'Do not deny her this honor!' 'Honor! I am denying her death from you murderous thugs,' I heard Tommy say, and he punched him. He just hauled off and socked him. The mob was horrified. 'Oh, Tommy,' I thought. He plunged the rags into a water barrel, and my Tommy, my brave, foolhardy Tommy, neared the bonfire again. It was hellacious even from where I stood. It was suicide."

Rami nodded assent. "Indeed."

"She was in the heart of the fire, now. Her sari had caught, as if her husband reached out for her. A flicker of orange caught her hair. It was long and streaming. I heard her call out—something that sounded like, '*Ram, Ram, sati, Ram, Ram, sati.*' Was that a call for help?" I finally looked at Rami.

"She was chanting, 'God, God, I am chaste,' " Rami said. "She must have accepted her...fate. You have to understand. When a wife decides to become a Sati, a chaste one, she is untouchable. The alternative is not appealing, Sary. A widow lives the life of an ascetic." He gestured helplessly. "Shaving her head, eating boiled rice, sleeping on the ground. To many, death may seem preferable..."

I looked at Rami with despair and shook my head.

"The woman was trying to regain the back side of the pyre again. It was the—the body that caught fire and blazed up so." *It had blossomed like a noxious flower, blooming blazing petals with black curling leaves of smoke.*

"Then there was Tommy, coaxing the woman

down that way. The crowd for once became just onlookers, holding their breath. As if they too wanted to see what would happen next."

Still in the hellacious scene, I looked through the rajah for a moment, but then I could wait no longer.

"Tommy—What happened to him? That is as far as I remember! And where is Jude?" I caught my breath until he answered.

"It is said—" The rajah spoke gently.

"No 'it is said'! You *know* the truth. I want to know it now! No!" I dashed away a glass of offered tea.

"Sary!" He grabbed my hands. I calmed. "Sary, your brave Thomas did get to the pyre. He did try to talk the woman down. He attempted to meet her half the way…"

He hesitated.

"It is said, he saw a way around to where it hadn't caught yet. That is true. The woman, changing her mind or only fooling them with her chant of willingness, was looking to leap, but there was a burst of flame as more husks were tossed. There are many stories, but it seems the fire circled, cutting him off. At that moment, the woman jumped. That was one version. She was—" He halted, his face anguished.

"No one really knows," he said softly. "The mob scattered when the logs became unstable, no doubt partly from your Thomas climbing on them and the mob's actions. Plus, a suttee, no matter what you might suppose, is at least frowned upon, if not semi-outlawed. They were afraid of being caught." He thrust long fingers through his hair.

"Don't stop there," I threatened.

"The pyre collapsed, sending burning wood rolling

down into the gathering and bits of cloth and flaming ashes flew to the winds. That is what my informers reported. The aftermath consumed many in the panic— the smoke, the heat, the mob all trampling each other, the flaming body rolling off—and when they tried to escape, part of the way was hampered by your own troupe."

"And—and the widow?" I took time to wonder.

"Some say she escaped down a passageway. She was safe either way. When your husband touched her, she was made unclean." He smiled ironically. "They would have had to begin the purification all over. Others say she went up like a flaming ghost in the center right before it collapsed."

My face was stone. "And Tommy?"

"No one saw him. After the collapse, many sought him." He placed his hand gently on my shoulder. "After the collapse, many sought him."

"Oh. No…no! He did not die. Not Tommy. You do not know him. He is cleverer, quicker than that. Why, onstage, he could…"

"Perhaps the god Agni—the God of Fire, ordained it."

"What drivel! Your gods…your gods!" I lashed out. "Tommy lives! He must. He was a hero! Not like your backward murderers!"

I paced, not sure what to do with feet that wanted to run, hands that yearned to flail. The rajah studied me, not without compassion—a kindness it was fortunate I did not see. "You must hear all this to heal."

"Heal? I have no wish to heal! Not while my Tommy and Jude are out there." My breath caught.

A shadow passed over the rajah's face—a flash of

annoyance. For a second his eyes turned to black ice.

"When the pyre collapsed, sending flames and burning logs into the crowd, they turned."

"Turned?"

"On him. They took him away…" He gestured helplessly. "Or he ran. 'S'truth, I do not know. They were—stirred up. I heard many stories." At my look, he added, "And yes, I have sent my enquirers. A hundred! The fire caught several buildings—a whole block went up."

"No more. I will hear no more of your merciful country."

At that kindle point, he made the mistake of touching my hair.

He remained solid as a tree, allowing me, still in wedding finery, to shove and push and beat at him until I sagged, my breathing hoarse and ragged. He clasped my wrists in two strong hands.

"Wearing yourself out. It is too soon." He meant after my recovery, or maybe the shock of remembering. It hardly mattered. Fear and frustration, tamped down like gunpowder until then, exploded without my will. Still I struggled, kicked, cursed, and threw things until, exhausted and raw from weeping, I rasped, "You've kept me here all this time. While I could have been searching, asking!"

"I will send word once more to find him, this…this…not-husband."

"And my boy?" Weariness dragged at me. I smelt cloves, perfumed oils, camphor, and sandalwood, and sensed his bare satiny smooth chest beneath his wedding tunic. I wanted nothing more than to rest, curl, nestle, and think of nothing.

Angrily, I shook him off, straining through mental fog, and paced the room.

Jude was missing from that last narrative.

As if he read my thoughts, he murmured, "This will gladden your heart, perhaps, beloved." I faltered. Rami's face shone with love. "Your theater troupe, my agents reported, did manage to back out of the area. This we heard months ago."

I sucked in a gasp.

"The mob turned their fury into either feeding the fires, running from the collapse, or fighting amongst themselves in place of battering what amounted to an armored fleet, your caravan of doughty Rolls Royces, armed to the teeth. You were a juggernaut."

"I don't care about that. My boy! I don't care a fig about the mob or—" It was on my tongue to say, "Or what happened to the troupe!" But that was not true.

"My little boy?" My heart lurched. "Six…almost seven…"

"Almost nine, *mera pyara*…now."

"Jude…is—alive?" I searched his face.

"I—believe so."

"You believe so!"

"There is reason. I have been searching. I had news very recently. I wanted to tell you, when I was sure…a wedding present, if you will."

His face took on its usual hawkish attitude, belying his age. "A troupe—your troupe, it is believed—was sighted near the Chinese-Tibetan border…"

"Chinese border," I repeated stupidly. "And Jude?"

"Several conveyances, your cars, were found abandoned and stripped. Props, costumes, and a foods truck…They were unmistakable."

"The cook's rig."

"Yes." He nodded gravely. "There were sightings of a battered caravan regrouped outside of Nepalganj Road on our northern border, heading presumably toward Kathmandu. In Nepal," he explained.

"Yes, I know where Nepal is!" Tommy and I had studied world maps avidly. I laughed without humor. World travelers, we had been always eager for the next town, the next hill.

"What else?"

He waved. "Something, someone, overheard one of your troupe in a tea shop, near where roustabouts and performers congregate. China and Kathmandu were mentioned. There was a man—I believe one of your slaves. A short person—very short," he emphasized, holding his hand three feet from the floor.

"We had no slaves! That was Malcolm!" I grinned as I hadn't in days, recalling the man billed as Malcolm The Midget. "Tommy's comic strong man in the old days, and a valuable player," I protested.

"So be it. My scouts questioned all in the teashop, followed leads as thin as a cat's whisker. After weeks, they heard they had indeed crossed the border. We questioned a temple priest in the last village, who avowed he saw a bright green truck with a faded banner with the words—let me see…Sir Thomas…or…The Amazing Sir Thomas. The actual words had been scraped off, possibly for safety."

I could still see the panels in my mind's eye announcing: Sir Thomas' Traveling Troupe Of Thespians, Acrobats, Magicians And Feats Of Astounding Strength!

"Of course it was them." I walked to the balcony as

if I could see them far off. "They left without me. But where are they?" I keened to the wind.

"I wish"—he held out hands in supplication—"I could tell you. They saw no boy at the teashop." He hesitated.

"Why was I not with them?"

"Kind people of a religious order found you wandering half naked, parched and starving; you had suffered a concussion, our physician decided. Being a foreigner, these others took you to the British Consulate. They refused you entry, saying they had no records of you. You were not a British subject and, in their words, 'it would be most inappropriate.'

"Our court physicians agreed that the head injury plus the repugnant suttee and the shock of your friend's heroics must have erased your mind. I was frightened, not willing to goad you into recalling, at least not until I found the boy I saw on stage, until I had answers. They said you might go mad, be forever lost into another world. You had terrifying nightmares."

"So you knew all along…"

"There were reasons…"

"So you say…"

"You wonder why I did not release you when you were also in danger, here? Where would you go? I could not identify your name. You were billed as 'Madam Sarabande.' Your troupe scattered. Apparently, you traveled extensively, but from whence you came, we did not know."

He spread his hands, helpless. "How would we? Superficially, you were in India the better part of a year, judging from a few playbills we found. You spoke with a colonial or American accent, yet with British overtones, and also had picked up an overlay of Hindi. Where would I have taken you? Which embassy? Would they have released you back onto the streets? Placed you in an asylum? No." He flipped his long hair. "It was better here, and selfishly, by that time"—he looked me full in the face—"I loved you."

His youthful face took on a grave maturity. I saw the noble, fiercely loyal older man he would become.

I quirked a smile, comprehending how my escape attempts must have rankled. Rami had been patient, doing his best between the rock of his brother and the hard place of my oblivion...and falling in love along the way...*as had I.*

My eyes finally met his.

The rajah regarded me with such compassion I needed to look away. Then he had to continue.

"Your Tommy was a true hero. Is that not enough? He will go directly to *Bhagavan* now. As you say— Heaven."

"Not Tommy. I don't want him in Heaven, I want him here! Safe! He is too real—too alive. Never would he just...leave."

"My point." He spoke gently. "This Thomas would have been found by now...or have been making enquiries, storming the castle, if you will."

I fanned my hair side to side. My beautiful, raven-haired, hopelessly romantic, not-of-this-world Thomas, my beloved, he must be alive...and my baby, Jude. Though not a baby now—as the rajah said.

"I do not believe he perished in the fire but, to their lasting damnation, at the hands of men."

I shook my head. As if that made a difference. I watched him stonily. "I will never believe that. You still have not told me everything. I feel it! And now, tell me! My boy?"

"India is vast. This city is vast. We have been turning Bharatpur, Rajasthan, and beyond upside down, and now, would you settle for your son?" Rami cocked his head.

Hope and distrust warred. I groped behind me and sat hard.

"You see, it appears he has been seeking you."

I broke down in howling sobs.

Slowly, he folded me against him, and if tears ran down his face too, it is not recorded.

"Shh-shhh…" He bent his head, stroking my hair until I quieted, hiccupping and heaving, afraid to hope, afraid I had not heard right. "He is well—is he—?"

"We found him weeks ago. Not him, physically, but where he might be. He left the troupe near Nepal on a mountain pass. Scouts found him safe with a Tibetan monk. They weren't certain at first. He was wearing the clothing of a monk and would not speak. He was smart." I nodded fiercely. "Our soldiers can seem terrifying thugs. It appeared he tore away from the group and was making his way back. We had to keep him safe from my brother. He was still in danger. Then, of course, my brother died.

"Sary, my beloved little foreigner, your son was to be a—wedding present. Belated perhaps, but—?"

Chapter Thirty-Two
Is He a Prince!

I returned to the seraglio to sort out the cyclone swirling within. I saw their faces—resentment overwritten by overweening interest as they flocked like pigeons to crumbs of toast, pecking at me with their unbearable need for novelty.

"Does not he like you? The rajah? You were not there long." They preened. "You did not wed. He must not care for you after all. So sad."

Padmavati stood, arms folded across her flat chest, looking on with her usual severe expression. Even Asha seemed puzzled.

"I have a son!" I blurted as they trailed me, peppering questions. I was restless, waiting to see what came next, missing the rajah—Rami—grieving for Tommy's whereabouts; I couldn't stand them another second.

"You have a son?"

"Is he handsome?" They twitted like brainless birds.

"Is he a prince?"

"Is he living?" This was the all-important question.

"Of course!"

"But where is he? I see no son!"

A woman just losing the first bloom of middle age, a thread of white silk stitching her raven hair, mimicked

259

looking under a table, behind a chair, causing much mirth.

Another with a thin face and tall sinuous body, called Shyamala, snickered and turned on her heel. Shayamala was the one who used to trip other girls in *ghalli dandi*.

"Indeed! Of course, you have many sons! We see them everywhere!" She called back over her shoulder, waving an arm wide.

"Is he a truly royal?" Rashmi, a plump maiden, ventured shyly.

"No! Of course not! No," I said more gently. 'His father was—was common."

I sensed blatant glee.

Another story!

I eyed them sourly.

Yes, another story I would never reveal...Ev'ret, bull-like Ev'ret, big as a barn door, thick as a plank. My brilliant son's father. Childlike Ev'ret—unintentionally brutal, tragically witless—and Big Bear flooded back once more, where my journey really began, when I was a slave for my brother, a widow, an accidental gold miner, and a mother...

Cold, untamed hills, rough and undomesticated miners, hunters, panners, and doxies...the cat-claw women, who tried to kill me with their suspicions. I did tell the seraglio of lovely England, after Big Bear gave up its gold, and the perils of Africa hunting for diamonds after the con man stole my fortune, and of the bounty of uncut diamonds that underwrote Tommy's magnificent troupe in an act of contrition that turned out so ruinously, and finally—how I came to be here...

Ohh, go away! I wanted to say. *I am not an exhibit.*

Yet if widows in this country, from frightened child-brides to grizzle-haired matriarchs, were either sent to ashrams to wither over the sins of their husbands or burned in suttee, how could these women believe anything I told them of the outside world?

I looked up at the touch of a hand, and there was Asha. "Sar-ree, what is his name?" she asked timidly.

"Jude," I said through tears. "His name is Jude."

Asha, my first and only ally, cast a chastened face.

"I'm regret, Sar-eee, for what they say. I believe you. But where is this son?"

And then...

Jude walked in.

Epilogue
Ever After…

It is said…

That years later, when an extraordinarily handsome yet reclusive silver-haired maharajah with the nose of a hawk and fierce wing-like brows toured the world, a striking woman with hair the color of corn silk accompanied him, but the most renowned part of her was her bewitching, enchanting green gaze…emerald eyes. The news of her was bandied about.

Their notorious love affair was legend, though the couple was also celebrated for their exclusivity, feted, sought after as they made world pilgrimages and were seen at the best events: racing at Deauville, Ascot, and Salisbury; sitting at the high stakes table at Monte Carlo; dining privately with the kings and queens of Europe; skiing at Zermatt or St. Moritz; even calling on New York and a squalid little place called Big Bear, in the mountains of far-off California.

The exquisite companion was famed too for her generosity in private charities, though she tried to keep her good works anonymous.

Just as exquisite, enchanting, and accomplished were their many children, ranging in age from six to fifteen, who accompanied them everywhere. They were marked for their arresting green eyes, made even more attractive shining from coppery, bronzed faces.

A hulking young man, nearly six feet, or seven it is rumored, named Jude—or perhaps it was Jud or Justin—guarded this delightful pack, along with his wife, a petite and shy thing half his size. They called her Ash or Alice or something like that. She was older than he. He had shoulders as wide as a barn.

Then, with the arrival of the Great War, attentions were drawn elsewhere, and the legend was scrambled in the tumult of conflict.

There were also rumors of a different sort.

There were sightings of a handsome theater entrepreneur, of matinee-idol good looks and hair of Irish black, who led a traveling troupe of celebrated thespians, accompanied by a captivating blonde actress. These sightings covered Nepal, Tasmania, Russia, and Timbuktu…and from New York to Paris. The traveling troupe was famous for their extravagant use of fake diamonds and emeralds each member finding some reason for wearing them. Never had there been so many tiaras in a production…and talk was they were real.

There may be some truth in that, for the members retired wealthy, some living abundantly in highest society or others more modestly. A tiny man named Malcolm, who owned a successful traveling carnival, became a silent partner with Barnum and Bailey's acclaimed circus. But these were rumors…

A word from the author...

I am married and write novels and scripts in Pacific Palisades, California. In my wilder days, I was a fashion illustrator, dabbled in acting and earned my SAG card, went on to getting shot with rubber bullets as a "stunt" performer training troupes from Camp Pendleton at Stu Segall Productions in San Diego, have sculpted, and love tearing my house apart and putting it together...I finally settled down penning novels where all one needs is a fertile imagination, a blood-spattered laptop, and a doorstop thesaurus...

Visit me at:

https://www.pinterest.com/sharonindiana/
https://ship11233.wixsite.com/bookshoponthecorner
ship11233.wixsite.com/sarys-diamonds-twrp
ship11233.wixsite.com/sarys-gold
http://ship11233.wix.com/the-monster-factory
http://ship11233.wix.com/beast-in-the-moon
amazon.com/author/sharon.roughwriter

Thank you for purchasing
this publication of The Wild Rose Press, Inc.

For questions or more information
contact us at
info@thewildrosepress.com.

The Wild Rose Press, Inc.
www.thewildrosepress.com

To visit with authors of
The Wild Rose Press, Inc.
join our yahoo loop at
http://groups.yahoo.com/group/thewildrosepress/